The Girls 2:
Dirty Little Secrets

Kenni York

www.urbanbooks.net

Urban Books, LLC
97 N 18th Street
Wyandanch, NY 11798

The Girls 2: Dirty Little Secrets
Copyright © 2015 Kenni York

ISBN 13: 978-1-62286-977-0
ISBN 10: 1-62286-977-X

First Mass Market Printing June 2016
First Trade Paperback Printing November 2015
Printed in the United States of America

10 9 8 7 6 5 4 3 2 1

Distributed by Kensington Publishing Corp.
Submit Orders to:
Customer Service
400 Hahn Road
Westminster, MD 21157-4627
Phone: 1-800-733-3000
Fax: 1-800-659-2436

Dedication

Every season comes to an end. Relationships are no different. This book is dedicated to all of the broken hearts and tattered souls looking for the love and approval of others, be it romantic encounters or friendships. Happiness lies within.

Dear Chicks,

You're not going to believe this. I don't even believe that I'm writing it so I know you're not going to believe it . . . or maybe you will. But I don't love myself. I look in the mirror every day and want to just shatter the glass. I smile, I say the right things, I make the right moves, and I play the game. And I think I've done it all this time so that you all, everyone around me really, could be more at ease. At first, I thought that being honest with you would help free myself of some of the anguish that's been built up inside of me for so long. This letter is proof of what I thought . . . but with each word I write I realize more and more how empty I am whether you know the truth or not. And that's all about me. So I've made a decision that I'm sure you're not going to like or agree with, but for once I am not hiding what I think, feel, or do. For once, I'm laying it out on the table so that nothing gets confused and there are no surprises. We've grown up together and shared so many moments, both good and bad. Over time, with everything that has happened to all of us, we've drifted apart, come back, and drifted again. The only difference now is that I will no longer be coming back. This will be the last time you hear from me. It's much better this way because I realize that when you are empty on the inside . . . when you are not at peace with yourself, there is nothing you can give to the rest of the world around you . . . You only risk disrupting the peace. Pray that my soul finds the peace that my person never experienced while I was with you.

Love,
Your friend

Chapter 1

Jada

Six Months Prior

People always say that you should be careful what you ask for. Jada was beginning to understand that more and more with each day that passed by. Pregnancy was kicking her ass. Now, in her second trimester, she was grateful to be getting over the all-day sickness but was struggling to find clothes that fit, foods that didn't disgust her, and a mood reminiscent of the way she used to feel on good days. As much as she wanted to have this baby, getting used to the changes was quite an adjustment. Standing there looking at the profile of her newly protruding belly in the dressing room mirror, she smiled. She was growing a person.

"Damn, girl, can you hurry up? It didn't take them this long to make the damn dress."

Candace was growing impatient as she waited in the cramped maternity boutique surrounded by waddling women. She was glad that her maternity days were over and had no intentions of reliving them.

Jada rolled her eyes at her reflection and began to peel off the floral dress she'd picked out. "Just a minute. Geez." She didn't know why she'd even bothered to invite the girl shopping with her in the first place. If only Jordan hadn't had to go into work for a few hours this morning. Thinking of her husband, she pulled her phone out of her bra and sent him a quick text.

What do you want for dinner today?

She quickly tucked her phone back into her bra and hustled to redress in her blouse and khakis before Candace could voice her impatience yet again. Things had been pretty strained among all of them since the day she'd announced her pregnancy. In fact, it was the last time the girls had all been together. Alex was living a new life given her relationship with Clay, Miranda was in rehab, and Candace was being Candace. Since having her daughter, she'd been dating a series of guys, none of whom seemed particularly special to her. But Jada was willing to bet that her friend had been doubling back to her former habits and sexing her baby's father. To avoid listening to her lie, Jada chose not to ask the girl about it. The last thing she needed right now was to be caught up in any of her homegirls' drama at this point in her life.

Walking out of the dressing room, she noticed that Candace had stepped out of the store to make a call. It was just as well. At least it gave Jada an opportunity to pay for her purchases in peace. She decided to get the floral dress as well as a maroon dress and a pair of blue jeans with the belly panel. A few minutes later she walked up on Candace as she was finishing up her call.

"Are you sure your folks won't mind?" *Who the hell was she talking to?* "Okay. I'll call you when I'm on my way. It won't take long."

"What? You're about to ditch me?" Jada spoke into her friend's ear, nearly scaring the life out of her.

Candace quickly flipped her phone shut and shot Jada a look. "Girl, you know that's how folks get shot, right? Just rolling up on someone like that. You better watch it before you and mini-you gets got."

"I ain't scared of you, chica. Now, who you ditching me for?"

"Nobody's ditching you. But after we leave here I'm going to stop by my homeboy's house for a minute."

Jada's eyebrow rose as the two of them began to walk toward Macy's to exit North Lake Mall the way they'd come in. "What homeboy?"

"He's like my best friend from high school, girl. I've known him forever, but we lost touch after I hooked up with Quincy. I ran into him a week ago when I was over at that strip mall off Rainbow where my sister works. Man, we go way back."

Jada looked away. She'd known Candace for a minute now and never once had she heard any tales about some long lost best friend that happened to be a male. It was all sounding like some bullshit to her. "What's his name?"

"Rico. And he's so sweet. He's good with Zoe too."

"You've had that man around your baby?"

"Yeah. What's wrong with that?" Candace turned her nose up as if Jada had said something completely out of line. "I'm telling you, me and Rico used to be inseparable, girl. He's like my brother. I trust him with my daughter."

"Y'all *used* to be inseparable. That was in *high school*." Jada stated high school with as much sarcasm in her tone as she could muster up.

"But the real is that you've obviously not been in contact with this dude for a hot minute, so you don't know who or how he is now."

"True friendship transcends time and is not affected by distance or lapse of time."

Jada gave her friend the side-eye. "You read that on a greeting card or something?"

"Ha-ha." Candace held the door open for her pregnant friend as they exited the mall. "But anyway, you know I wouldn't have nobody around Itty Bitty that might click on stupid. I don't play that."

Jada smiled at the girl as she sauntered out of the door past her. What she knew was that Candace was likely to paint the prettiest picture of someone she had no business dealing with as long as she was caught up in them. But once the magic of the moment passed away and she was tired of them, Candace's description of and references to them would become less than favorable. Jada wasn't buying this homeboy that was "like a brother" story at all. But if that was the story Candace wanted to stick to at the moment, so be it.

"Well, all I'm saying is be careful, love." It was the soundest advice she could give her without going into depth about her association with this dude.

"Of course." They approached Candace's car first, and the girl promptly turned around and embraced Jada in a heartfelt hug. "Let me get out of here so I can get home in time for my mom to get to her meeting tonight."

"Oh, she kept Zoe today?"

"Yep. I'm trying to find a babysitter that I can afford and trust. I'm not ready to send her to a day care yet."

Jada felt her phone buzz inside her bra. She had a bad habit of storing her phone there so that she wouldn't have to fish through her purse for it. She pulled it out and saw that she had a text message from Jordan. "Well, you'll find somebody. I'm sure it's hard to leave your kid with a stranger, whether it's a day care center or a private sitter. I think . . ." Jada's voice trailed off as she read and reread the text that she'd been sent.

But will you swallow it if I let you?

The message had nothing to do with the question she'd asked him earlier. She stared at the screen trying to decide how or if to respond. Candace was speaking, but she couldn't make out what she was saying since she was lost in her own thoughts.

Candace slapped her arm. "Look, you and Jordan can go on and have you sex-text convo. I'm out, girl."

Jada looked up and nodded. "Uh-huh. Okay, boo. Be safe." She walked in the direction of her car without looking back. After getting inside and starting the engine she returned to the text message. Reading it again she shifted from confusion to annoyance. Her little voice was telling her that something wasn't right. She didn't know what the hell was going on, but one thing was for sure, that damn text message was certainly not meant for her.

Chapter 2

Jordan

It felt good to be away from home for a minute. Everything about home was a constant reminder of how their lives were about to change. The myriad of baby clothes and paraphernalia, the *Atlanta Parent* and *American Baby* magazines that covered the coffee table and the magazine rack in their bathroom, and the calendar in their kitchen which marked Jada's doctor's appointments and the number of weeks she was all served to taunt him. He was going to be a father, and it seemed as if he couldn't escape the reality of that one thing. Even watching the way Jada's body was changing was beginning to take a toll on him. Jordan knew that his personal hang-ups and gripes were selfish and wrong so he tried his best not to show any of his feelings to Jada. But in order to keep her at bay of his true emotions he needed a break.

He'd lied and told her that he had to go into the office just so that he could get out of going shopping with her for maternity clothes. He'd never been fond of trailing her around on her shopping expeditions, and he surely was in no mood to peruse maternity shops. Instead of going into the office he decided to hook up with one of his oldest buddies from college for a little one-on-one.

Jordan met Martin at Midway Park. As usual, Martin was late. Jordan had been waiting twenty minutes for his homeboy to show up and was just about to call it quits when the shorter, balding guy finally appeared across the court.

"Late as usual, nigga. You gon' miss out on your own funeral, watch," Jordan said giving his boy a pound.

Martin Hood was a portly, light-skinned dude who got much love from the ladies during college because of his loveable and quiet demeanor. His boys knew that that "quiet" business was just a front. Once you got to know Martin he was full of life and jokes. The thing that Jordan liked about him the most was that Martin, although chronically tardy, was one of the most reliable dudes he'd ever met. Jordan would go so far as to call Martin his best friend.

"Man, I had to go with Ashley to check out this bakery," Martin stated tossing his gym bag to the ground and pulling out his baseball cap.

Jordan tossed his basketball at Martin. "What's up at the bakery?"

"Trying out cakes for the wedding."

Jordan stopped dead in his tracks. "What wedding? You never told me that you asked Ash to marry you, bruh."

"Ahh, bruh, you haven't been paying attention." Martin dribbled the ball and smiled at his boy. "I posted that shit on Facebook, and I e-mailed all the homies an announcement."

"You know I'm not on Facebook. I don't even know nothing about no Facebook, and I ain't seen no e-mail either, bruh. Not to mention Jada hasn't said anything about receiving an invitation in the mail."

"Come on, man. Bring some offense." Martin began to run to the hole while dribbling the basketball. "Invites are going out next week. You gon' get one. Make sure you text me your mailing address."

"What?" Jordan said reaching for the ball and missing by an inch. "You not gon' have your boys be in the wedding?"

"Naw, we keeping it as simple as we can. Just me, her, the preacher, and family and friends can watch as we do our thing."

"Can't see how I missed this, man. Ole baby-face-ass Martin getting married!"

Martin shot the ball from the three-point line and was amazed that he actually made it. "Yeah, you been so caught up in baby-land you probably missing a whole lot of shit."

Jordan ran for the ball. "Man, it's a little overwhelming. It's like the whole relationship just shifted. Everything is about the baby. I mean, *everything*. From the food she cooks 'cause the doctor put her on a diet to control her blood sugar . . . right down to the way we have sex, *if* we have sex, so that she can be comfortable."

Martin laughed. "It can't be that bad, man. Y'all both getting what you wanted, right? You wanted to have a baby."

Jordan shrugged. Martin wasn't even married yet so he didn't have a clue how crucial this whole thing was. "Yeah, man. I'm excited about the baby and all . . . It's just a little overwhelming."

Martin knocked the ball out of Jordan's hand. "You'll be all right, man. You need to go ahead and shake it off 'cause it's affecting your game."

"Nigga, you wished you *had* game," Jordan countered.

"Bring it then."

"Man, shut up and run me that ball."

Once their friendly game of 21 was over and both men were exhausted and sweaty Martin reached for his water bottle while Jordan reached for his cell phone. He checked the time. 2:30 p.m. He wondered if Jada was home or if she was still out shopping. The thought of going home right away didn't appeal to him much. He checked his Yahoo! Messenger mindlessly and saw that he had an instant message from one of the interns at the radio station where he worked as a DJ during the week.

Mona: What you doing, Boss Man?

Jordan liked it when she called him that. At first he thought it was sign of respect, but then he realized over time that she was really doing it flirtatiously. The attention he was getting from her was enough for him to entertain her random instant messages and e-mails.

Jordan: Just finished playing ball with my boy. What's up?

It didn't take longer than a second for Mona to respond.

Mona: Nothing. Just saying hi . . . Couldn't tell if you were really online or not. Why you didn't invite me to hoop? I'm nice.

Jordan: Yeah, right. Girls don't hoop like dudes do. You don't want none of this, youngon.

Mona: What you know about what I want? Anyway, I can ball. I'm real good with my hands . . . and other things too.

It was the furthest she'd ever crossed the line with him. Feeling that they were just engaging in harmless banter, Jordan didn't feel compelled to put an end to the direction their conversation was going in.

Jordan: What else you good with?

Mona: My mouth. Can I show you?

Jordan's phone buzzed in his hand as a text message came through. As he clicked to read it Martin pulled him out of his daze.

"Whatever you over there talking 'bout sho' got you grinning like a dang Cheshire cat," Martin joked. "Jada musta said something you like."

Jordan glanced down at the text that had just come from his wife asking about his dinner choice. Figuring he could just call her in a minute to let her know, Jordan pressed a button and looked up again at Martin. "Don't worry 'bout what's going on over here with my phone. You just worry about making sure you get my invitation to me on time. Next time some important shit happens with you try picking up the phone."

"Like *you* ever pick up a phone," Martin argued. "You stay more busy than anybody. Between work and being booed up with Jada you don't never have time for jack. Shoot, I'm surprised you even called me up to ball today."

"Sometimes you need to get out with ya' boys," Jordan said as he struggled to send his reply to Mona while keeping up with the conversation with Martin.

"A'ight, man," Martin said rising from his seat on the concrete. "I gotta get back to the house. We have plans, and I don't want Ashley to get pissed with me for being late. You know how that goes."

Jordan pressed the send button quickly, rose from the ground, and stuffed his phone into his pocket. "Yeah, bruh. I know exactly how that goes."

They gave each other a half hug and a pound before each headed toward their respective cars.

"Aye, congrats, man," Jordan called out to Martin. "If I ain't tell you, I'm happy for you. I know you and Ashley been through a lot. It's good to see y'all hanging in there."

Martin nodded. "Yeah, you and Jada are our inspiration." He laughed.

Jordan shook his head. It wasn't the first time someone had referred to him and his wife as such. Especially in Jada's circle, they were the only couple that was able to sustain. On the outside looking in, it probably seemed as if they had it all. But on the inside just trying to make it, Jordan was starting to feel more and more like he'd made a mistake in marrying so young. They had their whole lives ahead of them. They both were at the beginning of lucrative careers. As much as he loved Jada, the thought of the dynamics of their relationship changing when they were still so newly married scared him.

"A'ight, man. Be safe," he told his boy as he reached his car. What else was there for him to say? The moment he admitted to anyone that maybe he wanted out he'd seem like the biggest asshole in the world. Perhaps it was just best for him to continue to suffer in silence. Jordan realized that relationships went through stages. Maybe they were just in an awkward stage that would soon change. In the meantime, he was content with using his disappearing acts and increasing mindless flirting habits as his defense mechanism.

***

He hadn't gotten a response back from Mona. After the game with Martin Jordan drove to his mom's and chilled there for a bit. He was stalling for time because he knew that once he got back home to Jada there was no way he was going to be able to get away should Mona decide to resurface. He wasn't completely sure that he wanted to get up with her, but the possibility of it excited him. The shit-talking was giving him life. It helped him escape the routine he and Jada had fallen into, which was driving him crazy.

Reluctantly, he returned home in the early evening. Part of him hoped that Jada would already be asleep even though it was only 5:00 p.m. That pregnancy fatigue was real, and it seemed to strike Jada more often than the nausea. He let himself into their quaint little cottage home apartment and knew he was going to be in trouble the moment he closed the door behind him. He could smell the scent of onions and garlic and could hear the sizzling from the doorway in the quiet of the house. Although the smell was pleasant, Jordan's stomach wasn't ready for it.

He threw his gym bag on the ground and walked into the kitchen where Jada was placing a large juicy steak onto a platter surrounded with baby potatoes, tricolored peppers, and broccoli sprouts. She was barefoot and dressed in a simple blue slip dress. Her hair was pulled away from her face as the sweat beads formed around her forehead and the nape of her neck. She had a look of intense concentration on her face as she worked.

"Hey, you," Jordan greeted his pregnant wife. He leaned in to kiss her and she offered her cheek instead of her pretty pink lips. "How was your day?"

Jada placed the cast-iron skillet she'd sautéed the steak and veggies in into the sink and ran warm water into it. She shrugged her shoulders as she poured dish detergent into the pan. "Typical Saturday. Went shopping with Candace. Came home and washed clothes. Watched a movie. Cooked dinner."

"Eventful," Jordan joked as he pulled a bottle of water from the refrigerator.

"You know what I didn't do?" Jada asked turning off the water and beginning to scrub the skillet clean.

"What?"

"Receive a return text or a call from you."

Jordon guzzled his water before responding to her. Judging by the tone of her voice she was in a bad mood, and he didn't want to escalate it into a horrible mood by starting a petty argument. Her emotions were raw these days due to the pregnancy. She bugged out over every little thing, and he wasn't in the mood to go there with her today.

"My bad, babe. Martin was hating 'cause I whooped him so we had to run it back," he lied. "Then we got to talking 'bout him and Ashley getting married. I got your text, and I meant to hit you back, but I was talking to bruh and I just forgot."

"And when you left the park?" Jada asked in a scarily calm-before-the-storm-type of tone.

"I rode by Mom's place. Hadn't seen her in a minute and I just wanted to see my mom. Is that okay?" He shouldn't have caught an attitude at the end, but the interrogation was grating his nerves.

"That's fine," Jada said picking up the skillet to dry it with a dish towel. "But I'm just wondering if ol' girl actually did swallow whatever you put in her mouth or was that something that was going on at your mom's house?"

Jordon tossed his water bottle into the trash and frowned at his wife. "What you talkin' 'bout, babe?"

Jada took her time wiping dry the skillet as she looked at Jordan with piercing eyes. Her nostrils flared as she spoke. "You know, today actually was a little more eventful than I put on.

You see, you *did* text me, asshole. Only I'm quite sure that the text you sent me wasn't meant *for* me. Your question was 'if I do will you swallow' and I'm asking you now . . . Did the bitch who the text was meant for actually swallow whatever the hell you put in her fuckin' mouth?" Her tone grew louder as she finished her question.

Jordan's heart pounded. He remembered the text all too well, and now he understood why Mona hadn't responded. She'd never gotten the message. He wanted to kick himself for getting their messages mixed up and creating this entire mess. Now he stood there watching his wife basically caress a cast-iron skillet like some psycho. He was pretty sure that there wasn't going to be any happy ending from this.

"I'm sorry." He didn't know what else to say. He couldn't possibly tell her that he hadn't sent the message because she had the proof sitting in her inbox. "I was just messing around online . . . talking trash. I guess I got your message mixed up with whoever I was talking shit to. It was nothing."

"You're *sorry?*" Jada asked, narrowing her eyes.

"I'm very sorry," Jordan replied sounding pitiful.

"You were just *messing around* online?"

Jordan nodded.

"It was *nothing?*" Jada asked, tossing the towel onto the counter and grasping the handle of the skillet tightly.

"Yeah, babe. It wasn't shit. Just talking shit on somebody's Facebook wall. That's it."

Jada nodded and remained silent for a moment before moving closer to him with a scary smile on her face. "Do I look like I'm stupid?" The second the word *stupid* escaped her lips she swung the skillet with all of her might.

Jordan ducked in the nick of time and quickly backed out of the kitchen.

Jada kept swinging the skillet, all the while ignoring the horrible pain she was feeling in her wrist. "You stupid son of a bitch! You think I'm stupid? Or are you actually that dumb to be putting this type of shit on some slut's public Web page for all the world to see it?" She swung and finally grazed the side of his arm.

"Fuck!" Jordan hollered. "I said I was sorry. Put that shit down, babe," he said jumping up onto their sofa.

She pointed the skillet at him and shook her head. "I don't know what's wrong with you, but you had better fix it. I'm not putting up with this shit from you, Jordan. You wanna fuck around with some skanks out in the street and do stupid shit to ruin your career like posting dirty comments on hoes' pages, then you go right ahead . . . but you gon' have to do all that without me. So you better make a decision, brother, 'cause I will leave your ass before I stick around for this shit."

Jordan held his hands up in defeat. The thought of her leaving him scared him. Jada was the best thing that had ever happened to him and even though he was feeling some kind of way, he knew that he didn't want to be without his wife. "I'm sorry, bae. It was stupid, and I was wrong. I'm sorry. You know I love you, and you know I didn't mean nothing by it."

Jada cocked her head to the side and surveyed her husband's shaken demeanor. She could see that he felt guilty and that she'd put a little fear in him. She needed him to know that she meant business. Shaking her head she turned away and returned to the kitchen.

Jordan could hear her fumbling around with dishes. Taking a deep breath he lowered himself to the ground and took a seat on the couch. Quickly he pulled his phone out to make sure he'd deleted any and all messages, including texts and instant messages. It wouldn't do to have her scroll through his phone in the middle of the night and find any more incriminating stuff.

"Come eat!" Jada called out.

From the sound of her voice he could tell that she was in the dining room. He tossed his phone onto the sofa and buried his face in his hands. He had a decision to make. Should he be honest with his wife fresh off this argument and tell her that he'd already eaten at his mom's house, or should he keep the peace and force himself to eat the meal she'd prepared? He rose from the sofa and took his time washing his hands at the kitchen sink before making his way into the dining room. Jada was already seated, and his plate was waiting for him at his usual spot. He took a seat and smiled at his wife.

"It looks good, babe." He meant it. The potatoes au gratin and the steak and veggies looked very appealing to his eyes. He loved his wife's cooking, but his stomach still hadn't fully digested the fried fish, okra, baked beans, fries, and hush puppies that his mom had whipped up.

Jada blessed the food and started to eat. The air in the room was stale as they both remained silent. Jordan took small bites of his food and was hoping that he'd be able to find a way to excuse himself without pissing her off. Jada was still fuming over his foolish behavior. She looked over and noticed that he was pecking away at his food verses devouring it the way he usually did.

"You don't like it?" she asked.

"Huh?" Jordan looked up at her. "Why you say that?"

She rolled her eyes. "Because you're barely touching it, like you think it's nasty or something."

Jordan shook his head. "You know everything you touch is the bomb. I'm just not that hungry."

Her eyebrow rose. "Why not?"

"I ate a little something at Mom's," he finally admitted. "But it's cool. This is good, boo. You know I'm gon' eat it."

"Don't bother!" she snapped. "I specifically asked you what you wanted for dinner. Instead of answering me, you out flirting with some trick. You knew I was gon' be cooking dinner for you, but you went and fed your face at your mom's house. You're an inconsiderate ass."

Jordan knew that he'd pissed her off this evening, but he was still the man of this house. He was just about sick of the way she kept berating him. This wasn't the Jada he'd come to know and love. Pregnancy was not a good look on her. "A'ight, you can chill now," he told her in a stern voice. "You don't have to keep bringing up the shit we just squashed. If we done with it, be done with it. And I told you I'm gon' eat the damn steak so you can let that go too."

Jada looked at him in shock at his tone. She couldn't believe his nerve. How was he going to come home and ruin her whole day, then turn around and try to put her in her place? Suddenly her appetite was gone. She rose from the table, and Jordan jumped up after her.

"Where you going?" he asked, only half-worried that she was about to actually leave the house.

"To my room," she told him. "I don't have the appetite to sit here with you and pretend that everything's all good. So you can suffer through your second dinner by your own damn self." She left the dining room and wobbled to the bedroom.

Jordan let out a loud sigh and sank back into his chair. He just couldn't win with her these days. It was really beginning to affect their relationship. He pushed the food around on his plate for a little while longer and tried his best to eat half of the meal. Once he realized that he wasn't going to make it, Jordan rose from the table and took both of their plates back to the kitchen to put in storage containers. He cleaned the kitchen and dining room up, figuring that Jada would appreciate the assistance.

There was nothing but silence coming from the bedroom, and he prayed that she had finally calmed down. He carried a lit frankincense incense into their bedroom and placed it in the usual spot on the dresser. Jada was lying in the middle of the bed surrounded by pillows and reading a book. He didn't say anything to disturb her. He pulled a pair of boxers out of his drawer and went to take a shower. As the water ran over his body he huffed. He was horny, but he knew that following their blowup there was no way that she was going to give him any tonight. But he was becoming used to that. Jada rarely ever felt like being intimate these days. It was just another thing that was affecting their relationship negatively.

After getting out of the shower and drying off he returned to their bedroom. Jada had put her book aside and turned out the light, signaling that she was going to bed. Jordan's eyes darted over to the clock on the dresser. It was only a little after 7:00 p.m. He wasn't ready to go to sleep so early so he grabbed the remote and plopped down on the side of the bed where she'd left very little space for him.

As the light from the television brightened the dark room Jada slapped one of her pillows. "Do you *mind?*" she asked with an attitude.

"What?" Jordon asked. "It's too loud?" He lowered the volume.

"No, I just don't want to be disturbed by the TV. Period."

"What you want me to do, Jada? It's not even 8:00 o'clock. Just because you're turning in super early doesn't mean I have to, babe. If I do that I'll be up in the middle of the night, and that's really gon' piss you off."

"Go watch TV in the living room," Jada suggested. "In fact . . . here." She sat up, struggled to reach the bottom of the bed to retrieve the spare blanket, and then handed it to him. "Take your pillows too and you can just sleep out there."

"*Seriously?*" He looked at her as if she was crazy. "You're punishing me now?"

"No. You want to stay up, and I don't. Plus I'm not comfortable all cramped up in the bed together."

"Cramped up?" This was news to him. "Since when do you feel like we're cramped up?"

"Why do you think I have all these pillows everywhere? I'm trying to get comfortable, and it's just easier when I have the whole bed for that instead of trying to keep me and my belly on one side of the bed."

Jordan swore under his breath and clicked the television off. He threw the remote onto the nightstand, then grabbed the blanket Jada offered him, along with his two pillows. This was the most ridiculous thing he'd ever heard, but he couldn't argue with her any longer tonight. Rising from the bed he rolled his eyes and hoped that this pregnancy would speed by quickly. As he left the room he heard her shifting around and knew that she was repositioning herself in the middle of their bed.

"Can you close the door?" she called behind him.

Jordan pulled the door closed without saying a word. Jada was officially getting on his nerves. He made up the sofa and turned on the TV, settling upon a rerun episode of *The Game*. No matter which way he maneuvered his body he just couldn't get comfortable on the couch. If someone had told him that having a baby meant no sex, a moody wife, and he'd be on the couch for God knew how long, he would have never agreed to it. Married life was turning out to be depressing.

Chapter 3

Miranda

Flashback

Fuck them, Miranda thought as she sat in her Nissan Maxima just outside the entrance to Stephanie and Corey's apartment complex. Corey was bugging about hitting her off and Stephanie had the audacity to be judgmental. She had half a mind to find a gun and go up in there and shoot them both dead in the fucking head. She was sick of people treating her like she wasn't shit. It was time to start showing these muthafuckas that they couldn't mess with her. The only flaw in her plan was that she didn't own a gun. But that was okay. She knew that she could cop one from any booster or crackhead on the street. Getting a piece would be the easy part. Executing the plan would be the hard part.

"What the fuck am I doing?" she asked herself. "I'm not about to put a bullet in nobody." She was tripping, and she knew it. She was just so pissed with the couple for how they were treating her, and she was in desperate need of a hit. Her mind was playing with her. It was time for her to go home before she did something stupid, but the thought of her empty, lonely apartment only made her angrier and more depressed. Before she could turn the ignition and get out of there she noticed a car exiting the open gate. Her eyes grew wider once she realized that it was Stephanie's Nissan Sentra speeding down the road. Where the hell is she going this late? Miranda wondered. There was only one way to find out. Quickly she put the car in gear and moved to catch up to a safe distance behind her friend.

They didn't go far. Stephanie parked her car at a convenience store right down the street and hopped out. Miranda parked her car across the street in the parking lot of an all-night Laundromat and killed the lights. There were no other people in sight. She squinted hard as she watched Stephanie pull a couple of trash bags out of the car. She felt her stomach turn the moment her friend began rummaging through trash bags in the Dumpster. What is *she looking for? Miranda wondered. Surely they weren't starving. Corey and Stephanie had plenty of money to blow so Miranda knew the girl couldn't have been Dumpster diving. Finally she realized that Stephanie was pulling trash from the Dumpster and placing it into the trash bags that she'd brought. The rationale of it escaped Miranda's understanding. Once Stephanie was satisfied with her work she tossed the bags in the Dumpster, got back in her car, and made a U-turn toward home.*

Miranda didn't follow her. There was no reason to. She was pretty sure the answers to her questions could be found in those garbage bags. She popped the trunk, and then hopped out of her car. After rummaging around for a minute she found a pair of work gloves that Norris always kept in the truck. She closed the trunk, then slid her hands into the oversized gloves as she crossed the street. It was clear that Stephanie had a secret, and she was about to find out what it was. After quickly looking over her shoulder to ensure that no one was watching she peered inside the Dumpster and pulled out the bag on top. The smell of garbage was repulsive, but Miranda was on a mission. She'd gone through two garbage bags before feeling as if she'd hit the jackpot.

Her fingers felt the thin plastic of what she knew was a card. Thinking that it was a credit card she pulled it out, only to see that it was a driver's license. Unfazed, she tossed it back into the pile and kept digging. Then it clicked. The name on the license was familiar. She doubled back through the garbage and pulled the ID out again. Montae Stokes. She thought for a moment, then realized just why the name was so important. It all made plenty of sense now. It wasn't Stephanie who had something to hide. It was Corey. But like a good wifey, Stephanie was doing the deed for him. Miranda wanted to kiss the license, but the thought of the germs crawling on it encouraged her not to. This was it. This was how she was going to get back at Corey's sorry ass and Stephanie's judgmental ass. She stuffed all the trash back into the garbage bag and made sure to place Montae's ID on top before carefully placing the winning bag back into the Dumpster on top of all the others.

She yanked the gloves off of her hand and whipped out her cell phone. Tonight she was about to be an anonymous Good Samaritan.

"DeKalb 911. What's your emergency?" the operator asked.

"Um . . . This isn't exactly an emergency," Miranda stated. "I mean, I think I have a lead on the Montae Stokes murder."

"Hold on, let me dispatch you to our tip line."

Miranda was placed on hold for a few moments before hearing another voice in her ear. Carefully she gave her location, then advised that she was a homeless person Dumpster diving and saw who she knew to be Corey Polk's girlfriend disposing of garbage at the convenience store. She told the interviewer that she'd gone into the bag hoping to find remnants of steak or something from the wealthy drug dealer's home but found Montae Stokes's ID instead. Before the interviewer could ask any questions she encouraged them to get someone out there quick before the evidence was gone, then disconnected the call.

Quickly she returned to her car and waited in the still of the night to see if anyone would follow up on her tip. Just when she was about to curse the justice system she saw an unmarked car stop at the Dumpster. She knew they were officers by the make of the car and their disposition. Her heart rate quickened as she watched them pull out trash bags with their noses turned up. They didn't have to look far or for long. What they needed was right there on top. She saw the taller cop wave the card in the air with his gloved hands.

"Gotcha," Miranda said out loud. *"Y'all fucked with the wrong one this time."*

Current Day

"How are you feeling today?" The therapist looked at Miranda with eyes of concern.

Nervously, Miranda wrung her hands together and rocked. The last thing she wanted to do was sit here and discuss her feelings. Her body felt like it had been hit by a truck. She ached all over and desperately wanted to crawl into the bed she'd been assigned by the rehabilitation facility. Unfortunately, she'd also been assigned to this whack-ass therapist and had to talk to her twice a day: once for a private session and once in a group session later in the day. Either way, Miranda wasn't feeling it.

She'd agreed to the rehab program once the reality of Stephanie's death had hit her. It was a sobering moment, and the girls had been so proud of her for committing to it. Although she said she'd do it, it had taken her three months to actually do it. Truth be told, it had taken Jada coming by the apartment and finding her passed out on the floor of her bathroom for her to get there. She'd been taken to the hospital, and from there she'd been shipped off to rehab.

Whatever the reason and however the transition she was here now, but all she wanted was a hit to take the edge off. Since she obviously wasn't going to get that she would have settled for being left the hell alone.

"You know this session is really whatever you make it, Miranda," Doctor Dunham told her as she removed her glasses from her face as if that move was going to shake her into talking.

Miranda shrugged. She wasn't studying this woman. This was her fourth solo session and the fourth time she'd spent the hour and a half saying nothing. What the hell was there to say? The woman knew everything there was to know about her. She knew that she was addicted to cocaine. She knew that she had been brought over from DeKalb Medical following an overdose. She knew that she had her girls listed as points of contacts versus any family members. She knew that she was alone. Most importantly, the Ph.D.-holding smarty-pants should have known that Miranda wasn't going to talk, especially about her feelings. It was pointless. Miranda knew that no one really gave a damn about her feelings.

"I want to help you, Miranda," Doctor Dunham stated. "But I can't do that if you don't do your part. This program was designed to . . ."

The therapist was talking, but Miranda checked out. She could see the woman's lips moving, but her mind was elsewhere. Honestly, her mind only stuck in one place when she wasn't craving a hit to put her out of her memory. Sleep never came. Insomnia forced her mind to replay the scene over and over again, never giving her a moment to be free of the living nightmare. Any time she tried to close her eyes it was as if she was standing in that funeral home again, staring at the still, lifeless body of the girl she'd once called her friend. That image only forced her to remember that Stephanie was placed in that casket because of her. This was something she couldn't discuss with anyone, including the therapist. Hell, she could barely stomach the memory and the reality herself. Doctor Dunham's constant inquiry about her feelings annoyed her. Miranda didn't want to feel the feelings she was experiencing, much less talk about them. The incident and her feelings haunted her daily. All she wanted was to escape it all.

Chapter 4

Corey

"You have nothing to worry about," Attorney Greg Phelps said to his client as they conversed in the private room at the DeKalb County Jail.

Corey threw his head back. "Aye, be straight up with me. Don't give me no bullshit, man. Tell me the real, ya' feel me?"

Phelps held his hand up. "If you have no evidence you have no case. It's as simple as that."

"Simple?"

Phelps smiled. "Simple," he reiterated.

Corey jumped up from the table and shoved it forcefully, penning his attorney in his chair with the table against his abdomen. Cory glowered at him. He was in no mood for any legal bullshit that this penny-pinching cocksucker was trying to feed him. He had too much on the line to be getting fucked around by the system. "Those bastard-ass GBI men in black fucks have Montae's ID with my prints on it. I'd call that evidence."

"Circumstantial," Phelps said nervously. "Means little to nothing. Just places you as a person of interest. Shows you were connected to him somehow, possibly there at the scene, but doesn't say you murdered him. Please . . ."

Corey frowned at the attorney and released the force he held on the table.

Phelps pushed the table away and cleared his throat. "A little trust'll go a long way here."

"Trust?" Corey asked. "You start trusting everybody that smiles at you then you're fucked, ya' feel me? So tell me, if this shit is so circumstantial, why the fuck have I been locked in this bitch for the last three months?"

"They had an eyewitness."

"What?"

"They had someone who said they saw you do it."

"Bullshit!"

"Must have been because that person is now MIA."

Corey shot him a look. "What?"

"GBI can't find their witness. Person just vanished so they have no one to testify against you."

Corey shook his head. "So, if they lost their witness, then again . . . Why the fuck have I been locked in here for the last three months?" his voice resounded through the room, raising the attention of the guard who poked his head into the room.

Phelps waved the guard away. "Because although the feds can't pin this on you, the state still intends to try, so they're holding you without bail until your court date."

Corey was livid. "This is some bullshit. When's the court date?"

"Two weeks," Phelps answered. "But I'm telling you that it's all circumstantial. With no eyewitness to present, you're as good as off. You'll be a free man."

Corey wasn't so sure about that. Maybe Phelps was telling the truth. Maybe they would dismiss the case and let him walk on the murder charges, but he knew it was only a matter of time before he'd have to face the music of the streets. More was going on than others truly realized. While Montae's folks were sure to come gunning for him once word got out that he was let off, *if* he got let off, there were others that would be looking for him too. He was going to have to explain a lot of shit to Castello and his crew. Surely the GBI had started sniffing in their direction once they hit his stash house and his place out in Roswell. Thinking about the Roswell crib made him feel emotions he wasn't ready to deal with. It reminded him of Stephanie and the fact that he hadn't even been able to say good-bye to the love of his life.

If he was getting out, it was time for him to start putting together a plan. He needed his crew's ear to the ground to see what kind of moves Montae's crew was planning to make. He needed to get his story straight for Castello and a plan so he'd be prepared for whatever the fallout was going to be with him. His business was very much a concern, but the most important thing he needed was to find out who exactly put the bullets in Stephanie. Once he found those bastards, they were going to have to feel the heat of his wrath. A lesson had to be taught in the streets. He was still the king, and no one was going to fuck with his family.

Corey looked over at Phelps. "I hope you right about this."

Phelps nodded his head. "I'm telling you . . . It's open and shut. Simple."

If it was one thing Corey knew from the dangerous life he led, it was that nothing was ever quite that simple. But he was down to take whatever stroke of luck he could get. He had things to do on the outside, and sitting in that cell waiting on some fucking suits to conjure up a case against him wasn't helping matters. In two weeks, let Phelps tell it, he was going to be able to get some shit popping. Until then, he planned to spend every moment getting his strategy together.

Chapter 5

Clay

"What the—" Clay tripped over the six-inch stilettos lying in front of the door as he tried to make his way into his apartment. Slamming the door, he kicked the shoes and rolled his eyes. He should have been used to coming home and tripping over heels by now. Ever since Alex moved in with him she'd taken the liberty of leaving her things wherever she pleased. It was one of the differences between them. He was organized and orderly, whereas Alex was creative and thrived in dysfunction. Maybe leaving her stuff everywhere had been okay when she lived with Kacey, but it was irking him that his girlfriend was becoming an apparent slob.

He sauntered into the kitchen and noticed that there was a bag on the stove. He took a sneak peek inside and found two takeout cartons of Chinese food. They usually took turns being responsible for dinner. It had been one of Clay's ideas. Since Alex was off on Fridays, today was her day to get dinner. She didn't exactly have any culinary skills, so it was so like her to order takeout. It was clear to Clay that she'd opted for delivery tonight.

As he pulled out a lukewarm egg roll, his beautiful, tall, ebony girlfriend skipped into the room. "Hi, precious!" she planted a big kiss on his lips. "I got you shrimp egg rolls this time."

He took a hearty bite of the appetizer and smiled. "Thanks, babe. How was your day?"

"It was okay. I mostly worked on my project for school and talked to Candace."

"How's Zoe?" Clay asked, inquiring about Candace's little girl.

"She's good, I guess. We didn't really talk about the baby. Candace has this new boo thang that she was going on and on about. You know how she does."

Clay raised his eyebrow. He certainly did know how Candace got down. It was no big secret that she'd been messing around with Stephanie's boyfriend, Corey, before the girl's unfortunate murder. It was also no secret that Zoe, Candace's daughter, was had out of wedlock with a married man. What really threw Clay was that even through all of this, Candace was married herself. Sure, she was divorced now, but half of the drama she kept up in her life had been going on while she was very much a married woman. Clay didn't want to come off as judgmental, but it was fair to say that Candace was one of Alex's friends that he liked the very least. He didn't trust her and didn't want her negatively influencing the woman he'd come to love so much.

"So did you finish the project?" Clay asked her, changing the subject.

Alex shook her head as she pulled his takeout carton out and placed it in the microwave. "Not yet. Almost though. Wait 'til you see this dress, precious. It is too hot."

"How hot?" He knew that Alex was all about fashion. Sometimes her fashion statements were a little over the top, but he loved how passionate she was about her craft.

She wrapped her arms around his neck and stuck her tongue inside of his mouth seductively. Over the last few months they'd gotten to know each other very well and very intimately. The transition of taking their relationship from friendship status to lover status had taken no time at all to accomplish once Alex took her blinders off and realized how much she really did love her best and oldest friend.

Clay reached behind her and tossed his egg roll into the plastic bag it had come out of.

He then held her tight and darted his tongue against hers. He could feel his nature rising as he caressed all of her curves. He'd been waiting years to feel her, to experience her body, and to show her how deep his emotions ran for her. Now that she was his he made sure to show her how he felt about her every chance he got. He never wanted Alex to forget how much he loved her. She'd spent a lot of time chasing after paper and dudes that had very little real interest in her. He wanted her to be very clear what it was like to have a completely attentive, reliable, and accountable man in her life.

The microwave dinged as his hands reached up under her tank top and gently slid up and around to cup her free-hanging, perky feminine mounds. Feeling her nipples harden against his touch he pulled her shirt over her head so that he could lick each nipple purposefully.

"I thought you were hungry," Alex said, giggling at the way he was devouring her breast.

"Um-hum." Clay squeezed her round butt as he continued to fondle and lick her beautiful breasts. "I'm hungry for you."

The faint sound of music hummed from the bedroom. Alex popped his head playfully indicating that he should let her go. He shook his head and grabbed her tighter. She squealed with delight but was serious about answering her phone.

"Precious, let me see who it is," she said pushing away from him.

He watched her scurry off to grab her phone. He couldn't believe that she'd rather yap on the phone with who he was sure was one of her girls instead of making love to him. That just wasn't going to work out. Clay exited the kitchen, rounded the corner, and walked the short distance to their bedroom. Alex was standing in front of the vanity mirror of their dresser talking on her pink, bedazzled phone. She looked up in the mirror and saw him standing in the doorway behind her. She held up a finger indicating that he should give her a minute. A minute wasn't the only thing that he planned to give her.

Clay wasted no time coming out of his button-up shirt and crisply starched jeans. He completely undressed himself as she continued to chatter on.

"That would be good," Alex said. "We haven't hung out in a minute and that gives me plenty of time to get my project finished so I won't be goofing off . . . oh, that's nice. I'll have to ask Precious about it though."

"Ask me what?" Clay whispered in her left ear before kissing the sensitive area of her neck.

Alex flinched. She hadn't even noticed him creeping up on her. Looking up into the mirror now she could see that he was butt naked and obviously was in no mood to hear the word no. She smiled at the image of him reaching around and grabbing her breasts while she tried to maintain some composure while talking to Jada on the phone. Jada was saying something, but Alex's mind was gone. The feel of Clay's hands all over her body and his lips attacking her hot spot rendered her speechless.

"Hello? Hello?" Jada hollered on the other end.

"Tell her you have to go," Clay ordered.

Alex shook her head and tried to focus. "Umm . . . okay, girl. So . . . ummm, next Saturday is cool with me and I'll check with—"

Clay took the phone right out of her hand. Her mouth gaped open as he put the phone to his ear to bid Jada farewell. "Alex can't talk right now. She'll call you later." He pressed the end button and tossed the phone onto the dresser, daring Alex to say something to him about it.

She shot him a "well, okay then" type of look and reached out for his manhood. Clay smiled and smothered her lips with his. They enjoyed a sensual kiss before he led her over to the bed.

"I'm about to put something serious on you," he told her.

"Oh yeah, rudeness?"

He slapped her ass and guided her onto the king-sized bed. "We'll see how rude I am in a minute."

No further words were necessary. Together they created a magical moment all their own. Alex appreciated how gentle and attentive Clay was. Being with him was much different from the sordid sexual experiences she'd had with her old boyfriends T and Mario. Clay made her feel like she was the most beautiful and important woman in the world. She loved him more and more every day.

Their Saturday morning ritual was becoming more and more like second nature to Clay. They started the day with breakfast prepared by him, then did their laundry together. After that, they'd go out and catch a movie, do some shopping, or run errands. He enjoyed the time he spent with Alex, but he had to admit that her princess mentality seemed to be expanding. That morning alone he was fuming on the inside because instead of helping him fold their clothes she was engrossed in one of her many fashion magazines that she refused to ever get rid of. The box of magazines she had in their living-room closet bothered him, but he never complained.

"That is not cute," Alex said pointing to an unhealthy- looking thin model in a multicolored asymmetrical dress. "They should not have ever placed that monstrosity on that girl's body."

"Babe, can you give me a hand with these towels?" Clay asked, referring to the small stack of folded towels sitting on the floor directly below where she was currently balled up with her magazine. He rose from the couch with a basket full of their clothes, then headed toward their room to put it up. He noticed that Alex hadn't moved or responded to him. He stopped and turned back to look at her. "Alex?"

"Hmmm?" She didn't even bother to look up.

"We're going to get massages in an hour right?" he asked her.

She nodded. "Yes, precious one."

"Then can you help put the clothes away so we aren't late for our appointment."

Alex waved him off. "Oh you can just get those when you come back from putting the clothes away."

That was it. Clay couldn't take it anymore. He dropped the laundry basket onto the floor, then walked over to Alex and plucked the magazine out of her hands. She sucked her teeth and looked at him in disbelief.

"Okay, that was sexy when you did it with the phone last night, but for real, for real, you being a little rude," she told him.

Clay threw the magazine onto the stack of towels, then pointed to it. "Here. Read it all you want so long as you pick these towels up and put them away while you're doing it."

Alex reached down to grab her magazine. "What's wrong with you?"

"*This* is wrong with me, Alexis." He held his arms outstretched.

Her eyebrow shot up. "What? You feeling some kind of way about the apartment? What does that have to do with your crappy attitude?"

"No, I'm feeling some kind away about *your* inability to help maintain the apartment."

"*Excuse* me?" Alexis couldn't believe that her boyfriend was standing there berating her.

"We've been living together for a few months, and I swear, you get lazier and lazier."

"I am *not* lazy," she argued. "Why would you say that?"

"Because you don't want to do anything, babe."

"I go to work and school. I think I do plenty, thank you very much." She rolled her eyes and flung open her magazine with a flare of attitude.

"I'm talking about doing stuff in the house. You don't wanna help do the clothes, you'd rather sit here flipping through magazines you've looked at a thousand times." He pointed to the heels that were still sitting on the floor near the front door. "And you won't even bother to put your shoes where they go. Those have been there for *three* days now!"

Alexis glared at him. "What? You're my daddy now?"

"Would your dad be able to push you to clean up after yourself?"

Alexis jumped up from the couch and stared at her boyfriend. Clay was sexy, but she wanted to tear his head off at this moment. "I don't know why you're trippin'. Just 'cause I didn't jump when you asked me to put the towels up? You all hyped up over some shoes? If it's that serious here . . ." she walked over to scoop up her heels, "I'll move them. You happy?" she asked cradling the shoes in her arms.

"What about food?" Clay asked.

"What about it?"

"We're going broke trying to maintain bills and your lavish takeout expenses all because you won't get in the kitchen and fry some chicken when it's your day to do dinner."

"I don't really cook like that," Alexis pouted. She was over being talked down to. "You knew that when you got with me, so I'm not seeing why it's a problem now."

Clay didn't like to see her face all distorted and ugly. He knew he'd hurt her feelings, but if he couldn't be honest with her, then they were never going to make it. "The problem isn't that you're not a good cook. The problem is that you won't *try* to cook. You know how to make some things. I mean, it ain't like you were sitting over there starving when you lived with Kacey."

She shot him a look. "Like you don't remember the many times I called you over to bring me dinner."

Clay shook his head and pulled her into an embrace. "Look, I didn't mean to come at you harshly or whatever, but we're a team now, so we both gotta act like it."

"Fine," she mumbled.

He kissed her on the forehead. "And if there's anything that I do that bothers you, you should let me know. I want us to be able to talk about anything. We're still cool like that, right?" He tweaked her nose.

Alexis looked into his eyes and smiled. "I guess so."

"Good." He pulled away from her and smacked her playfully on the butt. "Now put them shoes and towels away before we're late for our massages, woman."

Chapter 6

Candace

Things were starting to look up. Candace was finally back to work at a new law firm, Regal & Snyder, located on Peachtree Street downtown. She was enjoying her legal assistant position and had plans of going back to school to secure a paralegal certificate. She had her own spot and her daughter was happily cared for by a sitter during the week while she worked. Her divorce from Quincy was long since finalized and her fling with Khalil would have been a distant memory if it wasn't for the fact that she was caring for his daughter. It was a fact that Khalil only copped to when it was convenient for him.

Candace was seeing someone new. Rico Perry was a dude she'd gone to high school with and running into him at Stonecrest Mall a few weeks ago had brought back many old, fond memories. They'd been cool in school, but Rico had chosen now to admit that he'd had a crush on her back in the day. He'd been a grade level behind her, and she assumed that that was the reason he'd never said anything then. She had originally decided that it was best to keep him a secret from her girls. No one really trusted her judgment in men these days, given her track record. She couldn't blame them, but she also didn't care to hear any of their opinions about who she was spending time with and why. But things were starting to get serious between the two of them, and Candace was thinking more and more about completely coming clean. She'd started with Alexis who hadn't seemed all that enthused about two high school chums reconnecting. Alex's despondence encouraged her to put off telling Jada for the time being, especially since she was the more critical one in the group.

Candace checked her reflection in the mirror as she applied gloss to her lips. She was pleased with her round shape and alluring curves. Dressed in a fitted racer-back tank top and tights, she knew that Rico was going to find her figure inviting as well. The baby made a loud slurping sound, which caused Candace to turn around to look at her. She was lying in her playpen playing with her toes. Feeling that it was a supercute moment Candace picked up her cell phone off of the bed and clicked a couple of pictures of Zoe.

If anyone had told her a year ago that she'd be a mother Candace would have laughed at them. Motherhood was never something that she'd intended to do with her life. It didn't play into her desire to keep her figure tight and belly flat, travel, come and go whenever she pleased, eat out often, and sleep late on weekends. A year ago, Candace had a completely different agenda that had steadily become unraveled with every move she made. But looking down into the playpen at Zoe she knew that she really couldn't imagine life without the precious little gift.

Being a parent forced her to think differently, and it definitely changed her routine. Everything she did now was for the sheer benefit of her angel. At least that was what she told herself and anyone else that would listen. She hadn't been dating much, partly because she didn't want to have just anyone around Zoe, partly because she was having a hard enough time keeping her vajaja in check and not giving it to Khalil whenever he decided to slide by, and partly because she hadn't encountered anyone worth being bothered with. At her new job there were several older men, all attorneys, that sniffed around her way now and again, but Candace was adamant about not falling into an office romance. She'd had enough trouble with having Khalil so close to her work environment previously.

Candace reached down and caressed Zoe's head. The fine hairs felt like silk against her fingertips. She finally understood what people meant when they said there was no love like a mother's love. She'd never loved someone so much with all of her being before. Zoe kept her grounded and had completely changed her life. She kissed the baby, feeling that sense of relief that the little one had lived through the unfortunate event that had occurred the night of Stephanie's death. She'd been so sure that she was going to lose the baby as she'd sat in shock, bleeding on herself at the scene of the crime. Candace knew that she'd never forget the searing pain that had spread from her heart to her womb as she'd watched her friend gunned down in the street and left to breathe her last breath while surrounded by a pool of her own blood.

She shook off the memory. It occurred to her at least once a day. The role that she played in the whole mess made her ashamed of herself, but she knew that whether she'd been messing around with Corey or not, it would not have necessarily changed what happened. Whoever shot Stephanie had done so intentionally and were going to murder her that night whether Candace had been there under shady pretenses or not. It was the worst outcome possible. She'd tried over the months to envision other possible scenarios for how the whole encounter could have played out. Anything would have been better than the reality of Stephanie exiting Corey's secret apartment only to be massacred. Even Stephanie walking in on Candace and Corey in the act of their ultimate betrayal and them sitting there fighting and arguing it out until they were all spent would have been better than not having still among them the friend, mother, and sweet spirit that defined Stephanie.

The doorbell rang, bringing Candace out of her trance. She looked down at her cell phone to make sure she hadn't missed a call. No one ever just showed up at her house unannounced and unexpected. She left the baby in the playpen and hurried out to the living room where she took a look through the peephole to see who dared to just pop up on her. The moment his beautiful skin, long locks, and Afrocentric appearance come into view she felt her stomach churn. What the hell is he doing here? she wondered. *Certainly he's not here to bring diapers.* This was confirmed by his empty hands. She wanted to ignore him in hopes that he'd just turn around and go away, but she was sure that he'd already scoped out her car in the parking lot. She cursed her luck and reluctantly opened the door.

"What are you doing here?" she asked with her left hand on her hip and her right hand holding the doorknob, itching to slam the steel door in his face.

He smiled at her as if everything between them was cool and easy. "Hello to you too, beautiful. Are you going to let me in?"

She turned up her nose. "For the purpose of what?"

"Come on now, with the attitude. Let me in." Those hazel contacts covering his eyes only added to the effect of the fake look of innocence he was giving her. He licked his lips and smiled at her again. "Come on, sweetheart."

She rolled her eyes and stepped back against her better judgment. She didn't really have time for whatever bullshit stunt he was up to. She needed to drop Zoe off so that she could swing by and pick up Rico for their date. She needed some time outside of the house and away from Zoe for a little while. Although she loved her daughter with every fiber of her being, she still greatly appreciated the little adult time she was able to get.

She watched Khalil as he made his way over to her couch and comfortably took a seat. *Great,* she thought. *Obviously he intends to stay for a minute.* She wasn't too thrilled about that realization.

Khalil looked around the room and then craned his neck to look back toward the bedroom. "Where's Z?" he asked placing his hands on his knees.

"In the back in her playpen. Here, I'll go get her." Candace began to walk toward the bedroom.

"Hold up for a minute. Can we talk?" Khalil asked. He motioned for her to join him on the sofa.

Candace wanted to tell him to fly straight to hell on a one-way, first-class flight but tried to mask her contempt for him. They were coparenting, and although Khalil was sucking at it, Candace felt that it was her obligation, as Zoe's mother, to make sure that her father was welcomed into her life. Now, whether Khalil actually handled his business was on him, but Candace didn't want to have to explain to her daughter a decade from now why she'd let their personal differences affect her and Khalil's father-daughter relationship, so she tried to remain cordial at best. Slowly she walked over and sat on the sofa, making sure to leave some distance between them. The last time he'd come over she'd made the mistake of leaving herself way too open, and before she'd known it, Khalil was going down on her like it was his first pussy feast. If he thought that was going to happen again he could go fuck himself. Candace was tired of peddling backward with the man.

"How you been?" he asked her nonchalantly.

"Busy," she told him. "Just like I was busy before you just popped up over here."

"Busy doing what?"

"Taking care of your daughter." She crossed her arms. "That's something you should try to do more of."

"Now what's that's supposed to mean?"

"Exactly what I said. She's a baby, Khalil. She has needs. Like diapers, wipes, formula, clothes . . . all that good stuff. You promised me and my folks that you were going to be a responsible father—"

"I don't need anyone's parents to mandate me to do anything for my seeds," he commented cutting her off. "I'm a grown-ass man, Candace. I don't have anything to prove to your mom and dad."

Candace's eyebrow rose. "What about me and Zoe? You have anything to prove to us?"

He shook his head. "I do the best I can, sweetheart. Trying to take care of these other three kids, deal with this mess with Sheila—"

"Well, you created that mess," Candace interjected.

"And I'm trying to work on this book thing."

Candace was surprised. "What book thing?"

This was the first she'd heard about any literary endeavor.

"I'm writing a book," he said. "Based on my life and my experiences. It's about all the stuff I've learned from various women in my life."

"Women you've fucked?" Candace asked.

"Why you have to have such a filthy mouth?" Khalil asked, frowning. He reached over to touch his fingertips gently against her lips. "You're too beautiful to be having such a foul mouth. Plus I don't want my daughter picking up on that type of language."

Candace slapped his hand away and chuckled. "Right."

He shook his head and crossed his right leg over the left while leaning back. "Anyway, the book is about some of the different relationships I've had with women and the things I've learned from them. Like each chapter covers a different relationship, starting with my mom in chapter one."

Candace was curious. "Am I in the book?"

"It's full of the women that have impacted my life, beautiful. Of course you're in it."

She didn't know how she should feel about that. "And what kind of light did you paint me in?"

He grinned devilishly. "You'll have to read the book to find out."

Candace's phone buzzed. She looked down to see that she had a text from Rico.

Where are you? You on your way?

She knew that she had to hurry up and get Khalil's ass out of her house so that she could get over to Rico. They'd been hanging out for a while and things were good. She didn't want to do anything to mess that up, especially because of Khalil. Bored with talk about his phantom book that would probably never come to fruition she rose from the couch. "I'm going to go get Zoe for you now."

She left him in the living room and returned to the side of the playpen in her bedroom only to find the little angel fast asleep. She started to leave her there, but realized that she had to move her anyway to get her in her car seat so she could take her to her parents. Candace stuffed her cell phone into her bra and smiled at her daughter adoringly. As she reached over into the playpen she felt strong hands grab her from behind and pull her back. "What the hell!" she exclaimed out of shock.

"Shhh," Khalil whispered in her ear. "Let her sleep. Don't disturb her."

"It's fine. We were getting ready to go any-way." She wiggled a little to encourage him to release his hold on her.

Khalil had one arm across her chest and the other around her waist. He held her close to him and knew that she could feel the rising of his nature against her round ass. He leaned down and kissed her ear seductively before speaking. "You're not going anywhere."

"*Excuse* me?" She was becoming enraged. "Let me go, Khalil."

"You don't want that. You know you don't," he said gyrating against the back of her body.

"Get off of me." She grabbed at his arm cover-ing her chest.

Khalil ignored her. He took his left hand and squeezed her right breast with just enough force to make her wince for all the wrong rea-sons. Over time he'd come to learn exactly what to do to get Candace where he wanted her. Her body was his playground, and he knew which openings to tunnel through in order to get her to submit to him completely. His charm and his sexual expertise were the key attributes that lured her into his bed time and time again despite all of the drama they'd been through over the last year. The fact that he was married, had lied to her and her parents, lied on her to save his ass, ignored her often, and failed to be there for her and Zoe when she needed him, became distant memories the moment his hands began to take over her body.

Candace didn't want to fall prey to it tonight, but she could already feel the stirring between her legs. She'd had sex with Rico only a few times at his parents' house, and she had to admit that his dick game was nothing in comparison to Khalil. Khalil fell short as a father and as a boyfriend, and she used that term very lightly where he was concerned, but he never once left her feeling disappointed or dissatisfied sexually. Just the thought of the way he pleased her made her want to throw herself on the bed and open her legs for him without protesting further. But she didn't want him to see her as a punk. She didn't want to be conceived as a pushover, thus encouraging his behavior. She needed him to know that she wasn't his sexual slave and that he couldn't just run through and hit it real quick when it was his daughter that really needed something from him.

"You need to stop," she said, slowly losing her resolve. "I have a date."

"Forget that nigga," he said kissing the side of her neck while squeezing her nipple through her tank top.

"Khalil," she said in protest as she tried to turn her head away to ward off his advances. "Stop. This isn't right."

Her cell phone rang from its spot in her bra. Before she could reach up to pull it out Khalil grabbed it and pressed talk. Candace knew that it was either her mom or Rico calling to see where she was. Either way, she was afraid that Khalil was going to say something stupid and embarrassing to the caller. The last thing she needed was for anyone to know that he was up in her house like he lived there, answering her phone. She found the strength to knock his arm away and reached for her phone before he could say anything.

"Hello?" she answered breathlessly while shooting him an angry glare.

"Aye, where you at?" It was Rico. He sounded perturbed.

Candace looked over at the time on the clock on her dresser. She should have been gone thirty minutes ago. She cleared her throat. "I'm still at home. Got behind a little bit."

"We're not going to make that movie," Rico said. "So you might as well just come get me and we chill there."

"You want me to drive all the way back here?" She was further irritated now. Rico's parents lived in a beautiful, spacious home out in Snellville. The thought of taking Zoe to her parents' in Decatur, and then driving out to Snellville, only to make it back to her apartment in Doraville didn't sound very appealing to her.

"Yeah. You want to be alone, don't you?"

She could hear his background and understood why he was trying to get away. Rico had two younger sisters. Erica and Ebony were seventeen-year-old twins. She could hear their cackling in the background and the sound of loud music, which she was sure was some cheesy boy group that had the young girls going crazy these days. Between the twins and Rico's parents, Felicia and Rico Sr. who argued with each other day in and day out, the house was never silent. The times she'd hung out with the whole family she'd left with a massive headache. She preferred the visits when they were all at work and school, giving Rico and Candace the freedom to have sex or just chill in silence.

Khalil watched the frown lines in her face deepen and knew that whatever dude she was fucking with wasn't handling his business. He toyed with the string of her jogging pants and she slapped at his hand. He ignored her and struggled with her to pull the pants down. He dared her to say something to give herself away.

She held her right hand out as if to tell him to stop, but he wouldn't listen. She bent over and tried to back away from him before he could successfully get her clothes down. Her voice sounded strained and muffled as she tried to continue her phone conversation despite Khalil's trifling behavior. "Um . . . I don't know . . . I don't know about that."

"What you don't know?" Rico asked. "I'll shoot you some gas money, just come on and get me, please."

"Um . . . I . . . I still gotta take Zoe. Ugh!"

"What you doing?" Rico could tell that something wasn't right. "What's all that noise you're making?"

"Nothing . . . nothing. I dropped something. I was picking it up."

Khalil smiled wickedly as she fell back on her bed. He grabbed her pants and snatched them off.

"No!" she exclaimed. She couldn't help it and immediately became infuriated with Khalil for putting her in this position.

"No what?" Rico asked. "What the fuck?"

She didn't like him cursing at her, but now was not the time to go there with him. She tried to push Khalil away with her free hand, but he still managed to slip his strong hand between her thick thighs and stroke her kitty with his long, slender fingers. She knew that it was a wrap at this point. No longer able to fight him off she lay still as he parted her legs and fingered her while she stared at the ceiling. "I'm trying to do something," she said weakly into the phone. "I can't . . . I can't concentrate."

"Are you coming soon?" Rico just wanted to get to the bottom line.

"Mmm . . . not tonight," she purred. "I gotta go, Rico. Call me tomorrow." She ended the call before he heard anything further slip from her lips to belie the excuse she was giving him.

Khalil smiled victoriously. Whoever the hell Rico was, the brother wasn't getting any tonight. Instead, Khalil knew that he would be tapping this ass all over Candace's bedroom until his dick just couldn't rise anymore. He reached over and turned off her bedroom light. He didn't want his daughter to wake up and see what he was about to do to her mother. The sounds of Candace's pleasure filling the room were going to be detrimental enough. As he lowered his face to suck the cum that was slowly beginning to slip from her heated core, Khalil realized that he had a serious hold on her. No matter what Candace ever said or did, he knew that he could always get this pussy anywhere, anytime.

Chapter 7

Miranda

"I think my family understands," Bobby said. "I mean, they've always wanted to help me, but I just wasn't ready, you know? I wasn't ready. Nobody can help you when you're not ready."

Miranda rolled her eyes and huffed as she rocked in her chair. This shit was driving her crazy. They'd only been in the group session for twenty minutes and already she wanted to jump out of her chair, pounce on Bobby the meth addict, and scratch his eyeballs out. Some of the things they said in group session really annoyed her. Sure, she contributed nothing to the conversation ever but listening to the bullshit they were peddling between themselves was worse than sitting in the individual session with Dunham begging her to share her feelings.

The group was used to Miranda's silence and discouraging noises and facial expressions. On several occasions she'd been asked to respect the other members of the group, but it didn't change anything. Nothing they said could change the way she felt. She didn't understand why the others were fronting like these meaningless, empty words they were exchanging were really having some kind of effect on their mental and emotional states. It was bullshit. It was depressing. It made her want a hit to escape it all.

"When my sister caught me sucking her boyfriend's dick for that rock it, was over," Missy said from beside her. "She knew that I was using, and she was always trying to talk to me . . . see what was going on with me . . . But she had no idea that it was her boyfriend that was putting me on."

Miranda couldn't help but laugh. It was the most ridiculous thing she'd ever heard. The nervous laughter escalated as she replayed the words in her mind. Quickly the laugh turned into sobs. It was so ridiculously stupid and reminiscent of her own tragic story in a way. Missy's sister was like Stephanie. The memory of Stephanie finding her at the trap begging Corey's runner to let her cop something was probably one of the most humiliating moments of her life. The way she'd looked at her with pity and disgust made Miranda's stomach turn even now. Remembering that in the end her friend was dead made her tears fall faster. She'd never cried in group before, and the others were genuinely stunned.

Miranda closed her eyes and remembered Stephanie's judgment and tone. Although the girl was dead, Miranda knew that if she could go back in time to that moment on that stoop of that trap house in Decatur that she'd wring Stephanie's neck for making her feel like shit. Her fists clenched as anger replaced her despair. It wasn't fair. It wasn't fair for any of them to judge her. They didn't know shit, and they had no idea no matter what they ever said or did.

"Miranda?" Doctor Dunham called her name softly as the rest of the group watched her have her moment. "You have the floor . . ."

Miranda felt a hand on her shoulder, and she jumped.

"You'll feel better if you let it out," Missy said.

With her eyes still closed Miranda felt herself grow annoyed yet again. Who the hell were they fooling? She had no idea how discussing all the crap they did to themselves and others was going to make any of them feel any better. Besides, some of the shit she'd done to her friends was not anything she cared to discuss for various reasons. She swatted at her shoulder. She could still feel Missy's touch although her hand no longer rested there. Missy was a crackhead. Why was she supposed to take advice from a crackhead?

"We're all here to support you," Doctor Dunham tried to encourage her.

Miranda opened her eyes slowly and stared at the wall over Bobby's head. She focused all of her energy and emotions into that one tiny space on the ugly pale yellow wall of the community room they frequently met in for group. "They don't understand," she said slowly.

"They?" Doctor Dunham asked.

"They don't understand," Miranda repeated. "They may want you to be okay, to be like them, but they don't understand what's going on, where you are in life . . . mentally, emotionally. Not your family. Not your friends. Not your counselor. Not your doctor. No one. Unless they've been there. Unless they've scrounged through trash, been on their knees doing shiesty shit, abandoned all of their inhibitions and integrity just to get a hit, they don't understand. Unless they've been hurt more times than a few, physically and emotionally, they'll never ever ever understand. I don't give a shit what they say. And they can pretend to not know what the fuck's going on, but believe me, that's bullshit too. They know. They just choose to ignore it unless it begins to directly affect them. Damn what it's doing to you." She turned to the right to look at Missy with tears streaming from the corners of her eyes. "Your sister ain't stupid. If her man was dealing crack, she knew that shit.

She was just hurt that you were in her house giving him head. That's all. The fact that he was feeding you junk was a secondary thing, so spare me the regards for her fuckin' feelings."

Missy jumped up and glared down at Miranda, and Doctor Dunham hurried over to restrain her. Miranda didn't budge. She'd lived in fear for so long that she was over it. She wasn't afraid of a little scrapping if it came to it.

"Don't talk about my fuckin' family!" Missy shouted, pointing at her. "You don't know me and you damn sho' don't know them."

"Missy!" Doctor Dunham was trying her best to pull Missy away and direct her back into her chair.

"I know you," Miranda responded in an even tone. "I know you, and I know them."

"Fuck you, Miranda! You sit up here acting like you're above us and shit. You ain't shit, bitch. You just a junky like the rest of us. You ain't no better."

Miranda shrugged. "Y'all delusional as hell. Sitting up in here singing 'Kumbaya.' This is a joke."

"*You're* a joke!" Missy spat in Miranda's face, and Doctor Dunham swung the eighteen-year-old around.

"That's enough!"

Miranda finally jumped up. All of her crazed energy exploded the moment her feet hit the floor. She quickly snatched Missy's arm pulling her away from Dunham's protective hold. She pulled the girl by her shoulder-length, unruly cornrows with her left hand. The other group members hooped and hollered over the scene playing before their eyes. Some were scared, some were excited about the moment of raw emotion, and others were disturbed. Dunham's small shrill voice hollered for Miranda to release the girl as she tried her best to pry her fingers away from Missy's hair. Missy reached her hands out and grabbed Miranda's neck attempting to squeeze for dear life. While Miranda could feel the pressure, Missy's grasp wasn't strong enough to cut off her air supply. Her state of withdrawal was having an adverse effect on her body so Missy's physical strength was a lot weaker than she thought it was.

"Girls, please!" Doctor Dunham begged. She blew the whistle that was around her neck that she used to calm the group down during heated moments. No one was giving a damn about that whistle today, and Dunham was rapidly losing control. "This is unacceptable. They will lock you in confinement for this, ladies! Please."

Miranda didn't care about confinement or any other consequence that might come her way. She needed this bitch to know that she was not to be fucked with. Miranda was tired of people taking advantage of her emotionally and physically. The last time someone had disregarded her feelings they ended up dead. Miranda fully intended to show Missy that she was not the one. Miranda stuck her index and middle fingers of her right hand as far up Missy's nose as she could, and then yanked. Missy screamed out in pain as her nose ring came undone. She let go of Miranda's neck and stared into her dark eyes.

"Miranda, no!" Doctor Dunham was now tugging on Miranda's arm. "Bobby, run and get Poncho and Captain."

Poncho was the head of security, and Captain was the head of the center. Miranda knew that once they arrived she'd surely be in trouble, but she didn't care. All that mattered was this moment. Blood trickled down her arm as she continued to hook Missy's nose despite the girl's futile attempt to remove her hand and Doctor Dunham pulling on her. Missy was growing light-headed and had begun to waver back and forth. Within five minutes Poncho was behind Miranda grabbing her from her waist and pulling her away, forcing her to scratch the insides of Missy's nostrils as her fingers were ripped out of the girl's nose.

A nurse was there to attend to Missy, who instantly passed out. Miranda looked on emotionless as everyone crowded around the girl while the nurse tried to bring her back. Poncho forced Miranda's hands behind her back and placed them in restraints. She knew what was coming next but didn't care.

"Let's go!" he said pushing her out of the room.

Together they walked down the hall to the far end of the building where the female dorm-style boarding rooms were. They walked past room 106, which was Miranda's room that she shared with another girl, Alicia. She knew that it would be at least two days before she saw the inside of that room again. They turned right at the end of the hall and headed to one of the two isolation rooms.

Poncho opened the door, removed her restraints, and then pushed her inside. "You better hope that girl's not seriously injured," he said before slamming the door shut.

The sound of the lock made Miranda realize that she was alone. She was stuck in her own horror story, held captive by her addiction and the memories of how her life had spiraled out of control. They could lock her away forever in this empty room; it wouldn't matter. She was already locked in her own hell long before today.

Chapter 8

The Girls

"Has anyone heard from Miranda?" Candace asked as she wiggled her toes in the warm water of the pedicure foot bowl.

They were congregated at a nail salon in the heart of Decatur having a much-needed girls' day. Jada had decided a week ago that they all needed to get together and hang out. It was her way of trying to restore and strengthen their friendship following all the things that they'd gone through. Later they would be meeting their significant others at the Hibachi restaurant on Memorial Drive for an early dinner. They were all like family, and it was time for them to start coming together as such.

"I haven't," Jada answered. She stared at a bottle of hot pink polish trying to decide if she really wanted to add color to her nails. "But I think they said that they encourage them to not connect with anyone from the outside for a minute while they're there."

"That makes sense," Candace said nodding. "I mean, she's there to work on her. Reaching out to us and talking 'bout everything we have going on probably won't help her much."

"I don't know," Alex said, changing the setting on her massage chair. "If I was away somewhere and going through something, I'd want to call my girls and have visitors. I'd want someone to show their support for me, you know? I'd want someone to be there for me."

"You want someone to be there for you when ain't nothing wrong with you to begin with."

"Ha! Don't hate just 'cause I'm lovable, boo-boo."

"Loveable? Yep, that's the word I was thinking of."

Alex frowned at Candace and stuck her tongue out.

Jada remained silent. She was concerned about Miranda as well, but the issues going on at her home plagued her more. It wasn't something that she'd ever feel comfortable sharing with the girls. They'd either jump all over Jordan in her defense, or they would mock her since they felt that her relationship and life were so perfect. She was still feeling funny about her marriage and wasn't sure what was going on with her husband. Until she had something concrete to put on the table she figured it was best to keep her feelings and misgivings to herself.

"So we're finally going to get to see this new boo thang today, huh?" Alex asked Candace, changing the subject.

Candace smiled. "Yep. He's supposed to meet us there, so I want y'all to be nice to him."

"Why wouldn't we be?" Jada asked.

Candace eyed her friend. "Girl, you know you. You don't like nobody."

"That is not true. Y'all just be coming with some real trifling dudes. Don't blame me. Blame yourselves for your questionable taste."

"Ewww," Candace shot back. "Attitude! Calm down, girl. I'm just saying I like this man, so be nice."

"Uh-huh." Jada focused in on the nail tech that was beginning her pedicure. "So is this the same guy that you tried to convince me was your homeboy?"

Candace smiled innocently. "He was, sweetie. A relationship won't work if you don't start off as friends first. You have to have some kind of solid foundation."

"Listen to you," Jada said. "That's what you learned after three trifling relationships?" She giggled. "I'm just messing with you, girl."

"Not funny," Candace said. She knew that Jada considered her affair with Corey as her third trifling relationship. The first two were her failed marriage with Quincy and the second her affair with Khalil.

"Candace does have a point, though," Alex commented. "Just look at me and Clay."

"Poor Clay," Jada said. "It took forever for you to see that man, girl. Bless his little heart."

"He's a good boyfriend," Alex admitted. "He's a little controlling though."

"Controlling?" Candace asked sounding surprised. "Clay? He's cool as hell. How can he be controlling?"

"Not like a supernegative way. He's just like . . . you know . . . obsessive-compulsive, extremely organized, and überfocused."

"That's got to be quite a change from what you're used to," Jada said. "Don't be going around calling the man controlling. You're just not used to structure and having a man that's on top of his business. It's a good thing."

"Right," Alex said sarcastically. "You and Precious probably have more in common than I ever noticed." She laughed. "Anyway, Candace, go on, friend. Tell us about your new boo."

Candace smiled. She was more than willing to talk about her new beau. "Well, y'all already know that we went to high school together. He's a year younger than me and is really sweet and attentive. He makes me feel like I'm the most beautiful woman in the world, y'all. It just feels right when I'm with him."

"What does he do?" Alex asked as she handed the nail tech her left hand so she could start her manicure while another tech attended to her feet.

"Umm, well, he's looking into going to school for music production. He's really talented."

"That's cool. But where does he work?"

"He's between jobs right now. I'm trying to help him fix his résumé so that he can find something decent."

Jada's eyebrow went up, and she looked past Candace who was seated in the middle. Her eyes locked with Alexis, and they both shared a look of concern.

It was Jada that spoke on their sentiments. "He don't have job, girl?"

Candace shook her head. "Not right now. But he's looking."

"Did he have a job when you met him?"

Candace shook her head reluctantly. She really didn't want to discuss this with her girls, but she knew that it was going to come up eventually. "It's only temporary, so don't trip. He has potential. I know he'll find something soon. Sometimes you gotta stand by people you believe in and climb the stairs of success together."

"Who are you, and where is our friend?" Alex asked. "'Cause, honey, I have seen you walk away from a dude that didn't have a car, much less a job."

"Does he have a car?" Jada asked.

Candace shook her head again. "He's had some credit and license issues. He has some things to work out. That's all."

"Yeah, he needs to work out his life 'cause he has nothing to offer you," Alex said candidly.

"Don't go there," Candace warned. "I'm not so materialistic that I'm gon' pass on a really good guy just because he doesn't have a car."

"Right." Alex shook her head. "He don't have no job to buy one, either."

"All right, y'all, stop," Jada intervened. "If Candace is happy with her unemployed boo thang, then let her have that."

"I'd say thank you if that wasn't laced with sarcasm," Candace retorted.

Jada laughed. The thought of Candace laying up with a dude that had nothing was unbelievable. It was a part of the very reason that she'd previously bailed on her marriage to Quincy. When he lost his job it had sparked the flame of their other issues. Now here she was drooling over a dude that didn't have a job to lose. *Maybe she's growing*, Jada thought. *Maybe she's becoming less superficial and materialistic, which is a good thing.* But it was one thing to not be superficial and a completely different thing to be responsible with standards. Jada wondered if maybe her girl's standards were starting to slip. It would explain why she'd opened her legs to Corey months ago, being so unscrupulous as to have sex with her best friend's drug-dealing, shady-ass boyfriend.

"Where does this guy live?" Alex asked, still probing for information to prove that this guy was a loser.

Candace resented her for digging so deep but couldn't fix her mouth to lie about it. "With his parents," she said. "Just until he can get on his feet."

Alex was done. She'd had her share of bums, and if Candace couldn't see this guy for what he really was, then that was her problem.

Jada shook her head. *No standards,* she thought to herself. But who was she to judge? She was sitting there feeling that her husband was cheating on her yet hadn't made a move to find out or to do anything about it. She couldn't possibly school her girls on the status of their relationships when hers was falling apart at the seams.

Candace's phone rang. She pulled it out of her purse to check the caller ID. She didn't recognize the number and decided to send it to voice mail. The others noticed her action.

"What?" Alex asked. "Is that your boo telling you that he needs a ride?"

"I'm going to thank you to shut up," Candace snapped. "And anyway, he had a session at the studio with one of his homeboys. They're going to drop him off at the restaurant."

They each sat in silence thinking their own private thoughts. The salon workers spoke among themselves in their own language commenting on how catty the girls were to be friends.

"So how's Jordan?" Candace asked Jada, changing the subject.

Jada felt the tension seep into her body the moment she was asked about her husband. "He's fine. He'll be at dinner." It was all that she had to offer them.

"And the baby?"

"Fine," Jada stated. "We find out the sex next week. I'm hoping for a girl."

"I'm so happy you got the baby you wanted, Jada," Alex gushed. "If anybody deserves to be blessed with life it's you."

Her words were touching to Jada. "Thank you," Jada said smiling down at her feet as the nail tech filed her toenails. "I'm excited."

Candace noticed that she didn't say "we're excited" but decided not to say anything about it. "Yeah, you're more the mother type than me," she said instead. "I'm sure this will be a breeze for you, Martha Stewart. You're the homemaker, soccer mom type."

Was that an insult? Jada wondered.

"Uh-huh," Alex cosigned. "I know Jordan is living the life. He probably gon' be giving everybody and their neighbors cigars when you drop that baby."

Jada felt her chest tighten. If only Jordan really was that excited about the birth of their first child. She could feel an anxiety attack coming on and prayed that she did not embarrass herself in the nail shop. She wanted them to change the subject. Talking about it definitely was not going to help her to feel any better.

"Choose your color," the nail tech said to her.

Jada looked at the bottle of hot pink polish again, then decidedly picked up the white polish. "French tips, please," she said. It was better to be safe and not deviate from the script. She felt the same way about her relationship. It was best not to say anything to her girls right now. She just needed to go on as if everything was normal until she knew for sure. For now, it was best for her to just not think about it.

The girls stood in the waiting area at the restaurant as they awaited their other halves. The aroma from the buffet was enticing Jada. She was on the verge of saying screw it and asking to be seated despite the fact that their whole party hadn't arrived. As time went on in her pregnancy she noticed that she was becoming hungrier and hungrier. Thinking that it was normal she didn't see anything wrong with feeding her face the moment hunger struck. Lately she'd been eating large bowls of Fruit Loops and calling it a snack.

Candace's phone rang. She pulled it out of her purse and hoped that it wasn't Rico calling to say that he couldn't get a ride out. She'd just stood up for him back at the nail shop. It wouldn't do for him to bail on her and give her friends more trash to talk about the man they'd never met. Much to her relief she saw that it wasn't him calling. It was the same number that had hit her up earlier at the shop. She sent the call to voice mail yet again.

"Somebody's trying to get up with you," Alex commented.

"Yeah, well, I don't answer numbers I don't recognize," Candace said placing the phone back in her purse. "So if they really want something they better leave a message."

Alex opened her mouth to respond, then her focus shifted when she saw Clay enter the restaurant. "Precious!" she called out to him.

Clay sauntered over looking like the suave gentleman that he was in his classic khakis, blue, green, and white plaid button up, with matching plaid Skip's. "Hey, babe." He greeted Alex with a hug and a kiss before throwing his arms around Jada and Candace. "Hi, ladies. Good to see you again."

"Good to see you too, hon," Candace said smiling. She was happy for her friend. She'd finally hooked a guy with some manners and husband potential.

"How you doing, Clay?" Jada asked.

"Doing well," he responded. "I can't complain. How's the baby?" He smiled at her baby bump.

Jada rubbed her stomach. "Absorbing every bit of food I ever consume and pressing on my bladder nonstop. But other than that, thriving very well. We find out the sex next week," she repeated for him.

"That's exciting. I'm happy for you and Jordan." Clay put his arm around Alex. Seeing expectant parents made him feel some kind of way. It was what he wanted for him and Alex in the future.

"Thank you," Jada said softly as she felt her own cell phone vibrating inside of her bra.

Clay laughed as he watched her pull it out. "Convenient pocket," he said playfully.

Jada smiled and shrugged. "At least I never lose it up here." She pressed talk on her phone and walked away from the group to answer the call.

The trio chattered for a bit before the doors of the restaurant flung open and a short, almond-complexioned young man made his way inside. His neck was covered by chains that were cheap replicas of those donned by rappers. His black T-shirt did very little to cover up his blue plaid boxers that were exposed due to his army fatigue pants sagging. Alex tooted her nose, disgusted by his tacky demeanor. Clay was turned off by the way the young man had made such a display of entering the door by flinging open both doors. Candace, on the other hand, looked thrilled to lay eyes on him.

As the guy approached the group Candace held her hand out to him. "Guys, I want you to meet my boyfriend Rico."

Alex wanted to fall to the floor. She was dismayed by the sight before her. This guy was nothing like any of the qualities that Candace usually sought in a man. She wondered what in the world attracted her friend to him.

"What's up?" Rico asked. He held his hand out to Clay. "How you doing, man?"

Clay shook his hand respectfully. "Good. How you doing, bruh? I'm Clay, and this is my girlfriend Alex."

Alex forced her lips into a smile, but she knew that her eyes were dancing with confusion. "Hi," she said weakly.

Candace tightened her grip on the short man's hand. "How did it go at the studio?"

Rico shrugged. "A'ight I guess. Dre made a beat that goes hard, but you know my lyrics gon' make it sick."

Listening to him talk was making Alex sick. Looking at Rico she felt as if she knew him. Not personally, but she knew his type. Dating her ex, T, a proclaimed rapper who had nothing, she knew what it was like to be in a relationship with Rico's type. She made a mental note to pull Candace to the side later or call her up for a one-on-one to hip her to some game. Whatever she thought she saw in this joker was some bullshit and Alex didn't want her friend to get caught up in any of the drama she'd gone through with T.

Jada returned to the group with a solemn look on her face. This whole thing had been her idea, and now she had to change it up on them. "Hey, guys." She was about to break the bad news to them but was immediately taken aback by the appearance of Candace's guy. He was nothing like the other men Candace had been involved with.

"Jada, this is Rico," Candace said catching her friend's glance. "Rico, this is my girl, Jada."

Rico smiled. "How you doing?"

Jada gave a polite smile in return. "I'm good. Nice to meet you. Umm, ladies, I'm sorry, but I'm going to have to leave you. Jordan's not able to make it, and I just remembered that I promised my mom I'd do something."

Alex frowned. "Seriously, friend?" It wasn't like Jada to forget anything.

Jada nodded. "Yeah. I'm sorry. But you guys enjoy dinner, and I'll get up with you soon. I promise." She gave both of her friends tight squeezes before moving to leave.

"Call me, girl," Candace said. She was eager to get Jada's opinion about Rico even though she wasn't sticking around to actually get to know him.

"Okay," Jada said. She waved to the group and walked out of the restaurant.

Chapter 9

Jada

She was angry. She'd planned this outing a week ago, but Jordan picked the hour that he was supposed to show up to let her know that he couldn't make it. She felt humiliated and disappointed. Her little voice was speaking to her again. As she slid into the driver's side of her car she felt her breathing escalate to irregular spurts.

No, she thought. *No, I can't do this now.* She held on to the steering wheel and tried her best to remain composed, but it was not to be. The panic attack was coming no matter how much she willed herself to get it together. She heaved uncontrollably and wrapped her arms around herself. Her eyes grew wide as her body spazzed out. She hadn't even been able to close the door upon getting in the car before the attack took over her. Shaking and trying hard to fight against her panicked breathing, Jada didn't notice the older woman getting out of the car beside her.

The woman was initially annoyed that Jada hadn't bothered to close her door. But as she was about to try to squeeze past the open door she heard the sounds of trouble coming from inside the car. The woman peeked in and saw Jada convulsing in her seat. "Ma'am!" the woman called out concerned. "Ma'am, are you okay? Are you having a seizure, sweetie? Are you okay?"

Jada heard her but couldn't respond. All she could do was sit there feeling her body shaking and her tears clouding her vision. The woman could see Jada's belly and realized that she was with child. She figured that since she was still sitting upright that a seizure could be ruled out. Her spirit spoke to her, and the woman rounded the front of Jada's car and got in on the passenger side. Without saying a word the woman threw her arms around Jada. She could feel her body quaking under her embrace but held her as tightly as she could. She'd seen this on an episode of *Grey's Anatomy*. A surgeon had been suffering from a panic attack and asked two other surgeons to apply pressure to her body in the form of a hug. The woman hoped that watching television had proved to be beneficial in this instance or else this young girl was in serious trouble.

Within a matter of minutes the woman could feel Jada's shaking lessen to a mere tremble and her breathing was becoming more relaxed. The technique was working. Now that the crisis had been averted Jada felt ashamed and distraught. Her feelings now became released in the form of a hearty cry.

"It's okay," the stranger said to her. "It's okay. You just let it out. Sometimes we have to just let it out."

Jada didn't know who this woman was, but she was glad that she'd been there to get her through the emotional moment. It was funny to her how God worked. None of her friends had realized that she was falling apart, but the second she lost it in the parking lot this stranger, an angel, came from nowhere to assist her.

"Thank you," Jada said pulling away from the woman who smelled like lilac. "I'm so sorry."

The older woman smiled at her. "There's no need to be sorry, honey. You can't help that you were having a moment. It happens to the best of us. I'm just glad that I could be here with you. You're having a baby," she said looking down at Jada's belly.

Jada nodded. It was feeling more and more awkward sitting in her car talking to a complete stranger.

"Your emotions are probably all over the place now," the woman said. "Bless your heart. Whatever it is, suga, you gotta pray on it and let that go. That baby feels everything you feel and the worst thing we can do is fill our impressionable, innocent beings with the anguish of us adults."

"Yes, ma'am."

The woman smiled. "Do you go to church, dear?"

Jada shook her head. "I haven't in a while."

The woman pulled a card out of her handbag and handed it to her. "Take this, baby. I'm Evangelist Betty Peters, and I started my own church. We're just two months old, and we meet at my house, but the Lord goes wherever He's called upon. I want you to consider coming and joining us one Sunday. You and your husband. We're down-to-earth folk, come as you are. We're just interested in getting to know the Word and praising God for all He's done for us."

Jada took the card and nodded.

"My brother died this morning," the woman told Jada. "I been crying all day. Me and my siblings decided to meet up here for dinner so we could shake off some of this somberness surrounding us. Plus we needed to eat," she said chuckling. "But I know what it's like to be consumed with stress and hurt, honey. Just feeling the way your body was trembling and hearing the vigor of your sobs I can tell a hurt spirit. Anyway, I hope you'll come out and worship with us, but if you don't, I want you to remember that whatever's going on, God's with you, baby. This is a happy time in your life. He didn't mean for you to be consumed with sadness when He's given you such a great gift."

Jada looked into the woman's eyes and felt herself about to start crying all over again. The woman reached over and squeezed her hand lovingly. "I'ma be praying for you, suga. What's your name?"

"Jada," she said. "Jada Presley."

"Beautiful name. I'm gonna pray for you, baby. I'm gonna pray for you by name. I'm not going to hold you up now. Please get home safely and I hope you'll come on out and see us." She exited the car and gently closed the door behind her.

Jada pulled her own door shut and watched as the woman disappeared into the restaurant where she was sure her friends were happily eating and not giving her a second thought.

She looked down at the simple black-and-white business card and considered the idea of visiting the woman's in-home church. She knew that Jordan would never agree to it. She placed the card in her purse, put on her seat belt, and then turned the ignition. It was time to go home and deal with her problem.

Standing in her bedroom she didn't know where to start. Something was going on with Jordan, and she was going to get to the bottom of it. When he'd called her at the restaurant to say that he'd gotten caught up out in Riverdale with his cousins she knew that they were headed down a dark path. He'd never stood her up in the two years that they'd been together. Calling her while she was there with the whole group and forcing her to apologize on their behalf was rude. If he hadn't wanted to go he should have been honest a week ago when she'd first brought it up to him. The fact that he canceled on her at the last minute really made her question the sincerity of his excuse. Was he really with his family or was he somewhere else? With the problems they'd been having lately Jada wouldn't have been surprised.

She began to go through his underwear drawer, and then his T-shirt drawer. She wasn't sure what she was looking for but was certain that she'd know it once she found it. Moments later she opened the smaller closet that housed only his things. She looked inside of shoe boxes, pants pockets, and felt around on the top shelf. Nothing. His laptop was sitting on the table in the living room. She took a seat on the sofa and lifted the top of the computer. The log-in screen appeared, and it dawned on her that she didn't know his password. She'd never had a desire to know it before. She made a mental note to demand the password the moment he returned home.

Frustrated, she lowered her head into her hands and sighed. She was running out of outlets to find the explanation for her husband's current behavior. The baby fluttered, and she remembered that she was hungry. She could have stayed with the others at the hibachi grill, but she hadn't wanted to feel out of place or answer subsequent questions about her husband's absence. She shook her head and looked in the direction of the cabinet where Jordan hid his liquor. She really could have used a drink at that moment but knew that it was a definite no-no. Thinking about the fact that he was hiding the liquor in that cabinet made Jada wonder what else her husband was hiding from her in there.

She rose from the couch, walked over, then bent down to open the cabinet. Sitting on the floor in front of it she pulled out the half-drunk bottle of Crown Royal that stood in the front. Next she pulled out a bottle of Golden Grain. She smiled at the thought of the liquor's potency. But once she reached her hand inside again . . . Her smile dropped. She pulled out a black notebook and looked at it questioningly. She'd never seen the book before. Opening it to the first page she immediately realized that this was his journal. *What grown man keeps a journal?* she asked herself. She breezed through the first entry and concluded that it was about work, his goals, and how much he loved her. The next couple of pages were the same, and then the entries stopped. The rest of the pages were blank.

She was a little relieved to have found nothing and was about to put the notebook back . . . until she noticed a slip of paper hanging from the bottom toward the back of the book. She turned to the page and removed the orange slip of paper. It was a flyer for a sale at some store, but Jada was disinterested in it. Her attention was stolen by the first words on the entry that rested on that page.

There's just something about her. I can't describe how I feel when I talk to her. It's nothing like I've ever felt before. She understands things, and I don't have to apologize for my feelings or thoughts when I talk to her. I can just be myself. And she is so beautiful. I can't wait until I get to see what she feels like.

The entry stopped there. Jada couldn't believe her eyes. She flipped the pages one by one until she was completely through the book. There was nothing else written. It was clear to her that he'd placed that entry way in the back just in case she ever decided to open his little journal. The entry was dated. May 12, 2011. That was a little less than a month ago. Jada remembered the text message that Jordan had sent her by accident and his lame-ass explanation for it. *Online shit-talking, my ass,* she thought as she struggled to get off of the floor. She was furious. She pulled her cell phone from her bra and quickly dialed his number.

"What's up, babe?" he answered sounding annoyed.

"You have about thirty minutes tops to get your ass home before I start burning some of your shit," she warned him. "Then what's left will be sitting outside when you get here."

"What? What are you talking about?" The noise in his background was loud, but Jada was sure that he heard her loud and clear.

"If you value your marriage you'll get your ass home now or you can kiss my ass good-bye." She hung up. There was nothing else to say. Pissed, she waddled back into her bedroom and pulled her suitcase out of the closet. If he thought she was going to just sit there and ignore the fact that he was cheating on her he could go fuck himself. She wasn't that docile little housewife that everyone assumed she was.

As she threw random articles of clothing into her bag, tears of anger began to drop. She felt like she'd cried a river today. She thought about where she was going to go. She couldn't go to Alex's because she didn't want to disturb her and Clay. She didn't feel comfortable asking Candace if she could stay over because she assumed that her new boyfriend would already be there squatting. She refused to go to her mother's because she didn't want her to know that she and Jordan were having problems. The second she got wind of that the whole family would be in her business. Pulling out her cell again she dialed another number.

"What's up li'l sis?"

She knew that her brother would give her good advice. "I'm pissed," she said.

"Why? What happened?"

"I want to kill Jordan."

"What he do?" Antwan's voice was filled with concern.

"I think he's cheating on me."

"Why you think that?"

Jada stuffed a shirt into her bag angrily. "Because I found his little journal detailing his bullshit."

"You over there going through dude's stuff?" Antwan asked sounding amazed.

"Well, I knew something wasn't right," she explained. "I didn't expect to find the journal, but I did. So I read it."

"That nigga slippin' on his pimpin'. Writin' shit down. That's one of the first rules of doin' dirt. Don't leave no communication trail."

Jada huffed. She didn't call him to listen to him run down rules of the game. She needed somewhere to go. "Where are you? You at home?"

"Why?" he asked suspiciously.

"What you mean why? 'Cause I'm leaving. I'm not staying around for this crap."

"You can't live with me, and I know you're not going to Mom's house. Stop being silly."

Jada pouted. "I'm not being silly. What do you expect me to do?"

"Is that your house?"

"Yes!" she barked into the phone. "So?"

"So why the hell are *you* leaving your home in the middle of the evening with that baby in your belly? If somebody gotta go let his ass leave. But, Jada, on everything I love, if you leave that house I'm going to whip your ass."

Jada was confused. She plopped down on the bed next to her bag and stared at the wall. None of this was making any sense. "So I'm supposed to just sit here?"

"I give a damn what you do, and you better not do it outside of that house."

"Gee, thanks."

"I'm sure you'll figure out how to handle the situation without losing the upper hand."

Jada was feeling defeated. She sighed and ended the conversation. "Fine, but if I kill him you better bail me out of jail."

Chapter 10

Jordan

His heart was racing as he tried his best to save face and remain calm in front of his cousin Tony. He'd been playing spades with the fellas and drinking a few beers when Jada had called to threaten him. He knew that she was pissed about him bailing on their little group date, but this behavior was irrational and unlike his wife. If all of this was about his failure to show up this evening then he was going to suggest that she get counseling. Over-the-top behavior was not attractive to him. He started to pull out his cell phone and tell Mona about the drama he was dealing with but decided against it. He wasn't going to be able to respond once he got in the house, and it didn't make sense to start a conversation he couldn't finish. Besides, he didn't even know the full extent of the drama he was about to walk into so he figured it was just best to sit tight and wait to see what happened.

"You a'ight, bruh?" Tony asked glancing over at him as he pulled into Jordan's complex.

Jordan nodded and tried to appear unfazed. "Yeah, man. I just needa see what's going on with Jada. Everything's cool." He suddenly wished that he'd driven himself verses riding out with Tony earlier. He could have called Jada back in private to try to diffuse the situation or at the very least not have to worry about being scrutinized by his cousin. Jordan knew that he had to keep himself in check because he didn't want his marital issues being the talk of his family the moment Tony pulled out of the parking lot.

Tony parked next to Jordan's car in front of his cottage-style apartment home. "You want me to come in with you, bruh?"

Jordan sucked his teeth. "Man, stop playing. I'll get at you later. Thanks for the ride." He hurried out of the car before Tony could make another joke about his situation.

As he hopped down the stairs leading to his private sidewalk to get to the front door he took a deep breath. Whatever he was about to walk into he hoped that it was not going to end horribly. He felt it was a good sign when he didn't smell smoke coming from inside and didn't see his clothes strewn about outside like she'd threatened to do nearly an hour ago. He let himself inside the house and was surprised to find the house dark minus the row of candles that started at the front door. He'd nearly knocked the first one over when he stepped in. Jordan closed the door behind him and carefully followed the pattern of the first four candles. He was confused. If Jada was pissed, then why the romantic setting?

"Babe, I'm here," he called out. He stood still to see if he could hear any movement. Hearing nothing he continued to follow the row of candles all the way to their bedroom where he found his wife sitting on the bed dressed in a black nightgown and holding a candle. "Hey," he said from the doorway.

"That took longer than thirty minutes," she pointed out, referring to his trip home.

"I was riding with Tony. Had to wait a minute 'til he was ready. You okay?"

She shook her head. "No, I'm not okay." She reached behind her and pulled out a black notebook that looked familiar. "And this is why."

As Jada waved the leather-bound book in the air it hit him. That was his journal. He'd written some things in there that he'd never intended for Jada to find. He thought he'd been smart about it by putting the true stuff in the back of the book. He wasn't sure if she was mad that he was keeping a journal or if she was smarter than he thought and was mad because she'd found his secret.

"What you doing with that?" he asked nonchalantly.

"Learning about my piece of crap-ass husband," she answered. "You know, I didn't know that you had an interest in writing. All this time and I just didn't know that."

"Nothing wrong with jotting your thoughts down," he said shifting his weight from one foot to the other.

"Hmm. Let me share my favorite part with you." She laid the book down on the bed and turned to a back page that she'd dog-eared.

Jordan swallowed a lump in his throat and began to run down a list of excuses in his head as she read his words out loud. He had no idea how he was going to get out of this one, but he knew that no matter what lie he handed her, he was going to be in the doghouse for sure.

"And she is so beautiful. I can't wait until I get to see what she feels like," Jada said reading the last sentences of the entry. She turned and looked at him. "What the fuck was that?"

"I was starting a story." The lie just rolled off of his tongue.

"What?"

"I made it up. I was starting to write a story."

Jada's eyes grew wide with anger. "Do I look stupid to you? Do I look like some stupid-ass woman that doesn't know the difference between sugar and shit?"

"Come on, babe. I'm trying to tell you it's nothing. Either you believe me or you don't."

Jada was feeling his attitude. "Uh-huh." She held the book up over the flame from the candle. "Well, your story stinks and should be burned."

She lowered the book and the page caught the fire. Jordan leapt forward, snatched the book, and quickly put out the flame before things got out of hand. Jada set the candle on the night-stand and rose from the bed. She walked out to the linen closet and retrieved a blanket and pillow. Jordan followed her to the living room, carefully stepping around the candles.

"What are you doing?" he asked her.

She tossed the linen onto the sofa and turned to face him. "I'm putting you out of the bedroom indefinitely." She crossed her arms. "Now I'm going to ask you again. What the hell is going on?"

"Babe, I told you already," he said giving her a pitiful expression.

"Yes, you told a lie. Now try the truth."

"It is the truth."

She walked past him. "I'm leaving you," she said nonchalantly.

He turned around in a panic. "What?"

She stopped in front of the wall where their marriage certificate hung. In the blink of an eye she snatched it down, slapped the frame against the wall causing it to shatter, pulled the certificate out of the fragmented glass, and dropped the remainder of the frame to the ground. She held the certificate up for him to see. "You and me . . . us. We're over. You can't even be bothered to be honest after you've been caught. I'm giving you two weeks to find yourself somewhere else to live." She looked at him as if she expected him to say something.

"Come on," he begged. "Why are you doing all this? This is crazy."

"This is crazy?" she questioned. "You put your dirt in ink and told me it was a story in your defense, but *I'm* crazy?"

"Look, I'm telling you the truth, woman! It was nothing. I didn't even finish it. You saw that for yourself."

"You're a bad liar, Jordan," she said seething. "You're a bad liar, and I'm sorry that I ever, ever met you." She dropped the paper, and it landed on top of one of the burning candles.

They both watched as the marriage certificate went up into flames. Jordan grabbed the blanket from the sofa and hurriedly smothered the flames. His breathing was uneven, sweat dripped from his forehead, and his heart was racing by the time the fire was out. The marriage license was barely legible. A black mark smeared their names and only fragmented edges remained where their wedding date used to be. It was a symbol of how their relationship was now marred by his dishonesty and creeping.

"You trying to set the damn house on fire?" he asked Jada as he wiped sweat from his eyes.

"Why not? This marriage has already gone to hell; you might as well follow on behind it." She turned to leave the room.

Jordan grabbed her arm. "Bae, really? What the hell?"

She snatched her arm away and screamed at him. "You tell me what the hell. I'ma ask you one more fuckin' time, Jordan. What the hell is going on?"

Jordan was stuck. He knew she wasn't buying it. He thought that if he stuck to the lie long enough, no matter how weak it was, she'd give in and just believe him. He didn't expect her to go Carrie on him and try to set the place on fire. He walked over to the sofa and slumped down on the scorched blanket.

"You're little entry wasn't made up, was it?" Jada challenged from across the room.

Jordan shook his head no.

Jada crossed her arms. "You've been messing with someone else," she stated rather than asked.

Jordan shook his head again. "I've only been talking to her. I ain't fucked nobody. I haven't gone to see her. Nothing. Just talking."

"I read your words, Jordan. You marveled on and on about how beautiful this woman is, how good you feel with her. All while your pregnant wife walks around here taking care of your sorry ass and nurturing your unborn kid. What the fuck is that?"

"It was a stupid thing," he admitted. "It was stupid and thoughtless. But, baby, I swear it means nothing. All I want is you."

"All you want is me, huh?" she asked sarcastically.

"Yes, bae. I love you. You know I love you. There's no other choice here other than you. You're all I want."

Jada shook her head. "You stole my choice," she said softly feeling her eyes fill up. "I wanted to be married to a man that I felt would always protect me and love me, causing me no pain . . . Instead, you've got me married to a man who won't hesitate to lie to me. Why should I believe anything you ever say?"

Jordan shrugged his shoulders. "I don't know what you want me to say, babe. I'm telling you the truth. I'm coming clean here."

"Clean, my ass. Look how many times you lied. And you're still not being completely honest."

Jordan stared at the floor. *Damned if I do, damned if I don't,* he thought to himself. Now it was probably best to just remain quiet. Anything else he said would only be turned against him.

"We're broken, Jordan," Jada said after a long pregnant pause. "We're broken, and I don't know how we can ever be fixed."

Jada disappeared into the bedroom closing the door behind her. Jordan exhaled. He was glad that Tony hadn't come in to witness this psychotic scene. He knew that Jada was a force to be reckoned with, but this was the first time that he'd seen how crazy she could get. He knew that she was hurting, and it hurt him that he was the cause of her pain, but how could he tell his wife that their marriage had changed the moment she discovered she was with child? Sighing, he rose from the floor and blew out the candles. So much for the romantic mood he thought that she was setting. Jordan looked over at his blanket and pillow lying on the sofa. Apparently this was going to be his home for however long it took to get back in Jada's good graces.

Chapter 11

Corey

"On the charges of first-degree murder, we, the jury, find Corey Polk not guilty. On the charges of conspiracy to commit murder, we, the jury, find Corey Polk not guilty."

A mixture of emotions ran rampant through the courtroom as the juror issued the verdict. The mother and uncle of Montae Stokes were livid. They had been certain that justice was going to be served, but yet, they'd just heard the worst news ever since learning about Montae's death. Some concerned citizens who were also in attendance hoped to hear a guilty verdict but were surprised to hear that things had turned around in Corey's favor. They now feared that their neighborhood would once again be taken over by Corey's team. In Corey's absence, the hustle lessened but hadn't completely stopped.

They attributed the decline in visible drug sales to the fact that Corey was locked away. Now that he was a free man again the citizens knew it would be back to business as usual again.

Corey was elated to hear the verdict. His dick of an attorney had been right after all. He was about to be a free man. It was time to handle a lot of things that couldn't have been done successfully while he was in jail. The citizens had a right to attribute the change in their community to Corey's absence, but what they didn't understand was why. Although Corey's right hand was still sending out runners, they had to do this on a smaller scale due to the lack of money to invest in the business, thanks to the dudes that had robbed Stephanie. Though Corey's crew wasn't the only weed and dope pushers in town most other crews knew not to step in his territory until everything was said and done. It wouldn't be good to start a takeover war not knowing if the king of the DEC was going to resurface anytime soon. Yes, everyone knew to hold their positions, including Montae's squad, but for different reasons. They were laying low. After killing Corey's girl there was no way any of them would show their face in his hood for fear that one of his men would off them on sight. They too were taking a wait-and-see position.

At the back of the courtroom sat a man that no one recognized. They shouldn't have. He was as nondescript and unnoticeable as they come. He had a vested interest in the outcome of this case being that the dope Corey was pushing massive amounts of hailed from his family. The Black Dope Mafia was hitting Atlanta hard, and Corey was a key player in getting things moving. BDM originated in New York around the time that the Junior Black Mafia was nearing the end of its reign in Philly being the feds stepped in and indicted their founders and key runners. In an effort to take over the Eastern drug game, BDM was steadily working to build powerful hubs in Atlanta, Florida, and New Jersey. Founded by Thomas "Tommy" Castello, the organization was making moves and putting out prime product with direct imports from authentic cartels in the heart of Bolivia. No one had purer cocaine than Tommy was bringing in to the States, and the dealers were taking notice. The problem with that was that Emilio Martinez, a rival kingpin, was trying his best to make his mark in the city and make BDM a thing of the past. Even worse, the Drug Enforcement Administration was paying attention as well and with BDM's entrance into Atlanta, the GBI was conspiring with the DEA to bring the organization down.

Johnny "Knuckles" Lyles was sitting in the courtroom taking in the entire experience so that he could carry the information back to Tommy. They were a private group. They tried their best not to have their faces out and about too much, but today was a big day. They needed to know how to deal with Corey and what moves to make next. Thanks to his fallacy in getting rid of Montae Stokes, a punk runner who was moving for Emilio Martinez, the feds were looking at them harder. Given the way Corey had botched up the job by leaving behind evidence, the heat was on. They needed to ensure that Corey wasn't going to talk, locked up or not. And now that they'd lost their key witness, BDM feared that the feds would go harder at trying to pin an indictment on any other players. Corey could be the fuckup in their plan.

Now that Knuckles knew that Corey was getting out, things needed to be done, discussions needed to be had, and moves needed to be made. As the trial proceeded with the formalities to adjourn all parties, Knuckles rose and made his way quietly out of the courtroom. There was no need to communicate with Corey with so many eyes and ears around. He knew where to find him, and he knew when would be best. He just hoped that things would go smoothly and that any further bloodshed could be spared. Corey was a thirsty kid, and he possessed great potential, but Knuckles had no problem eliminating him if his association with BDM continued to be problematic.

"How's it feel to be a free man?" Phelps asked, biting into an apple.

Corey had just walked out of the back doors of the jail after being processed out. Breathing in the crisp fall afternoon air made him grateful for every moment spent outside of the stale, stifled atmosphere of the Fulton County Jail. He eyed his attorney as he stood near the gate munching his snack like a horse. He hated the man because of the fucked-up judicial and legal system that he represented, but he was gladder to have the short man in his pockets seeing as though he'd just helped him get out of a situation that could have turned his whole life around. The time that he was facing with that murder charge was unreal. But now he had a whole other battle to fight now that he was back out in the streets.

"Feels like I need a decent meal, a blunt, and some head," Corey said honestly. "If you can't help me with that, then we best be parting ways now."

"Can I drop you somewhere?"

Corey shot him an astonished look. Where the hell did he think that he was going to drop him off to? He didn't want anyone in the streets catching him with dude. Everything he needed to do he needed to ride solo. Corey peered down the street and noticed an old-school Mustang idling. He knew that Mustang.

"I'm straight," Corey told Phelps. "Anything else I need to know?"

"Yep. Don't leave the country."

"What the fuck?" Corey wasn't in the mood for fuckery.

"Don't leave the country. You're exonerated of that murder charge, but you're going to be tried for possession with the intent to distribute. Lucky for you the judge allowed us to post bail."

Corey shook his head. His troubles never seemed to end. "Yeah, so when that happens get at me. I'm not leaving the country or the state so you can relax."

"I'll be in touch," Phelps said.

Corey rolled his eyes and waved him off. "Yeah. Later." He looked at him and waited for the man to catch a clue.

Phelps raised his eyebrows and pursed his lips in an "excuse me" manner before nodding his head and taking off toward his modest Toyota

Camry. Corey shook his head as he watched the man pull off. *Where the fuck did he think he was taking me in his wife's car?* Corey thought. Putting his hands in his pockets and surveying his environment without appearing too paranoid, he hurriedly opened the passenger door and slid into the awaiting Mustang. The moment the door closed the Mustang peeled off.

"Where to?" Antonio asked as the jail grew smaller in his rearview.

"My mom's house. I need some food and a long fuckin' shower," Corey responded. "Put ya' ear to the ground and find out where them muthafuckers hiding at. Somebody's gon' answer for the shit that's gone down. What your stash looking like?"

"Man, we dry as hell, bruh. Not one bit of powder. Got that mid running all day but powder is a no-go. You know only you got the line to the connect," Antonio said sarcastically.

Corey nodded. He wasn't so sure that the connect was going to want to fuck with him after the way things went down. For the life of him he couldn't figure out why the hell Stephanie threw Montae's wallet out and how the fuck the feds were able to find it in the public Dumpster she'd put it in. What he did know was that the BDM, the connect that he answered to, was going to feel some kind of way about the ceasing of dope from his stash house and the money that was taken from Stephanie. Some of it was his, but most of it was owed to BDM for fronting him with the dope he'd been putting out at the time. Tommy Castello had trusted him and now because of his dead baby mama's futile attempt to help him and his inability to do a proper job of getting rid of Montae, Corey knew that he was going to have to come up with something to appease BDM. In the meantime, he needed to make sure that he put the word out that his family wasn't to be fucked with. There was only one way to do that.

"I need a new phone and some steel by tomorrow," Corey ordered.

Antonio nodded. "I got you. You already know."

Corey looked out of the window as they rode through the familiar streets of the neighborhood he ran. *I'm home, niggas*, he thought to himself as they passed down Memorial Drive. *Bring it!* Thinking about the fact that he wasn't returning home to Stephanie made his blood boil. The streets were about to be live. Corey was ready for war.

Chapter 12

Candace

The phone rang three times before going to voice mail. This was the seventh time she'd called him today. It was just like him to go silent and be MIA the moment she truly needed him. Candace wanted to kick herself for her moment of weakness weeks ago. She should have never let him into the house, much less into her body. She cursed his sexy lips, talented tongue, and probing hands. The man was definitely bad for her.

"Khalil, it's me again," she said to his voice mail. "I really need you to call me back. Or if you want to stick to the script and do what you usually do, can you just pop up over here and this time bring some diapers with you? Zoe's running out, and I don't get paid until the end of next week. Please." She disconnected the call and tossed the phone onto the bed.

She hated having to ask him for anything, but he was Zoe's dad. The least he could do was pitch in on the diapers. But, no, even that was too much for him to be bothered with. She wished that she could pick up the phone to call his other baby mamas and ask them how they dealt with his trifling ass because it was clear to her that she was getting nowhere fast with him. Maybe she should just start demanding cash from him whenever he had the nerve to do a drive-by. At least then she'd have a reserve for when times were hard. Now that she had to cover her own expenses, including childcare for Zoe, which wasn't cheap, she had to be more and more creative with stretching her dollars. It didn't help that she was putting more money toward gas these days with her frequent trips to Snellville to pick up Rico. It was all starting to become a bit too much. She prayed for the day that her boyfriend would find a job so that he could do what a man was supposed to do and help his woman.

Her phone rang, and she dove for it instantly. Thinking that it was Khalil finally calling back she pressed the talk button without paying any attention to the caller ID. "Hello? Hi."

"I'm trying to reach Candace Lawson," the unfamiliar male voice announced.

Standing at the foot of her bed Candace pulled the phone away from her ear to survey the number. It was the number she'd been dodging for the last couple of days because she had no clue who it was. How could she have made the mistake of answering now?

"This is she," Candace responded slowly.

"This is Agent Wilbur from the GBI."

Candace's heart felt as if it had plummeted into her stomach. She took a seat on the edge of the bed and was grateful that Zoe was peacefully napping. She knew that this phone call was going to have the potential to be unnerving. "How can I help you, sir?"

"We're calling to do a follow-up with you."

"Why? I told you all that I possibly could remember. There's nothing else to tell."

"Are you aware that Corey Polk has been freed?"

Candace was genuinely surprised. She hadn't been watching the news lately and none of the girls had called to tell her anything. But then again, Corey's affairs had nothing to do with her. She wasn't his girlfriend. "I didn't know, but what difference should that make to me?"

"I'm very clear on how street violence works, Ms. Lawson. I assume that you're not ignorant of it yourself. If Corey is half of the thug the streets make him out to be, then the death of his girlfriend isn't going to be something he takes lightly."

"So?" Candace still had no clue what any of this had to do with her.

"So he's going to be looking for some of the same people we're looking for. I need you to think long and hard. Is there anything that you may have forgotten or overlooked when you first told us your account of how the incident happened?"

Candace was silent for a moment. She hated being forced to relive that moment, especially when it already came back to her so frequently to begin with. "No," she said. "There's nothing else."

"Nothing specific about the car the perps were in? No names mentioned?"

"Nothing!" Candace snapped.

"Okay. Well, what about your relationship with Corey?"

This was getting a little too personal to her. "I don't have a relationship with him."

"But you'd showed up at the apartment to see him, correct? Not the victim."

"Right, yes. But I don't have a relationship with him . . . It's . . . It's complicated."

"Complicated? Hmmm . . . During any of your visits with Mr. Polk do you recall having met any older guys that may have been said to be a part of an affiliation?"

"Huh?"

Agent Wilbur took a deep breath over the phone. It pained him to have to talk to these young girls who acted like they knew nothing when it came to their street punk boyfriends. Their little acts didn't faze him one bit. "Has he ever introduced you to any of his colleagues?"

"No, of course not. Why would he do that? I wasn't his girlfriend."

"If we showed you a series of pictures would you be able to identify anyone that you may have seen Mr. Polk with?"

"No," she said annoyed. "I can't because I've never seen him with anyone. Again, Corey wasn't my boyfriend, Mr. Wilbur."

"Agent Wilbur," he corrected her. "I hope I haven't caught you at an inconvenient time, Mrs. Lawson. We're just trying to tie up some loose ends and put away anyone that was involved in the incident and anyone that may be doing any illegal trafficking. You're a big help to us."

Candace wasn't falling for the way the investigator was trying to butter her up. "There's never really a convenient time to discuss this."

Her nerves were getting the best of her as her hand shook while holding the phone to her ear. "And for the love of Jehovah, please, please, please, stop referring to my friend as the victim and her death as the incident. I don't know what else you want from me, Agent Wilbur, but I've told you everything that I possibly could. There's nothing left. Now if you don't mind I have an infant I need to tend to."

"Certainly, ma'am. We'll be in touch."

Candace hung up without saying good-bye. *I really wish that you wouldn't,* she thought as she looked over at Zoe who was now beginning to stir. It was time for her to be changed and fed. Candace laid the phone on her bed and walked over to the changing table where she kept the pack of diapers. She reached inside and pulled out a diaper, realizing that the pack was now empty. She was sure she had at least three more to get through the afternoon. Taking a deep breath, she did exactly what she didn't want to do. Knowing that she couldn't call her parents and ask for anything she dialed the only other number that she knew she'd get a response from and help without hesitation. The phone rang twice before there was an answer.

"Hello?"

"Jada, it's Candace. I need a favor, hon."

Chapter 13

Alex

Alex had been hanging with Jada when she mentioned that she had to make a stop real quick by Candace's house. They were dropping off a case of diapers. Alex didn't mind because she'd wanted to give Candace her two cents about her boyfriend ever since the day that he wandered into the Hibachi Grill with his pants sagging, looking like a fashion misfit. Her girl needed to hear some unfiltered truth so that she could hurry up and kick ole boy to the curb before either of their feelings got too invested in whatever it was they were doing.

"What's up, chicks?" Candace greeted them at the door. It was always good to see her girls, even when it was in a time of despair.

Jada hugged Candace and carried the case of Pampers inside the cozy apartment. "I'ma go put this in the back, okay. The baby's awake?"

"Yeah, she is," Candace answered hugging Alex and closing the door. "What's up, booskie?"

Alex smiled. "What's up with you, honey?"

Candace shook her head. "You wouldn't believe the kind of day I've been having. It's rough right now, girlie. I can't even lie."

Alex walked over to the couch and took a seat. "Well, I've been meaning to get up with you for a minute now."

"About what?" Candace said sitting in her only armchair.

Jada entered the room with Zoe in hand. She was in awe of how adorable the little girl was. "There's your mommy. There's your mommy right over there," she said to a fuzzy Zoe. "Is she hungry?" Jada asked Candace.

Candace shrugged. "I swear she eats like a grown man. I just gave her a bottle less than two hours ago."

Jada paced the living room and walked the baby in an effort to calm her down.

Alex got back to the conversation at hand. "So, um, about your dude."

Candace immediately became defensive. "What about him?"

"How deep into this thing are you?"

"Why?" Candace crossed her arms.

"Because you need to save yourself while you can, honey. One look at him, and I knew that he was not the man for you."

"And what makes you such an expert on who's right and wrong for me? Hell, up until earlier this year you couldn't even see the good man standing right in your face."

Jada looked over at the two and wondered where the hell the conversation was going. She could feel the hostility growing in the room.

"Say what you want but I'm telling you that ya' boy ain't no good for you, friend."

"Well, thank you for your concern, but no one asked you for your opinion."

"Isn't that why you wanted us to meet him?" Alex asked.

"No. I wanted you to meet him because he's my man, and as my friends, I thought y'all should know him. But I'm grown, boo-boo. I don't need either of your approval."

"Hey!" Jada exclaimed feeling insulted. "Don't put me in this. I didn't even venture my opinion."

Candace waved her off. "Knowing you, it was coming sooner or later."

"You're tripping," Alex commented.

Candace rose from her seat and placed her hands on her hips. "No, boo. *You* trippin'. Please don't run up in my house thinking you're going to school me about my man. You ain't never got nothing nice to say about anybody's relationship. You don't never like nobody's boo thang, but the second you hook up with someone, your head's all up their ass and in their pockets that you don't see them for the jerks they really are. Hell, I'm surprised that Clay is even with your ass. You're about as deep as a damn puddle of water."

"Candace!" Jada called out walking over with the baby. "What the hell?" She had no clue that today's visit was going to turn so ugly.

Alex rose from the couch. "Nuh-uh, Jada. Let her speak her mind. Let her get it all out because the truth of the matter is that she's jealous. Li'l miss thing out here fronting like she got her shit altogether when she knows that it's killing her that she's somebody's tired ol' baby mama and the only dude she could pull is a lame with no skills, no job, and no business about himself. That puddle of water, boo, is much like your boyfriend. Useless and will evaporate as soon as the sun shines, just like all the other dudes you've been with. He'll be gone when he's done fuckin' with you."

"No," Jada intervened. "No, we're not going to do this and certainly not in front of Itty Bitty."

"Give me my baby," Candace demanded.

"What?" Jada asked. She didn't understand why Candace was catching an attitude with her.

"I said give me my baby, please."

Jada handed Zoe over carefully, then looked at Alex accusingly.

"Thank you for the diapers but I think it's time for y'all to go now," Candace stated.

Alex shook her head. "I'm just trying to help you, girl. I know what it's like to be stuck with a broke-ass dude who claims he's going to be the next Jay-Z. It isn't going to happen, Candace. That boy is going to use you until you have nothing left to give. You see, you don't even have money to get your kid some diapers." Alex knew that the last statement was a little below the belt, but she felt that Candace needed to hear the real right now. The last time they let a girlfriend get below their radar, she slipped into depression and addiction. Alex didn't want Candace to suffer any unnecessary hardships when all she had to do was just listen.

"Bye, ladies," Candace said turning away and heading to her bedroom. "Please let yourselves out."

Jada cut her eyes at Alex. "You just *had* to go there, *didn't* you?"

"What? You know I'm a straight shooter, friend."

"A little tact would have been nice. I get what you were trying to do, but your delivery just then . . ." Jada shook her head and headed for the door as her words trailed off. "Let's just go before you do any more damage."

"If we're friends I should be able to tell my homegirl the truth, right?" Alex asked, following her friend to the door.

Chapter 14

Clay

Clay tapped his foot lightly as he sat on the couch waiting for Alex. She'd promised him that she'd be home in time for them to make it to his supervisor's birthday dinner. Alex hadn't understood why he wanted to hang out with any of his coworkers after hours and had shown resistance against going to the party to begin with. Clay had explained to her that Anthony was more than just his supervisor, he was his mentor. Clay's job as an entry-level accountant was lucrative, but he wanted more: more money, more control over how he made his money, and a greater position at a higher-grossing company. He was certain that if he learned all that he could from people like Anthony, who had his own consulting firm on the side, he'd get where he wanted to be. That type of rapport could only be built by networking outside of the office.

Clay looked at his watch. They were already thirty minutes late. He considered leaving her a note and going on to the party without her, but the gentleman in him just couldn't leave her behind. He wished that she'd give him half of the consideration he gave her. He considered calling her phone but didn't feel it was necessary to remind an adult of where they were supposed to be and when. Besides, he'd texted her once already asking about her ETA and had gotten no response.

His stomach growled as he sat in the quiet of their apartment. There was no use trolling through the cabinets or refrigerator. There was nothing there to eat because he hadn't gone grocery shopping. He'd purposefully refrained from shopping the week prior because it was a task that Alex rarely ever did unless he dragged her along with him. He wanted to see how long she'd go with nothing in the house before finally getting off of her ass and going to the store. He loved her, but Clay couldn't believe how soiled his little diva truly was. He took some responsibility in that fact as he remembered the numerous times he'd jump to her aid the moment she requested the slightest thing. He'd done it because he was in love with her. Now he was trying to help her gain a sense of independence because he loved her and wanted her to be a responsible person for herself and for the sake of their relationship.

No longer able to take it Clay rose from the couch and grabbed his blazer. He'd given Anthony his word, and there was no way that he was going to renege on it because of someone else, even if it was the love of his life. He headed for the door and was nearly knocked over backward as Alex came bolting in.

"Hey, precious! I know, I know, I know." She blew him kisses as she threw her purse on the sofa and ran toward their room. "Let me just slip into my black dress and we can go!" she called over her shoulder.

Clay stared into thin air. *This woman drives me nuts*, he thought as he closed the door quietly. He leaned up against it and crossed his arms. He wondered how long he was going to have to wait for her to get herself together. Much to his surprise she ran right back out with her black dress slipping down her shoulder, heels stuck under her arm, and body leaning slightly to the left as she tried to put in a silver earring.

She walked over and turned her back to him. "Zip me, please."

Clay complied silently.

"Ugh." She dropped her shoes to the ground and slipped her feet into them as she struggled with the clasp of her other earring. "Sorry it took so long. I didn't know that we were going to stop by Candace's house, and then that turned into a big thing. You know, she had the nerve to catch an attitude with me because I told her that her new dude was not a good look. I mean, come on, precious. You saw that dude. He was not Candace material at all. Talkin' 'bout he's a rapper. He probably can't even read yet, alone come up with some lyrics. And did you see how Candace whipped out her card and paid for both of them at dinner? Who does that?"

Alex was talking sixty miles per hour as Clay continued to stand in front of the door with his arms crossed, waiting. He was fuming on the inside, but Alex had yet to realize that anything was wrong. She checked her reflection in the mirror that hung on the back wall of the living room and pinned her hair up into a loose yet fashionable ball. She grabbed her purse from the sofa and headed toward the door, finally ready to head out.

"Okay, I'm ready," she said approaching Clay who was not budging. She stared at him blankly wondering what his problem was. "Come on, precious. We're gonna be late."

He smiled at her. "We're *already* late. We were late nearly an hour ago before you decided to put in an appearance."

Alex touched his face lightly and gave him her sincerest pouty face and innocent tone. "I said I was sorry. It was beyond my control, precious. Jada was driving. I was just riding."

"You could have let her know that you had somewhere else to be."

"What difference does it make?" Alex asked becoming annoyed with the discussion. "I'm here now. We're both dressed. Let's just go."

Clay was done. It was one thing for her to be inconsiderate. It was another thing for her to be inconsiderate *and* unapologetic about it. Her attitude was turning him off. Sure she'd said, "I'm sorry," but her tone and attitude belied her words.

"How about I go and you stay?" Clay commented coolly.

"*Excuse* me?" Alex asked with her hands on her hips.

"I'm just saying, you didn't really want to go in the first place, and I don't want you to do anything you don't want to do."

"But I rushed home and got dressed. Now all of a sudden it's all good if I don't go? You're tripping."

"No, I'm tired," he corrected her. "Tired of trying to redirect you."

"*Excuse* you! I'm not your child, precious. I don't need redirecting."

"Yeah. Well, you can just spend the evening at home with the person you care most about. You. I'm sure that'll make you happy." Clay turned around, opened the door, and then let himself out.

Seasons Lounge was filled to capacity. Anthony and his wife had gone all the way out to make the man's fortieth birthday celebration spectacular. Drinks were flowing, food was set out on platters in abundance, the music was easygoing and not too loud or rowdy, and beautiful women were everywhere. Any heterosexual man with class and a healthy sex drive would have been in seventh heaven, but Clay was miserable. Despite all of the buzz around him, all he could focus on was the fact that Alex was not giggling beside him.

"Clay! My man!" Anthony was on his third Cîroc on ice and was feeling no pain. He gave Clay dap for the second time that evening and frowned at him. "Didn't anybody tell you that this is a party?"

"Yeah, man. It's cool," Clay responded.

"Then why you over here looking like you 'bout to cry?" Anthony looked around. "Where's your lady?"

"She didn't come," Clay said taking a swig of the rum and Coke he'd been nursing for the last half hour.

"Y'all having problems?"

Now was not the time to talk about his relationship issues. He smiled at his mentor. "Nah, man. Why you over here worried about me and mine when it's your birthday? You should be standing on a table somewhere going buck wild."

"Man, when you get as old as me, 'bout the only thing you really wanna do on your birthday is have a good drink, a good meal, a good fuck, then be left the hell alone."

Clay laughed. It was the first time he'd heard his boss speak so candidly.

"Look, I got a lead on something I think you'll be interested in," Anthony said changing the subject briefly.

The DJ turned the track up as 50 Cent belted out the lyrics to "It's Your Birthday."

Clay leaned into Anthony in an effort to hear him better. "What's that?"

"Come . . . Monday . . . opportunity." Only every other word of Anthony's statement was audible to Clay over the blasting from the sound system. Anthony patted him on the back. "I got you." The man hurried off with his glass raised in the air.

Clay set his nearly empty glass on the counter and mindlessly watched as Anthony and his wife danced their hearts out. Others joined them on the dance floor seemingly without a care in the world. Clay's mind was elsewhere. He was intrigued by the opportunity that Anthony had mentioned and couldn't wait for Monday morning to roll around.

"Excuse me?" A sultry voice was in his ear as a beautiful, curvy, Dominican woman dressed in a revealing white Bodycon dress placed her left hand on his shoulder. "You look like you could use a friend."

His eyes tried to remain trained on her face but the exposure of her well-endowed cleavage was begging for attention. "Is that right?"

She smiled and caressed the side of his face gently. "Um-hum."

"And you want to be my friend?"

"If that's okay with you." She removed her hand. "Please forgive me if I'm a bit aggressive, but I'm the kind of person that sees what she wants and goes for it."

"Sounds like my kind of person."

She moved in closer and lowered her eyes seductively. "I was hoping you'd say that. You wanna dance?"

The woman's body was calling to him, but Clay wasn't down to give into temptation. As much as he was upset with Alex, he wasn't ready to throw away what had taken forever for them to start building. He smiled politely at the woman and rose from his seat. "Actually, I was just about to go."

She made a face indicating that she could barely hear him.

He leaned into her. "I'm leaving but thanks anyway," he said a little louder.

"Not before we get the chance to know one another."

"I'm sorry, pretty lady. You have a good evening." He moved to walk away.

The exotic beauty grabbed his hand and whispered into his ear. "You don't even wanna know my name?"

Clay laughed nervously as the sweet smell of the woman's perfume became intoxicating. "I don't really want to waste either of our time."

She placed her arms around his neck, and for the first time he could smell the alcohol on her breath. It was amazing what liquid courage could do. It clearly had provoked this very attractive woman to be so unattractively forward with a complete stranger. Any other guy would have taken her to the lounge's restroom and given her exactly what she was aiming for, not caring to know her name at all. Before Clay could pull the inebriated woman off of him without embarrassing her completely she forced her lips against his and tried with all of her might to slip her probing tongue past his lips while reaching down to grab his dick with her left hand. Others around them only thought they were an open freaky couple living in the moment. It was a moment that was going to last with Clay forever.

"So *this* is why you wanted to leave me at home?" Her voice was loud, shrill, and unmistakable over the loud music.

Time felt like it froze for a moment as Clay turned and came eye to eye with Alex. The chick hanging from him stood there with one arm still around his neck looking at Alex as if she was confused. Alex shot the chick a nasty look and crossed her arms in classic ghetto girl fashion.

"Is there a problem?" the beautiful stranger asked Alex.

"Uhhh . . . yes, ho. And *you* would be the problem," Alex responded.

Clay had never seen her get so turned up. He knew that it was time for them to get out of there now before an ugly scene ensued. He untwined himself from the other woman and stepped up to Alex holding out his hands. "Babe, calm down. Before you go off—"

"Before I go off you might want to tell me who the hell this bitch is holding your dick in her hand in the middle of this bar."

"Watch your mouth," Clay stated.

"Bitch?" the drunken woman piped up. "Oh, honey, trust me . . . You don't want none of these."

"You right, and neither does my man, so you can get to steppin'," Alex retorted smirking at the other woman.

The drunken bombshell eyed Clay as if she expected him to come to her defense. When he didn't she sucked her teeth and shook her head. "Forget both of you. I can have any man in this bar. I was just trying to make your day," she said to Clay.

"He doesn't need you to make his day," Alex retorted.

"Humph. Judging by the way his dick jumped when I touched him, he obviously did."

"What?" Alex asked, hyped up. She looked at Clay. "What the fuck did she just say to me? Honey, you don't know me. Please don't let the bourgeoisie fool you. I will mop the floor with your cheap-ass mail order dress on. Thirsty bitch!"

Clay grabbed Alex's arm. It was time to go. "Come on, man. This isn't the place for all that."

"Yeah, get out of here, you low-budget-model skank," the woman retorted. She laughed and turned toward the bar to signal the bartender for yet another cocktail.

Alex snatched away from Clay, grabbed his glass of rum and Coke from the counter, and tossed the contents onto the side of the woman's face, wetting her hair and staining her white dress. The crowd was now in an uproar, and they were the center of attention.

"You stupid bitch!" the woman called out turning around to swing on Alex who ducked just in time for the chick's mediocre punch to land upon Clay's jaw as he tried to pull Alex away yet again.

"Damn it!" he exclaimed.

Security was quick on the scene. Two big burly men approached the bar. One was holding on to the Dominican troublemaker and the other was standing before Clay and Alex.

"Okay, you two gotta go," the officer said in a brisk manner.

"We're leaving, sir," Clay stated, grabbing Alex's hand and heading toward the door. He was embarrassed beyond belief. He knew that on Monday he was going to have to explain to his supervisor why his girl had turned up and showed out.

Once they hit the pavement Alex snatched her hand away from Clay and slapped him upside his head with her clutch bag. "You dog!"

Clay shrugged it off and looked around at the line of folks waiting to get into the lounge as they checked out the scene Alex was causing. "Chill out and let's go to the car," he told her.

"No! I can't believe you, Clay. You're no different from any of the other trifling dirty dogs. Why don't you go find your li'l girlfriend and take her ass home."

"You're acting crazy. I don't even know that girl."

"Yeah? Well, she was sho' familiar with you with her tongue all down ya' throat and your junk all in her hand. What the hell was that?"

"That was a misunderstanding that I would have explained to you if you'd given me a chance."

"Right. I know what I saw."

"Can we go home, please?" Clay was over making a spectacle of themselves in public. This shit was for the birds.

"You go. I'm done with you."

"Alex, come on," Clay tried to appeal to her despite her edginess. "Let's just go home and talk about this."

Black tears ran down her cheek. "Fuck you, Clay. Fuck you and the bitch you left me at home for." She turned away and walked in the opposite direction.

Clay didn't know where she was going, but he wasn't about to chase her. The woman he loved should have listened to him and believed him. He was bending over backward to be the man that Alex needed, and she was giving him opposition at every turn. Tonight she was just going to have to be mad because he wasn't about to kiss her ass. Sadly, he turned in the direction of his car and prayed that she made her way home soon and safely.

Chapter 15

Miranda

"You said something that you were very passionate about," Doctor Dunham stated. "You said that they don't understand. Who is the 'they' that you were referring to?"

It was yet another tedious one-on-one session in Dunham's office. For the last couple of days Miranda had been confined for attacking Missy. During that time Miranda had cried herself to sleep, cried herself awake, and cried to be let out. She was going crazy. She was a prisoner inside of her own mind of hurtful memories and painful truths. It didn't help matters much that once she was able to return to the common area, she'd seen a news update stating that Corey was found not guilty for the murder of Montae Stokes. She'd figured that that was going to happen considering the fact that the witness the state claimed to have had disappeared. Now she wondered how long it would be before Corey figured out what happened and if he was going to come for her once he did. But it didn't matter. He could kill her if he wanted to. Her spirit had died a long time ago. Her body might as well follow suit.

Five Months Earlier

Now that she'd fucked them by providing the police with the slightest bit of evidence against Corey, it was time to take things one step further. The GBI had made no secret about the fact that they were looking for information about the murder of Montae. She'd given them the circumstantial tie to Corey, now she needed to make it stick. She sat in the middle of her living room holding her cell phone in her hand and getting high off of some weak-ass product she'd copped from a dude in Decatur. She'd been stalking the stash house for a minute, and the guy must have been watching her because he approached her with an offer that she couldn't refuse. He'd given her exactly what she'd been begging Corey and his boys to give her. Or so she thought. The feeling and taste of the dope was nothing like what Corey provided. It pissed her off even more that he'd forced her to run to some knockoff dealer instead of just doing his job.

Infuriated, she looked down at the phone and pressed talk *to dial the number she'd pressed in nearly twenty minutes ago. The line rang twice before an unenthused female voice greeted her.*

"GBI hotline. How can I help you?"

"I need to speak to Agent Wilbur," *Miranda said covering the phone up with her T-shirt to try to muffle the sound of her voice.* "I needa talk to him right now about Montae Stokes and Corey Polk."

"Ma'am, are you calling to provide a tip?"

"Better than that, honey. I'm calling to offer to be their star witness. But I needa talk to Wilbur. That's the only person I can talk to."

The attendant wasted no time tracking down the agent and patching him through. This was a high-profile case for whatever the reason and Miranda knew that they were going to be dying to hear what she had to say. That was the thing. She wasn't exactly sure what she was going to say, but she sure hoped that they bought it enough to act on it.

"Agent Wilbur," *a deep male voice boomed on the line.* "Who am I speaking with?"

"No names," *Miranda said getting a little nervous.*

"Ma'am, I was told that you had information about the Stokes murder. You are aware that this is a serious matter?"

Miranda didn't like the way that he was talking down to her. "Of course I'm aware. I called you, remember? I'm down to tell you whatever you need to know, but not before I know that I'm going to be safe when I do so. I don't want Corey coming back for me."

"Ma'am, I can assure you that once we convict Polk and his associates you won't ever have to worry about him again. So, you're telling me you have solid proof that Polk murdered Stokes?"

Miranda was a little caught off guard. Who the hell are Corey's associates? she wondered. "Um, something like that. I saw him do it with my own two eyes. I saw him kill that man at that club in the DEC." Miranda could hear the man murmur "Yes" under his breath.

"So you're an eyewitness? I need you to tell me exactly what happened."

"I was in the back. Corey came in with some other dude and shot him. Then they drug him out the back door of the club so nobody could see them on the street, and I ran out the front while they were moving the body."

"And you're willing to do a recorded and written statement, as well as testify?"

This lie was going on forever. "Yes, yes. Of course."

"May I have your name now, please?"

She considered giving him a fake name but didn't feel like committing to it. "I'd rather remain anonymous."

"If you're going to testify, you can't be anonymous. That's very difficult."

"Look, I have to look out for me here—"

"Okay, okay . . . I understand . . . The people we're dealing with here are very powerful so you're perfectly valid in wanting to maintain some anonymity."

Miranda was baffled. She couldn't understand for the life of her why the agent felt that Corey and his little street team were such a force.

"Tell you what, you give me your word that you'll have yourself in my office tomorrow afternoon and I'll make sure that we take every precaution in keeping you safe. Deal?"

"Deal." Miranda wasn't really sure what was going to happen now. "But in the meantime will he stay on the street?"

"Ma'am, now that we have you on our team and something tangible with Polk's prints on *it we're going to bring him right on in. We can detain him for a while until we get your official statement, and then an indictment will certainly follow from there."*

Miranda was feeling empowered. Corey was about to be arrested, and he wasn't going to know what hit him. Even if they only held him for a short while Miranda felt that she'd done something major. Payback's a bitch, *she thought, imagining how Stephanie would lose her mind the moment she learned that her man was in jail.*

"So you'll come in tomorrow afternoon?" Agent Wilbur asked.

Miranda's phone buzzed in her ear. She looked at the screen noticing that she had a text message from Jada. Quickly she read the message: Are you coming to dinner tomorrow night, chica? Get back to me. Get back to me. *Miranda had no intentions of going to that damn dinner. She was sure that it was nothing more than an intervention because Stephanie couldn't hold water. Truth be told she was surprised that the girls hadn't been swarming around shortly after her encounter with Stephanie at the trap. But it was just like Jada to put together some organized sit-down to try to tell her about herself. They could all kiss her ass.*

"Ma'am? Hello, ma'am? Are you there?" Agent Wilbur asked frantically, worried that he'd lost her.

"Yes, yes, of course," Miranda said laying out a line of her subpar coke, anxious to get the pig off of her phone. "Tomorrow midafternoon. Ask for you, right?"

"Yes, ma'am. Do you need the address?"

"No, I'm good."

"Okay, we're right off of Panthersville," Agent Wilbur said for good measure. "You can't miss it. We're counting on you. Your city and state are counting on you. You have no idea the help you're being to us. Thank you for coming forward." He felt the need to instill her with a sense of pride to ensure that she didn't back out of their arrangement.

"I understand," Miranda said rolling her eyes impatiently. "See you tomorrow." She ended the call and set the phone on the floor beside her. She snickered, knowing that she had no intention of ever visiting the GBI building. She was just ready to sit back and watch the news awaiting word that Corey had been picked up. She didn't even plan to pick up the phone to place a return call to the agent to advise that she wasn't coming. They'd figure that out soon enough.

Miranda's phone call did more than she'd ever intended for it to. Agent Wilbur was convinced in his belief that her testimony was exactly what they needed to bring Corey in and get to the heart of the BDM. The moment the GBI had learned that BDM was infiltrating Atlanta, Agent Wilbur was assigned to the case. The DEA was waiting to swoop in and put an end to the whole syndication of the organization. Agent Wilbur was just concerned with keeping his territory clean of this type of criminal, poisonous activity, and having this indictment placed on his résumé so he could soon move up in rank.

Agent Wilbur wasted no time in getting on the phone and working his magic to secure an arrest warrant for Corey. He was itching to pick up the two-bit punk, and quickly. His energy was manic the moment he'd gotten off of the phone with his mystery witness.

"Hey, trace the number she called us from," he said to Royce, the agent beside him who was one of their information specialists.

Royce had been going through some computer files for another case he was assigned to but had been listening intently as Agent Wilbur got hyped over his conversation with the informant that had called in. He'd gath-

ered just enough information from Wilbur's end of the conversation to know that this was about to be an open-and-shut quick conviction should the informant really waltz through their doors tomorrow with her detailed eyewitness account. Royce also knew the magnitude of the conviction and how it would be detrimental to BDM. He put his current project on hold and tapped into the agency's phone line to retrieve the last number Wilbur's line had been connected to before he'd called down for his warrant.

"No problem," Royce said cooperatively. "404-555-5111." He tapped his keyboard, surfed through some screens, and smiled victoriously as he found what he was looking for. "T-Mobile number registered to Miranda Wilson-Cox."

"My man!" Agent Wilbur said as he scribbled down the information. If she didn't come in as promised he was going to her. There was no way he was going to risk letting this conviction slip out of his grasp.

"Anytime," Royce said as Agent Wilbur walked away. Royce looked around to make sure that no one else on the floor was in close enough range to hear him. He pulled out his cell and dialed a familiar number. "Hey, it's Roy. You've got a major problem coming your way."

Current Day

Miranda rocked in her chair. Nothing she said and nothing she did ever seemed to work out right. Nothing she felt ever seemed to matter so she didn't see the point in discussing anything with anyone. But despite Miranda's disinterest in the program's mandated counseling, Doctor Dunham kept pressing. She could feel that the woman was about to break soon.

"There must be someone that you've always been able to count on," Dunham said. "Someone that's always been in your corner. There must be at least one person that you feel you can trust."

Miranda shook her head. How many times did she have to tell these people that in life you're all you really have? She strongly believed that no one could understand her and no one was ever really there for her. "No," she responded quietly. "No one."

Doctor Dunham was thankful just to hear the sound of her voice in comparison to the usual unproductive silence of her previous sessions. "When was the last time that you felt like someone was on your side, Miranda? When was the last time that you felt like someone cared about you?"

Miranda thought back. It had been an awfully long time, and her history was so filled with disappointment and pain that she could barely recall any positive moments. She closed her eyes and remembered that it had been Jada who was there in the hospital with her when Norris, her sorry abusive-ass husband, had broken her ribs and beaten her to the point where she'd had a miscarriage. It had also been Jada who had found her in her apartment passed out from an overdose. But where had her friend been the whole time she was spiraling down the road of self-destruction?

"I had a friend," Miranda stated opening her eyes. "I had a friend that sat by my bedside when my husband beat me and when I'd nearly killed myself . . . Jada."

"Tell me more about Jada."

Miranda shrugged. "She's very ambitious. She's probably more focused than anyone I've ever known. She's having a baby. She always wanted to have a baby. Jada has this perfect life . . . a career, a husband who loves her, the baby she always wanted . . . no drama. She's so picture-perfect that it's like watching TV with her. It's hard walking in the shadows of a person so different from you."

"But she's been there for you," Doctor Dunham countered.

Miranda nodded slowly. "Every time things were at full mass . . . every time it could have ended for me."

"Well, that sounds like someone who loves you to me," Doctor Dunham stated. "But I'm curious as to why you originally said you *had* a friend instead of have."

"Junkies don't have friends," Miranda said with tears in her eyes. "Because no one wants to be associated with someone who's engaged in something they don't understand . . . something that scares them. I had a circle of friends that distanced themselves from me because they didn't understand."

Doctor Dunham tilted her head over in thought. "Hmm. Is that what happened, or do you think that perhaps you may have distanced yourself from your friends? Especially this one who seems to always be your saving grace?"

A tear fell from Miranda's right eye as she stared at the psychiatrist. "All the more reason for them to try harder to hold on. When you really love someone you don't turn your back on them, no matter what. You don't judge them, you don't ignore them, and you don't leave them to kill themself."

"You feel like Jada left you to kill yourself even though she was the one that got you to the hospital when you overdosed?"

"I feel like she wasn't there for a while before that moment. Saving me from me didn't fit into her picture-perfect life, I'm sure, not that I'm her responsibility or anything. Doctor Dunham, I've been killing myself for a minute now. It didn't just happen the night I passed out in the bathroom."

Chapter 16

Jordan

They went on for weeks, barely speaking and ignoring the issues that they were having. Home life was so hostile that Jordan didn't even want to go back after work each day. He lingered around the office as long as he could, doing meaningless research or paperwork just so that he could avoid having to sit in his living room while his wife lay on the cushiony bed in their bedroom pretending that he did not exist. Worst of all, he was horny. Although he knew he was the cause of his home being turned upside down he still felt that she owed it to him to forgive and forget. If anything, their current situation was making him want to reach out to any one of the several women he often chopped it up with on Facebook or via text.

"What are you still doing here?" Mona asked, poking her head into his office.

He looked up from his computer screen and smiled. He'd been trying his best to avoid her all day, especially considering the fact that his interaction with her was what had sparked the tension in his marriage.

"Messing around, wasting time," he told her honestly.

Mona entered the office with her long honey-blond Brazilian weave flowing freely down her back. She stood in front of his desk and smiled seductively. "You know there are other more fun ways to waste time, rather than sitting here playing on the company's Internet."

"Like what?" he asked feeding into her dirty talk.

"Like playing with something else."

"What you got for me to play with?"

She giggled. "Why you been on silent lately? You ain't hit me up or nothing."

"Close the door," he told her realizing that they were still at work.

Mona turned around and shut the door. For good measure she turned the lock before turning back around to face Jordan. "What's good?" she asked.

"You claim you are."

She giggled again. "I'm trying to tell ya', but you act like you don't really wanna find out."

He licked his lips. It had been so long since his dick had been touched by a hand that it wasn't his fault that he couldn't control the throbbing that was now occurring. He was already in the doghouse. If Jada assumed that he'd already fucked someone else, he might as well go ahead and do it. There was no sense in being blamed for something that hadn't happened.

Mona rounded the desk in slow, sexy strides. "So, what you down for?" she asked.

"Who was out there?" Jordan was down for whatever, but he didn't want to risk the chance of losing his job for a meaningless fuck.

"Jazzy J's show just started," Mona answered, moving to stand in front of Jordan as he turned his chair away from his desk. "All the other interns are gone for the day. It's quiet on the floor. Everyone's in the studio."

Jordan nodded. His body temperature increased as he reached out and grabbed her right breast through the soft fabric of her shirt. She moaned a little at his touch, giving him the courage to grab both of her breasts with his large hands. The young girl was thrilled by the fact that she was being lusted after by the popular afternoon show radio DJ. She reached over and unbuckled his jeans. Jordan lifted up a little and helped her to ease his jeans and boxers down. Mona lowered herself onto her knees and took his erection into her mouth without a word.

Jordan's eyes closed, and his head flew back to rest on the top of his office chair. The sensation felt so great that he felt as if he was going to bust one in her mouth immediately. Jada never gave him head like this, especially after becoming pregnant. Every little thing made her nauseous now, and he knew not to even ask her. Before the pregnancy she tried her best to do it whenever she felt in the mood to do so. It really wasn't her thing, but it was such a big thing to him. Jordan valued head over most other wifely duties. If he had a woman that was putting it down on a regular basis, like Mona was at this moment he would definitely feel like the man of his castle. He wouldn't have ever had a need to talk shit to the chicks he encountered online or flirted with around the office. He loved Jada, and she was a good, loving, and nurturing woman. She just wasn't the freak he needed in his life.

As Mona worked her jaw muscles and squeezed his balls gently, the tension built up greater. He reached for her head and pushed her down, encouraging her to take the dick all the way to the back of her throat. The sound of her gagging turned him on. His cell phone buzzed on his desk. He didn't give a damn who it was trying to get at him. He was on his way to a much-needed orgasm. He bucked a few times into the heated moisture of Mona's mouth and felt himself begin to erupt slowly at first, and then a series of sporadic involuntary jerking occurred as he released the evidence of his excitement into the girl's mouth.

Mona pulled away with come dripping from her lips. She smiled at him shyly as she wiped her mouth with her fingers. Jordan didn't smile back. He wasn't sure if the sight of her on her knees with his come all over her lips and fingertips turned him on or disgusted him. His phone buzzed again and he quickly grabbed it up. Guilt set in immediately once he saw that it was Jada that had been texting him. Emergency, her text read. Jordan took a deep breath. He knew that he was going to be in deep shit.

He raced to DeKalb Medical Hospital the moment he'd gotten off of the phone with his mother, Vivian Presley. By the time he'd gotten Mona out of his office and himself cleaned up he'd called his wife back but was surprised when her phone was answered by his mother. Vivian had informed her son that his wife was in the emergency room because of some pains she was having in her lower back and abdomen. The entire drive to the hospital had been nerve-racking for him. All he could think about was how traumatic things were going to be if she lost the baby.

"I'm trying to find my wife, Jada Presley," Jordan said to the nurse sitting at the reception desk of the ER.

The woman nodded without speaking to him and checked the admissions database to see where his wife was. "Hmmm, she's no longer in the ER," she said. "She's been admitted and is in the main hospital on the third floor in room 320."

"The third floor?" Jordan asked.

"Yes, sir. Labor and delivery."

Jordan wanted to fall to the floor at that moment. Time stood still for a second. He wanted to cry out into the bubble of anguish that was clouding around him. This wasn't happening. Jada was only five months pregnant. There was no reason she should have been in the labor and delivery ward at this point in her pregnancy. At least there was no positive reason that he could think of.

Frantically, Jordan rounded the corner and walked the long hall toward the main hospital. He located the elevators and rode up to the third floor feeling nervous and shaky. He should have been home hours ago instead of sitting at the office avoiding his wife. He should have been right there with her instead of sitting in that office with his dick in Mona's mouth. How was he going to live with himself if something happened to his child or his wife when he'd been getting head by a woman that shouldn't have even been close enough to breathe on him?

He found room 320 and entered, fearing the worst. Jada was lying on her left side gripping the side of the bed and crying softly. His mother was sitting in a chair on the right side of the bed holding her hands together tightly. Even his sister, Ressie, was there, leaning over the right side of the bed rubbing Jada's back.

"There you are," Vivian said looking at her son with sullen eyes. "You okay?"

Jordan nodded, confused. "What's going on?"

"What's up, li'l bro?" Ressie asked, looking up at Jordan.

"Shit . . . wondering what's wrong with my wife." He walked over to the left side of the bed, kneeled down to be eye level with Jada, and rubbed her head. "Hey, babe."

"Your son is trying to come early," Vivian stated, watching her son interact with his wife. She knew this man, and she could read him well. Something was going on with him.

Jordan reached down and touched the side of Jada's belly feeling a bit of relief knowing that the baby was still inside of her. "Who told you you could do that, li'l man?" They'd learned the sex of the baby just a couple of weeks ago, and Jordan had been elated to know that he was having a son although the thought of parent-hood still scared him.

Jada closed her eyes, not wanting to focus on his face as he kneeled before her pretending to be so attentive and caring. *Where the hell has he been when I'd originally texted him to say that something was wrong?* she wondered.

One of the machines beside her began to beep loudly as a long strip of paper continued to flow to the floor. Jordan looked up at it and knitted his eyebrows. Jada was also connected to another machine via a long tube that was inserted into her arm. It all looked complicated and very serious to him. The door opened, and a nurse came in to check on things.

"Hello, everyone," the nurse greeted them. She looked at Jordan. "Are you Mr. Presley?"

Jordan stood up and moved back to get out of the nurse's way. "Yes. Can you tell me what's going on with my wife specifically?"

The nurse pressed a button on the fetal monitor and took a look at the strip of paper that it was providing. "She's trying to have this baby too early," the nurse reiterated what Vivian had just told him. "But her doctor is right down the hall and is about to come in now to talk to you." She made a mark on the strip and let it fall back to the ground. "Okay, Mrs. Presley. We're doing shift change now, love, so I'll see you if you're still here tomorrow." She looked back at Jordan. "Her new nurse should be rounding in just a few minutes as well. You all have a good night."

"You too," Vivian stated.

"Thank you," Jordan replied.

No sooner than the nurse walked out, Jada's obstetrician, Doctor Henry, entered the room. "Mrs. Presley!" she called out cheerfully. "What's going on in here? Good evening, everyone," she said acknowledging the family.

"Good evening," Vivian said in her dainty tone.

"Hello," Ressie said, amused by the doctor's upbeat personality.

"How you doing, Doctor Henry?" Jordan asked as the doctor walked past him to get to Jada.

"I'd be better if our girl was lying up on this bed right now." Doctor Henry smiled at Jada. "Turn over on your back for me, sweet pea," she instructed.

Jada moaned and slowly complied. Doctor Henry took her vitals for herself quickly, and then listened to the baby's heart rate. "What's been going on with you?" she asked Jada. "Are you doing anything strenuous at work?"

Jada shook her head no.

"You been sticking to your diet to manage the gestational diabetes?"

Jada nodded.

"Anything stressful going on?" the doctor asked.

Jada blinked through her tears and nodded slowly. Vivian's interest was piqued, and she shot a look over at her son who donned a guilty expression. Something was definitely going on between the two of them.

"Okay, here's the deal," Doctor Henry said, scanning the room and looking at everyone present. "This baby is nineteen weeks old gestationally. The idea is for us to make it at least to thirty-seven weeks in order for the baby to be full term and safe to be delivered. I don't have to tell you that going into preterm labor is not a good thing, especially this early in gestation. The survival rate . . . well, we're not going to even get into that."

"Is this going to force her to miscarry?" Ressie asked.

"I'm going to administer Terbutaline . . . It's a tocolytic medicine that she'll get through her IV to help relax her uterine muscles and stop the contractions. So we're going to keep her here for about two days, give her the Terbutaline, and observe her to make sure it works. By law and medical regulations we can only give her this for up to seventy-two hours."

"So what if it doesn't work?" Vivian asked.

"Then we'll try something else. But I feel confident that this will work." Doctor Henry took a breath and continued. "The other thing is that I noticed her blood pressure is up, another sign of high stress level. So . . . I'm going to prescribe something for that as well as do some testing for preeclampsia. We want to take all precautions because with hypertension this medication can be fatal to both mommy and baby."

"What the flip?" Ressie interjected. "There's no other option then? I mean, if it's risky . . . she's already in a risky situation as it is with the preterm labor and the high blood pressure. Why would we want to risk making matters worse by giving her a medication that could . . . be fatal?"

"It's the best course of action," Doctor Henry stated. "Given the gestational age of the baby it is the most effective course of action. And we'll give her minimum dosages of the Terbutaline.

Don't worry. If we see things going south at any point we'll reconvene and go a different route." She looked at Jada who had long since turned back on her side and closed her eyes. "Any other questions?"

"I think you pretty much covered it all," Jordan stated slumping over against the wall. "Okay, the nurse will be back with the Terbutaline and the Labetalol for the blood pressure." She patted Jordan on his arm. "Don't worry. We're going to take good care of your wife."

Jordan nodded. He wished that he'd done a better job of taking care of her emotionally and maybe then they wouldn't have been in this predicament.

Chapter 17

Corey

He'd been out for a minute and was trying to get things back together. Staying with his mom had been a temporary thing, and he couldn't have stuck it out a moment longer. Being business minded, he'd had an account opened in his mom's name a long time ago and every so often he'd given her money to stash in it. Now that he was starting over he was able to draw from that account. Money talked in this city so he'd had no problems getting set up in an apartment in Five Oaks located on Montreal Road in Tucker. It was a one bedroom with a loft and was good enough for Corey. He just needed his own space so that he could work some things out, and he had to move fast.

His boy had gotten him the gun and phone he'd requested so now he was mobile and strapped. His ride had been seized after he was picked up, and the judge wasn't freeing it from the impound because of his pending drug charges. This meant shit to Corey. He simply fronted the cash to buy a 2001 black Cadillac Deville from the dude that owned the used car lot on the corner of College Avenue and South Columbia Drive. Now he was waiting for the word on who popped his girl so he could pay their ass a visit before he was paid a visit by his BDM friends. It bothered him that they hadn't surfaced yet. Corey wasn't a procrastinator. He preferred for them to just go ahead and bring whatever heat they had in mind instead of feeling like he had to look over his shoulder every second of every minute. The shit was killing him.

Getting out of his car and taking a quick look around Corey walked down the long, steep driveway of the house he thought he'd never have to visit again. He'd waited as long as he could, but now it was time to have the confrontation that was inevitable. He rang the doorbell and waited patiently wondering just how this was going to go down.

Ms. Johnson opened the door slowly and stared at the dark-skinned young thug in disbelief. "When I heard you was out I prayed that God wouldn't bring you to this door," she said with a scowl. "How dare you come here!"

He wanted to tell her that she could trust and believe her house was the last place he wanted to be but getting buck with her wasn't going to help matters. "I came to see my kids," he said calmly.

"You think I'm going to let you in here to disrupt these babies' lives? You're even dumber than I thought. These children are better off never knowing you exist."

"You can't keep me from my kids, Ms. Johnson." He was starting to lose his patience.

"Were you thinking about your children when you was out in the streets selling your drugs and taking innocent lives?" Ms. Johnson shot back. "Were you thinking about your children when you got their mother shot?"

His jawline tensed as he tried to exercise some restraint and self-control. "You think I wanted that to happen to Steph? You think I'm happy about that? You think that I don't feel some kinda responsibility for how that went down?"

"You should!"

"You act like I pulled the trigger!"

"You pulled the trigger the moment you pulled her into your lifestyle!" Ms. Johnson shouted emotionally. Her tiny fists balled up in frustration, and her face suddenly made her look older than she was. The stress and anguish were more apparent than ever. "That girl loved you, and all it got her was dead."

Corey was hurt and angry. "Believe it or not, Ms. Johnson, I loved your daughter with all my heart. I loved that girl. This shit tears me up every time I think about it, and you best believe I'm not gon' sleep on this like nothing happened. I'm gon' handle it."

Ms. Johnson shook her head and covered her ears. "You watch your mouth! And don't . . . don't come 'round here talking this nonsense. I don't wanna hear nothing about your illegal activity."

Corey sighed. What the hell did she want from him? "Look, I just wanna see my kids."

His voice boomed loud enough to reach Damien's little ears. "Daddy! Daddy!" he shouted from inside the living room.

Corey's eyes lit up as he tried to peer over Ms. Johnson's shoulder. He looked at her and cocked his head to the side. "My son wants to see me," he said in a threatening tone.

Reluctantly she stepped back and allowed him to enter her home. As he walked in Damien ran into his arms. Ms. Johnson shut the door, not noticing the dark sedan that slowly pulled up in front of her house beside Corey's car. She crossed her arms and watched the interaction between father and son. She'd purposely been keeping Damien away from the radio and television so that his image of his father wouldn't be tainted by the ugly truth. She didn't want her grandson to know what kind of monster his father really was or that he had any link to his mother's death. It had been hard enough to explain to the child that he wouldn't see his mother again until he reached heaven.

"Where you been, Daddy?" Damien asked innocently holding on to his father for dear life. "Mommy's gone. She's dead now. Did you know that?"

Corey squeezed his boy and felt his heart aching. "I know, son. I'm sorry." He pulled back and looked his son over. He hadn't seen him in so long. The boy was growing up quickly. "You taking care of your sister and your grandma?"

Damien nodded. "Ariel cries too much. Grandma cries too." He paused and looked at his grandma whose head was held down in despair. "Mama used to cry too. She cried because you were gone all the time. I thought you weren't coming back," he whimpered. "I thought you was in heaven too with Mommy."

Corey grabbed the boy back into a tight embrace and fought the urge to release tears himself. He hadn't cried in ages, having been taught that real men didn't shed tears. It broke his spirit to hear his son's fear and feel his emotions. Stephanie's death affected everyone, but most importantly, their children were going to suffer because of her absence for the rest of their lives. He couldn't not do anything about it. He couldn't wait any longer. He couldn't bear to see his young son in such turmoil. Just the thought of his toddler daughter shedding tears constantly made him want to place a bullet in somebody's skull. Ariel could obviously sense that something was wrong. She was far too young to understand life and death, but she was human, and she knew she was missing the connection she shared with her mother . . . She was missing her scent, her voice, her touch, and her face.

Corey felt Damien's body shaking as he cried. Looking up, his eyes caught a picture of Stephanie. It was her high school graduation picture. He remembered that day. Seeing her short brown-skinned face smiling back at him was torture. He'd failed her. He'd failed their whole family. Kissing his son on the head he pulled away from their embrace and rose up. He turned to look at Ms. Johnson. "Ariel?" he asked.

Ms. Johnson sighed and led him to the back bedroom that used to belong to Stephanie. The kids now occupied the room indefinitely. Ariel was sound asleep in her crib that she seemed to be outgrowing. Corey's eyes misted over yet again as he touched the curly hairs on his daughter's head. He'd help to give these children life, only to have placed them in a fucked-up situation. He leaned over and kissed the baby's cheek gently before turning to face Ms. Johnson.

She shook her head. "This is their home," she said feeling that she knew what he was thinking. "The courts granted me custody, and the fact remains that *this* is their home."

"They safe here with you right now," Corey stated.

"Right now?" she asked confused. "What you mean right now? What? You think whoever you've gotten yourself involved with is looking to hurt these innocent kids?"

The thought hadn't occurred to him before she voiced it. He'd been thinking about getting custody of his kids once he cleared up all his other drama. But now a new fear was etched in his heart. He didn't want to alarm her further. "Y'all good. I'll be back to see my kids." He moved to walk away.

"You can't keep running over here bringing trouble to my front door. I might not like you, Corey, but I'm thinking about these children. You need to think about these kids too . . . don't bring us no trouble around here," she begged him, feeling herself running out of fight.

Her request was valid no matter how hurtful the reality of it was. Corey walked out of the bedroom with Damien at his heels.

"Where you going, Daddy? I wanna go with you," Damien pleaded.

Corey patted him on the head. "You gotta stay with Grandma, buddy. I'll get you later." He didn't want to shatter the boy's world any more than it already was by telling him he wasn't coming back any time soon.

"Don't go! Please, Daddy. I don't want you to be dead too." Damien began to cry.

This was the life he'd exposed his children to: having the fear that any time their parents walked out of the door they'd be dead. Corey remembered all of the times that Stephanie had asked him to get out of the game so they could go to some other city and start over. She wanted to have a safer, happier life. He'd been so money and power hungry that the idea wasn't even an option for him, although he'd told her he would consider it. If only he'd listened.

"Stop crying," he told his son. "Be a big boy and take care of Ariel and Grandma for me. Can you do that?"

Damien nodded although his sobs continued.

Corey looked back at Ms. Johnson. "I'll call you," he said before letting himself out of the house. He closed the door behind him and pulled out his cell. The moment the line connected he didn't even give Antonio the opportunity to say hello. "Nigga, you better have a name and location for me right now!"

"I mean, I got a location for where they trap at," Antonio stated nervously. "But that ain't no guarantee that the dudes that pulled the trigger on Steph gon' be there, man. You know you gotta think this one through, bruh." He could sense that his leader was getting a little hotheaded and feared that he'd act recklessly, bringing him along for the ride. He was down to push dope for his dude, make moves for him, and he'd even been with him when the job was done on Montae, but he wasn't about to do a bid because Corey wanted to act without a real plan. That shit wasn't going to fly. He was growing tired of playing the flunky.

Corey climbed the driveway at record speed. "Tired of sitting around, my dude. We gotta move on this. Can't nothing else be done until this is taken care of." He opened his car door and slid into the driver's seat. What he saw almost made him drop the phone, but he handled it with a calmness that surprised even him. "Aye, man, I'ma call you back. But you get at me if you can get that. Time is of the essence," he said as he closed his car door.

"A'ight, man," Antonio said skeptically. "Doing my best, bruh."

Corey ended the call, tossed his phone into the cup holder, and started up the car. He took a deep breath without looking over to his right. He prayed that time was on his side and that he would get to handle that business he'd just discussed with Antonio. "Where to?" he asked.

"The W downtown," Knuckles replied. "Hit the ground floor of the parking deck."

Shit was about to get real.

After traveling through the hotel's service entrance, the kitchen, and then taking the service elevator up to the tenth floor, Knuckles and Corey finally made it to their destination. Corey was nervous as hell. He assumed that Knuckles was taking him there to kill him ruthlessly in the bathroom of a lavish suite so that housekeeping would find his bloody body laid out in the tub the next morning. During the two years that he'd been doing business with BDM he had only met with Knuckles on two occasions: once when the organization had first recruited him, and then again when the shit with Montae started popping off. Knuckles had advised him that he needed to handle the situation the way street punks handled their beef, but that they needed some proof that he'd done the deed. That was why he'd kept the man's wallet; for some kind of tangible proof that he'd pulled the dude's card and had disposed of him. It turned out not to be the kind of proof BDM was looking for, and they certainly were not pleased with the fact that the police had picked up on him so soon.

The duo entered the hotel room and Corey gasped the moment his feet hit the carpet. Sitting on the comfortable posh sofa in the sitting area was the head of BDM himself. Tommy had a grim look on his face as he sat next to a young dude who Corey had encountered on several occasions. He was the one that kept the police off of Corey's ass as well as the one who actually passed the dope and cash between Corey and BDM. He was the middleman.

"Sit," Knuckles told Corey.

Corey obliged, taking a seat across from Tommy and his middleman.

"I'd offer you a beverage but this shit here isn't a social call," Tommy said in his raspy voice as he gripped the arm of the sofa.

Corey nodded. He wasn't in a position to say anything. All he could do at this point was listen. Talking would probably only push the nail further into his pending coffin. Besides, his heart was in his voice box now and there was no way he could formulate words with the fear that was running through him. Knuckles stood behind Corey's chair with his arms by his side ready and waiting should a move need to be made. Feeling the heavyset man towering over him made Corey sweat.

"Surely you understand why we couldn't communicate with you during your recent jail stay," Tommy stated.

Corey nodded.

"You also know we have much to communicate about. I'm out of several kilos and $40,000, Corey. I'm not very happy about that."

Corey nodded again.

"I also have the DEA throwing a precelebration party with the GBI, thinking they're about to bring my ass in behind your stupidity. I'm not very happy about that either," Tommy advised.

Corey swallowed hard.

"I should whoop your ass, then skin you like the pathetic doe you look like right now," Tommy told him. "I should let Knuckles hang you from the ceiling and set you on fire from your balls. But that's not going to get me back my money or my dope, is it? And it certainly isn't going to get the feds to stop digging up shit in my backyard."

Corey felt himself growing lightheaded from holding his breath waiting for the moment that Knuckles capped him. But Tommy's last words made him think that he actually stood a chance of getting out of that hotel room alive to accomplish his primary goal.

"First things first, where's my dope and my money?"

Corey cleared his throat. "I'm not sure. I mean . . . I know where the stash house is so I think it might be there."

"You *think?* You think your adversaries are stupid enough to keep that kind of cash sitting in the hood where they can be knocked over by 12 and that shit be seized? All dumb fucks like you keep money at your homes and operation bases?"

Corey shrugged.

"Look who the fuck I'm talking to," Tommy huffed. "The more I teach your ass the dumber you seem. Keep up, boy! I need my money to make it to me, or there's going to be more problems than a few. It's the principle of the matter."

"Yes, sir," Corey said weakly. "And I'm working on handling that. I lost something too."

"You comparing the breech in my business to the loss of your bitch?" Tommy asked. "Money is greater than pussy any day, son. Pussy will get you fucked in the game . . . but of course, you already know that, don't you?"

Corey had mixed feelings. From a business standpoint he could understand Tommy's position. The feds had seized his dope, and Montae's crew had stolen a great chunk of his money from Stephanie. Additionally, it didn't help that Stephanie's dumb-ass idea had gotten them into the hands of the feds. But on the other hand, Stephanie was his family. He'd lost his family, his woman, and Tommy had very little sympathy for that fact.

"Get out your fuckin' feelings," Tommy said, "and focus! Let's talk about the job. Did anyone see you?"

Corey shook his head. "It was just me and my lieutenant. I swear I didn't see nobody else around."

"Just because you didn't *see* them doesn't mean that they weren't there. Did you check to make sure you weren't being followed and that no one was there?"

Corey knew where he was going with this. "No . . . We didn't."

"Thanks to my nephew and the good ole' media we all know that a witness came forward. That is no good."

Corey was afraid for his life again as Knuckles shifted his weight behind him. "But whoever it was . . . They're ghost. My attorney said they just vanished. Charges against me were dropped, witness is history . . . We're good on that."

Tommy shook his head. "Dumb ass! Do you think they're really going to let that ride? You got off. Great. But they're not walking away from this. Not as long as this witness is still living and breathing and able to talk. If they can get up the slightest dirt that makes its way back to me in the slightest bit, *that's* a problem."

"But they don't even know who the person is."

"While you were taking a vacation my nephew was working. Royce, tell 'em what you know."

The middleman looked at Clay. "The witness is Miranda Wilson-Cox, whose previous address was 2117 East Chadwick. She was friends with your girlfriend."

Corey's head began to spin. What the fuck did Miranda have to do with any of this? "She's a fuckin' crackhead!" he spat out. Suddenly it dawned on him how salty she'd been when he'd had to shut down servicing her. He was worried that she was going to run her mouth to Stephanie and he hadn't wanted to deal with any of the unnecessary drama. Had the bitch been stalking him? Had she actually been there the night they took out Montae? Was she on some get-back shit?

"Seems like you have quite a mess here," Tommy stated. "The GBI went to pick her up after she failed to show up for her planned meeting with them. She was already gone, of course."

Corey was confused. "Gone? You mean . . ."

"Knuckles had a talk with her. She was ghost after that. But don't worry . . . He didn't kill her. He encouraged her to kill herself. That didn't exactly work out either."

"What?"

"Seems she made her way to a rehab center where she's currently under lock and key. The GBI is trying their damnedest to find her. Royce has tried to put them off by erasing information about her from the Social Security database and Georgia's vital records department, If that bitch was there and fingers you after all this, *you're* gonna have a problem . . . *We're* going to have a problem now that she's met our friend here."

Corey gulped. "So what are you saying?"

"I'm saying that your client, friend, or whoever she is needs to be dealt with."

The thought of having to murder one of his girl's closest friends was disturbing but Corey knew what he'd signed up for the moment he got involved with BDM. They were all about the money and if blood had to shed to keep their paths clear to make the money, then so be it.

Corey wasn't as coldhearted as some thought. Compared to Tommy and Knuckles, Corey was a teddy bear.

"I don't have to tell you what would happen if you decided to switch sides, do I?" Tommy asked.

Corey shook his head. "I'm not a snitch. I wouldn't do that shit."

Tommy nodded. Corey could say whatever the hell he wanted. Tommy knew that a man would do just about anything to save his own ass once it looked like he was about to burn. Tommy had been in the game for a long time. The feds had been trying to pin a case on him for as long as he could remember. Even when he was a kid like Corey running the streets for his mentor, Coney Martinez, Tommy had proven to be a rare breed. He'd done a bid upstate for Coney but hadn't once dropped dime on him. Once he was out, Coney supplied Tommy with everything he could ever need to run his hustle flawlessly just before stepping down and getting out of the game. It was Coney that had put Tommy in touch with his direct connect, his cousin, in Columbia, supplying Tommy with the purest coke the USA had ever sampled. Being loyal and keeping his mouth shut had earned Tommy a dynasty like no other. No, Tommy was no snitch like these normal young dudes of today. He wasn't your average man.

He was a beast.

"I don't want to have to see you again," Tommy told Corey. "I see you again, that means you and I have a problem."

Corey nodded his understanding.

Tommy motioned toward the door. Their meeting was over. Corey jumped from the chair and brushed past Knuckles to get out.

"Corey," he heard Tommy call behind him before he could turn the knob on the door.

He turned around slowly wondering if it had all been a bluff and if the big man was about to shoot him dead in his face the moment their eyes made contact.

"You don't have long, my friend," Tommy warned him. "Get it down and get it down quickly."

Corey nodded and hurriedly escaped the room. He rushed to the elevator, dying to be as far away from the BDM members as possible. This was turning out to be a lot more than he'd bargained for.

"You think he has the heart to do it?" Knuckles asked Tommy as he took the seat Corey had previously occupied.

"You shitting me? I'd be surprised if he even finds the fucks that shot his bitch. But he better hope he does and gets me my money. Keep your eye on him."

Knuckles nodded. He knew exactly how this story was going to end.

Chapter 18

Candace

"Come on, woman. I'm hungry," Rico barked.

Candace was in her kitchen trying to keep her mind occupied. So much was bothering her, but she didn't feel comfortable telling Rico about any of it. He wouldn't have understood. She scooped out a hearty helping of her lasagna and placed it on a plate for her boyfriend before taking the plate out to him. "Eat up," she told him.

"That's what I'm talking about."

"And when you're done fill this out," she told him, motioning to the packet sitting in the middle of the table.

"What's that?" he asked.

"It's a job application," she said sliding into the seat across from him. "They're hiring debt collectors at my job. It's an easy, breezy position, and I'm in good with the hiring manager, so you're as good as in there."

"For real?" he said taking a bite of his dinner and reaching for the application. He'd been putting in applications here and there for the longest and nothing had worked out for him yet.

"Yeah, so make sure you fill it out completely, okay?"

Rico smiled. Hooking up with Candace had been the best decision he'd made lately. It gave him somewhere to go to get away from his parents and their dysfunctional relationship, wild sex because Candace was a freak with it, and plenty of food because the woman liked to cook whether she was good at all the dishes she tried or not. Now here she was helping him get money in his pockets. There was no way he was ever leaving her. She was exactly what he needed.

"Let's get married," he said to her taking a bite of his salad.

Candace poured herself a glass of wine and laughed. "Yeah, right. So now you want to be a comedian, right? You're something else." She looked over at the swing that Zoe was dangling in happily.

"Naw, I'm for real. You love me, don't you?"

Candace looked up and studied his face. Was he for real? "I love you," she said out of nowhere. They'd never really discussed their emotions like this before. She'd assumed that he was really digging her, but never had they discussed being in love or the possibility of getting married.

"And I love you too, so I don't see what the problem is."

She still wasn't convinced. "You think it's just that simple?"

"It is. When two people love each other and want to spend the rest of their lives together it don't get no simpler than that."

"I have Zoe," Candace said bluntly. "It's more complicated than one and one makes two."

"I love Zoe," Rico shot back. "Zoe's not an issue. I treat her just like I would my own kid."

Candace conveniently forgot about the way he hadn't bothered to lift a finger to help her get provisions for the child not even a month ago when her own father was MIA. "Um, you do realize that with Zoe comes Zoe's father."

"No, it doesn't. That nigga ain't ever around. So he might as well keep doing what he's doing. I'll be her daddy."

It all sounded like music to Candace's ears. As much as she kept harping on being an independent woman doing it for herself she had to admit that she was growing tired of struggling alone. The thought of having a helpmate was appealing, but she wasn't sure that marriage was the right move for them to make right now in their relationship. "I don't know," she said cutting her lasagna slice into pieces.

"What you don't know?"

"I mean, we haven't even been dating that long. I've been married before, and it didn't work. That was mainly because we had no business getting married as quickly as we did. We didn't really know each other."

"Don't compare me to that nigga," Rico snapped. "I'm not dude."

You ain't lying, Candace thought. *Quincy came with a house, a car, and no debt. You come with just about nothing.* "I know that. I'm just saying that I don't want to make the same mistake twice."

He was sold on his decision and wasn't about to backtrack now. He was determined to get Candace to see things his way. "You think being with a man that loves you for you no matter what happened in your past is a mistake?" he asked reaching across the table and taking her hand.

During the time they'd been together Candace had been honest with him about everything, including cheating on Quincy with Khalil, laying up in Khalil's house and getting caught by his wife, sexing Lydia, a woman she'd met at Trapeze, the sex club, sleeping with Stephanie's boyfriend, and being there when her girl was shot. She had no secrets from him and despite everything she'd shared with him he was still there. She knew that any other dude would have bailed on her once they'd gotten wind of even half of the drama that came with her. Rico had a valid point. He obviously loved her no matter what. But were her feelings for him deep enough to make such a sacred commitment? She'd vowed to herself that the next time she got married it would be a truly for-better-or-for-worse, no-way-out situation. Did they have what it would take to sustain a marriage?

"I know you're the one for me," Rico said, laying it on thick. "The way that I feel when I'm with you, man . . . I've never felt this for anyone else. You make me wanna be a better man, Candace."

Her eyes lit up at his words. She was making an impact on him. "Well . . . If we do this there are some stipulations that cannot be overlooked," she told him slowly, beginning to sway. "You know me. I'm a chick with standards. Either you're down or we can't do this."

Rico nodded and gave her his full attention. "Go."

"The smoking."

"Huh?" he frowned at her.

"The smoking, Rico. I mean, you don't ever do it while you're over here, and I respect that, but I'm not stupid. I know you be smoking weed, and I just don't want to live with or be married to a dude that smokes. Especially weed. I don't want my daughter around that."

Rico's nostrils flared slightly. "Wow . . . I didn't expect that."

She gave him a matter-of-fact facial expression. "I'm not backing down off that."

He picked up his fork and took a bite. "I been smoking for years, babe. That's like asking you not to go shopping. That's some shit you like to do. Some shit you're used to. Your hobby. The shits the same for me and smoking."

"That's a habit you have, not a hobby," Candace corrected. If he didn't want to agree to her terms then he could just kiss his proposal good-bye because she wasn't going to accept it.

"Fine, habit, then. So you know it takes time to break a habit."

Candace nodded. She understood that. "Okay, yeah . . . So you get a period of two months to withdraw from it."

"Before we get married? Come on, Candace. Work with a brother."

"Two months after it's over. No matter what. Not even a cigarette."

He shrugged. "Done."

She smiled. "Cool."

"Anything else?" he asked.

She bit her lip. "Yes. Two more things. First, we need to join a congregation."

"A what?"

"A congregation, baby. At the Kingdom Hall."

"And when was the last time you went to the Kingdom Hall?"

Candace shot him a dirty look. "That's beside the point. I mean, I know that I need to get back into the Word. I can admit that. But if we're going to do this then we need a solid, spiritual foundation."

Rico's mouth went to the right as if he wasn't buying what she was saying. "You want me to be a Jehovah's Witness? I'm not 'bout to be going out knocking on folks' doors trying to give them no pieces of paper telling them if they don't get right they going to hell."

"We don't do that!" Candace protested, feeling offended.

"I know you don't. You don't even go to the services."

"*Excuse* you! I'm saying we don't tell folk they're going to hell. Who does that? And don't try to make this out to be about me. I can admit that I've been slipping. But I want to be a better believer, a better woman, and a better mother for Zoe. So if you want to get with me, then you're gon' have to get with it."

"My family's Christian."

"Good for them. Witnesses are Christians."

"Uh-huh, but we go to church and observe holidays. Y'all don't."

"You observing holidays ain't got nothing to do with your faith. You do it because you like having a reason to celebrate and get gifts. That has nothing to do with building up His kingdom."

Rico dropped his fork. "Hol' up. Since when did you get so religious?"

"I think we've gotten away from my point," Candace said trying to keep her attitude in check. She hated it whenever anyone tried to belittle her walk with Jehovah. "Look, I'm telling you we need a spiritual base. I'm telling you that spirituality has to be rooted in a Witness setting. That's what I want for my family. If you're down, great. If not, then we can't get married."

"So I'm supposed to throw away years of what my family traditions have been in order to please you? Where's the compromise in that?"

"There's no compromising in spirituality. And anyway, I'm not knocking having family traditions. I'm just saying the whole materialistic aspect of holidays and stuff isn't of God."

"Okay, Miss Holier-Than-Thou, if you so dead set on not compromising with spirituality and you wanna do everything by the book and shit, then how come it's okay for us to have sex? You always down for a good fuck, and I ain't read my Bible from cover to cover, but I know fornication is a sin."

"I never said I was perfect," Candace stated. "And I stated that I want to be a better person, did I not?"

Rico was all out of comebacks. He couldn't believe the stuff that she was throwing at him, but if he wanted her to agree to marry him he needed to give her what she wanted. "Fine," he said. "Fine. If you go, then I'll go."

"No oppositions?" she asked wanting to make sure that he was truly serious.

"Naw, no oppositions."

Candace smiled and took a sip of her wine. Maybe they stood a chance after all.

"So what's the third stipulation?" he asked her.

"Oh, that one's simple." She pushed the application sitting in the middle of the table closer to his side. "Make sure you fill this out so you can get this job. We need two stable incomes if we gon' do this thing. My girls already clowning me about you not having a job and wanting to rap.

I can't show up with an unemployed husband. That ain't gon' work for me at all, point-blank period."

Rico's eyes grew narrow. He looked across the table at the woman he was trying to make a deal with. "What you mean your girls clowning you about me?"

The moment his question resounded through the room Candace wished that she could take her statement back. "Um, it was nothing . . . We were just having a discussion, and they were just concerned is all."

"Concerned about what? Why the fuck you discussing me with your friends?"

"'Cause that's what girls do. We discuss our relationship issues."

"Wasn't aware that I was an issue for you."

Candace held her hands up. "Wait a minute, wait a minute . . . Hold on, Rico. Calm down. I didn't mean it like that, babe. Really. The girls just have my best interest at heart, and they wanted to make sure that I was making a good decision by getting into a relationship with you. I mean, I have my own set of problems, and I need someone by my side that can help me and not hold me back."

"So your girls got you wondering if I'm holding you back?" Rico was upset. "'Cause I'm between jobs?"

"Like I said, they just have my best interest at heart." She realized the words were true and made a mental note to call and patch things up with the girls as soon as possible. "You know Jada's the mama of the group and she just wants to—"

"Check this out, Jada don't know shit about me. She didn't even stick around that day to get to know me in order to even have an opinion about me. Quite frankly, I ain't studying nothing her or ya' other girl got to say. At the end of the day I'm ya' man, and that's how it's gon' be. Girls be real quick to put another chick down or clown her dude when they jealous and insecure with themselves."

"Um . . . It wasn't really like that. They just—"

"So I'd thank you not to discuss our business with your li'l friends anymore," he said cutting her off again. "They ain't got shit to do with what we do over here. Unless you fuckin' one of them too 'cause you know how you get down."

"Okay, you know what? I'm just about tired of you taking shots at me, Rico." She was close to telling him to go shove his proposal up his ass.

Sensing that she was really pissed Rico tried to calm down. "My bad. I ain't mean it like that. I'm not trying to come for you or nothing, I'm just saying . . . Let's keep our business between us. I'd rather you didn't sit around telling them jealous birds our business and listening to any of their whack-ass advice."

Candace decided to pick and choose her battles wisely. They were trying to make a positive move and arguing over her discussions with her friends wasn't beneficial to what they were trying to do at all. She decided to tell him whatever he needed to hear to get them past this moment so that they could make the final decision that would impact their lives forever. "Okay," she said softly. "I'm sorry. You're right. Our business is our business. So you'll fill out the paper, and I'll turn it in to HR for you. Cool?"

Rico nodded and remained silent for a moment. "Cool," he finally said. "So how about we go 'head and make this thing official sooner rather than later."

"How soon?" Candace asked feeling a little pressured.

"Soon, soon. We can skip that whole wedding fiasco bit and save some money by just going to the courthouse and getting it done."

Candace liked the idea of saving money but knew that her parents would have a fit when she told them she'd eloped. But that was a bridge she was going to have to cross whenever she got to it. "Okay. I'll do some research to see how much the license is and what time they do it and stuff."

"Let's do it next week," Rico said. "I don't wanna wait."

"You don't wanna wait until you start the job?"

"You said the job's as good as mine, right? So why wait? Let's get married next week, baby. I don't wanna wait another minute longer to start my new life with you."

Candace sat back in her chair and eyed him. He appeared to be dead serious. A giddy feeling overcame her. In the midst of all the frustration and drama she was enduring Rico had ridden in on his little white horse and saved the day. They had a lot of logistics to work out, but the prospect of having a complete family excited her. She had a second chance to be a wife and lead a good, healthy life. She looked over at Zoe who was finally asleep as the swing continued to sway back and forth. Her baby deserved to have a complete family instead of a stressed out mom and an absent father. Candace cut her eyes back over to Rico who was waiting for her to respond.

"Okay," she said sweetly. "Let's do it."

Chapter 19

Jada

The room was silent. She'd been floating in and out of consciousness for days now it seemed, and she could have very well been hearing things wrong. The medication they'd given her to stop the contractions had her shaking uncontrollably. At times it was so hard to focus on anything that someone was saying because of the trembling being so aggravating. But while Candace was sitting on the edge of her hospital bed with that stupid grin on her face Jada wanted nothing more than to steady her hand so that she could reach out and slap the girl, assuming that she'd heard her correctly.

It was Jada's last day in the hospital. The doctor had said that they would release her in the morning because the contractions had successfully been stopped. She was being placed on bed rest for the next month so she wasn't exactly out of the woods yet. Right now she just wanted to relax and get her thoughts together while her in-laws were away and Jordan was at work. Candace's visit would have been a little more welcomed if she hadn't come with this crazy shit.

"You don't have nothing to say?" Candace asked her.

Jada lay on her right side and stared out of the window. She couldn't think of any tactful words to share so she decided to remain quiet.

Candace patted her leg. "Come on, girl. Can I get a congratulations or something?"

Is she kidding? Jada wondered. She continued to stare out of the window. She hadn't gotten fresh air in days and was excited about getting out of the hospital room.

Candace was growing impatient with her friend. "You okay, girl?"

Jada nodded.

"Then why you not talking to me, chick? I just told you the most important news of my life. and you laying up here like you mute or something."

"What do you want me to say?" Jada asked.

"Umm, I just told you that congratulations or something like that would be nice."

"Congratulations," Jada said without feeling. She hoped that her girl would just let it go now and move on to something else.

"You all dry with it. I'ma let it slide though because I know that you're going through something right now. But when you get back to you usual upbeat self I expect you to get your party planning skills on and throw me a reception."

I bet you do, Jada thought. The last thing she was in a position to do was throw a party, especially to celebrate a decision that she found completely ridiculous. It perturbed her that Candace continued to make illogical decisions, then expected everyone around her to pretend that she was the luckiest girl in the world. Jada wasn't in the mood to play make believe today.

"Anyway, so I rented a small U-Haul to move Rico's things out of his parents' place," Candace said. "So he's moving into my apartment as we speak. It's been so long since I've lived with a man. I hope he don't do no crazy stuff, like leave the toilet seat up or leave the cap off the toothpaste."

"Did he do any of that anytime that he spent the night?"

"No."

"Then you should be fine, considering how much time that dude was staying over your place," Jada said rolling her eyes.

"It really wasn't that often. And sometimes people switch up on you the second you start living with them."

"It's possible."

"I needa go shopping for a ring. I can't be married without a ring. That's not cool."

Yep, because that ring really makes a difference, Jada thought. "While you moving him in and shopping for a ring, have you told Khalil?"

Candace sucked her teeth. "Told him what? Khalil ain't my man, and I don't owe him any explanations for what I do with my life."

"He's still your daughter's father."

"He don't act like it." Candace didn't want to admit that she'd overlooked Khalil. She knew that he had a habit of dropping by whenever he pleased, and now that she and Rico were getting married it wasn't going to be cool for him to continue doing that. It also wasn't going to be cool for him to be expecting to sex her in the house where her husband now resided. Deep down, Candace knew that Jada was right. She needed to let Khalil know about this change immediately.

"What about your parents?" Jada asked.

Candace shook her head. "They don't know yet. We're going to invite them over for dinner the night after and break the news to them together."

"Good luck on that."

"What you mean by that?" Candace was defensive.

"Just what I said, suga. Good luck." Jada wasn't about to argue with her about this. It was pointless. Over time, Jada had come to realize that no matter what she said to her girls, no matter how pointedly she warned them against something, they were going to do it anyway. Now that she was stressed to the max with her own relationship issues the last thing she needed was to be getting riled up about Candace's or Alex's mess.

"It's going to be good," Candace said. "This time is going to be different. Oh, and I wanted to just apologize for the way things went down at my house when you and Alex came by."

Jada waved it off. "Water under the bridge," she said.

"You guys are important to me, and I value your opinions. But Rico is important to me too. I just want everybody to get along. I don't know what it's going to take for y'all to like him and him to like y'all."

Jada's interest was now piqued. "Excuse me?"

"What? I just want everyone to be cool. Y'all my family."

Jada sat up straight. "No, what you mean you want him to like us? What reason does he have to *not* like us? Hell, he doesn't even know me."

Candace shrugged. "He's a man, girl. I was telling him how y'all were concerned about me being with him, and he just got all upset and started going off, saying stuff about not listening to my jealous friends."

"Jealous friends? We're supposed to be jealous of you now and y'all's thrown-together relationship?"

"Don't attack me, girl. These aren't my words. I'm just telling you what he said."

"And I hope you set his ass straight." Jada could feel her blood pressure rising.

"I told him y'all were my girls and that you just had my best interest at heart. He asked me not to discuss our personal business with y'all anymore, which makes sense, and we just left it at that."

Jada shook her head.

"What?" Candace asked feigning innocence.

"Your boyfriend is a little punk bitch, that's what. How is he over there throwing a tantrum because we don't want our girl being used by some leech?"

Candace laughed. "Why he gotta be all those names though? Remember, he's about to be my husband, girl. Calm down."

Jada wanted to throw her out. Her friend simply didn't have a clue. She wondered how defensive Candace had gotten when Rico was sitting in her face going in on her girlfriends. Jada lay back down. It boiled her blood to think of the things this girl would do just for the sake of having a man smiling in her face. It was really becoming sad and kind of pathetic. Between her girls and Jordan, Jada was going crazy. She needed a vacation from everyone's bullshit before the stress caused something fatal to occur.

Chapter 20

Miranda

Relationships. All it seemed like they ever talked about was relationships. Whether it was your relationship with your parents, your friends, or your significant other, Doctor Dunham wanted to explore the depths of it. Much like all the other things they discussed, this too seemed pointless to Miranda. Sitting in another private session she toyed with the bottom of her T-shirt. It was too big for her. She'd lost weight since being there. She wasn't eating much. It wasn't because the food was nasty; honestly, she didn't know if it was or not because her taste buds seemed to be out of whack. It was just that her appetite was nonexistent. She was probably the smallest she'd ever been in life. One of the staff members had made a comment earlier about her looking as if she was going to waste away to nothing. Miranda hoped that the notion was possible. She figured it would make things so much easier were it so.

"The others are starting to receive visitors now," Doctor Dunham stated. "It's important in your progression that you know you have an outside support system."

"I don't," Miranda said.

"I was thinking you may want to reach out to your girlfriends. At least your friend Jada."

Miranda shook her head.

"What about your parents?"

Her parents. The thought of them made her shutter. She hadn't spoken to them in so long they probably thought she was dead, which was just as well. The less they knew about her and what she'd been going through, the better. If they saw her on the street they probably wouldn't even recognize her as their own flesh and blood. Disappointing them anymore than she already had wasn't something she wanted to do.

"Not calling my parents," she said with finality.

Doctor Dunham nodded. "When people love you, Miranda, they worry about you. I'm sure your parents are quite concerned about you. But I know that when you're ready to face them . . . When you're ready to face that part of your life you will."

You don't know shit, Miranda thought to herself.

"Family is a bond that's unbreakable," Doctor Dunham stated. "Family loves you even when you've strayed. Remember that."

"Family can hurt you more than a complete stranger," Miranda countered, taking the shrink by surprise. "Family can try to break your spirit and your body. Let me tell you about my family. My family landed me in the hospital, raped me, beat the shit out of me, stole from me, and had the nerve to walk out on me when all I ever tried to do was love and support him." Thinking about all the things Norris had done to her made her shiver. "Fuck love. Fuck family. Fuck trust. It's all a bunch of bullshit."

"I'm sorry that all of that happened to you, Miranda. But you can't turn your back on love or your entire family because of one person's ill doings."

Miranda stared at Doctor Dunham's degrees on the wall. "You got your master's from Georgetown," she stated.

"Um-hum." Doctor Dunham followed Miranda's glance.

"And your Ph.D. from Stanford."

"That's right."

"All that education . . . all that training . . . and you *still* don't know shit." She returned her eyes to meet the psychiatrist's. "They didn't teach you to listen to what the hell your patient is saying? How are you going to form a conclusion when you don't even retain the information that's being given to you? What?" She read the shock in Doctor Dunham's face. "You're surprised that I can make sense just because I'm a fuckin' junkie? I haven't always been a J, Doc. I haven't always been depressed and withdrawn. It happened over time, like I said before, or did you miss that too?"

"What is it that you want to say, Miranda?" Doctor Dunham asked without changing her even tone.

"I'm trying to tell you that the whole time I'm walking around with bruised eyes, ribs, and feelings, who the fuck do you think was seeing me? That's right, boo, my family. Maybe I didn't come out and say, 'Hey, I'm getting my ass kicked,' or 'Hey, I'm on crack,' but these were the people that saw or spoke to me often and said nothing. They did nothing."

"What did you want them to say or do?"

"Something!" Miranda snapped. "Anything to show that I wasn't alone . . . that I had somewhere else to turn to. Sure, the girls ambushed me once, but that wasn't in the name of helping me. That was them trying to figure out how stupid I really must've been to stay with a dude that was putting his hands on me. So, yeah, I can turn my back on love and all that other shit because it's been done to me plenty of times."

Doctor Dunham nodded. Miranda wanted to knock her glasses off of her face. What the fuck was she nodding at?

"I told you—" Miranda said wiping her eyes with the back of her left hand, "no one understands, and when they don't understand, they'd rather distance themselves and pretend that there isn't a problem."

"What I'm hearing is that you wanted someone to save you from your husband and from your growing addiction."

Miranda looked down. "No. I needed someone to save me from myself."

Chapter 21

Alex

She'd been in hiding and was tired of it. She hadn't talked to the girls, hadn't returned any of Clay's calls, and hadn't wanted to so much as think about the turmoil that was her life. Candace had texted her to advise about Jada being in the hospital, but she hadn't even been able to pull it together enough to swing by and holler at her girl. Thank goodness her old roommate Kacey hadn't moved out of their old apartment and hadn't gotten a new roommate. She'd been camping out on the floor in her old room, feeling like a squatter. The entire situation was depressing. Alex missed her comfortable bed, she missed having meals she didn't have to prepare for herself, and she missed Clay's presence. But the memory of that hoochie tonguing him down like they were in the privacy of a hotel room was driving her mad. What she really wanted to do was go home and set his car on fire—with him in it.

Tired of sitting at Kacey's home bored and alone, the girl was never ever there, Alex decided to kill two birds with one stone. She needed some advice about her issue, but she also needed to show her support. As she stood at Jada's doorstep she felt a little bad about the fact that she hadn't brought the girl a card, a plant, or something. She'd taken the train and a bus to get to Jada's house. She was tired and exhausted and wished more than ever that she had the luxury of borrowing Clay's car.

Jada opened the door looking sheepish in her lavender pajamas and hair pulled back in a messy ponytail. Alex's visit was unexpected. "What? Your phone not working?"

"I missed you too, friend," Alex said giving her friend a hug.

Jada hugged her back and allowed her to cross the threshold. She closed the door behind her and returned to her place on the sofa where she'd been getting ready to take her medicine before she'd heard the knock at the door. "Where you been hiding?" she asked Alex.

Alex sat on the sofa by her and dropped her purse beside her. She thoughtlessly kicked her feet up on the ottoman in front of them. She was wearing platforms, and her feet were tired from the long trek she'd had to make from the bus stop to Jada's front door. "I've been at Kacey's."

Jada reached for her glass of water. "Why? What's wrong with Kacey?"

"Nothing. I just temporarily moved back in."

Jada placed her medicine in her mouth and swallowed it down with the water. "Why?" she asked weakly. "Where's Clay while you playing sleepover with Kacey?"

"Probably sexing the chick I caught him in the bar with."

Jada's pill hadn't gone all the way down. She began to choke mercilessly upon hearing Alex's statement. She raised her hands in the air to try to help her choking spell. Tears welled up in her eyes as she struggled to get herself together. "What the hell are you talking about?" she asked barely able to breathe.

"Girl, this Negro blew up at me one night . . . that day we went to see Candace and she tripped out."

Jada nodded.

"Yeah, so that evening he blew up at me because we were late to get to his boss's birthday party, and then he just straight walked out on me. He left me at home, friend, and went to the party by himself. I was real pissed for a minute, then I tried to be the bigger person, right? I was ready to apologize and admit that I could have been a little more considerate seeing as though I knew we had plans. So I catch a ride to the lounge where the party was. I walk in and guess what I see? Clay all wrapped around some half-naked hoochie with their lips practically glued to each other."

Jada was in shock. This was not the Clay that she knew. She wondered how much of the story Alex was embellishing. "Oh my God. Please tell me that you didn't go up in there showing your ass."

"Oh, I showed my ass, and then some. How he gon' try to play me like that?" Alex crossed her arms and pouted. "All that trash he talked about T and Mario when he's just bad. All dudes are dogs."

Jada was feeling her on that but didn't feel like now was the time to share her own hardships. "You need to talk to him, girl. Clay's a decent guy. Maybe there was something else going on and it just looked like—"

"Friend!" Alex exclaimed cutting her off. "Really? Do I look stupid to you? I know what a kiss looks like, and they were damn near fuckin' at that bar when I walked in. She was all grabbing his crotch and stuff. Ugh! Whose side are you on?"

"Yours," Jada said weakly while wondering whose side her friends would be on if they knew that Jordan was screwing around on her. "I'm just saying . . . Things aren't always as they seem."

"Well, it seemed like I was ready to whoop that chick's ass when I threw that drink on her and things were just like that! I was ready to go in on that ass."

Jada died laughing. She held her belly as she doubled over in amusement. "No, you did not! Please tell me you didn't turn it out like that."

"Yassssss, girl!" Alex giggled. "They put all our asses out. Ole' girl knew that she was about to be getting the floor mopped with that dingy-ass dish towel of a dress she had on."

Alex was behaving way out of character. It was that moment that Jada realized that her friend had real feelings for Clay. She'd never wanted to fight any chick over a dude ever. This whole possessive thing was new for her. But still, Jada was having a hard time digesting the fact that Clay was out whoring around like that after everything he'd gone through to get with the love of his life. It made Jada chuckle once more because the same could be true for her own trifling husband. It was all a bit much to digest.

"His dog ass," Alex stated pouting again. "But what really sucks is that I miss his ass. What the hell is that about?"

"You're human," Jada replied leaning back and wishing that Alex would move her feet. "And you love him. That doesn't just go away overnight."

"It should. It shoulda went away the moment I caught him."

"Talk to the man," Jada said once more. She figured she probably needed to start taking her own advice.

Alex leaned over and lay her head on the swell of Jada's belly. "Friend, why is this happening to me? Clay was supposed to be it for me. He was supposed to be my Jordan."

"The hell are you talking about?" Jada asked fighting the urge to slap Alex upside her head for lying on her stomach like it was a cushiony pillow.

"Come on, girl. You know you got it easy peasy over here with your boo thing. I just want my happily-ever-after."

"Is that what you think this is over here?" Jada asked astonished. How wrong her friends were to assume that she didn't have hardships just because she wasn't crying about them all the time.

"You're over here all pregnant and barefoot, living the good life."

Jada was over it. She pushed Alex's head away and repositioned herself. "That's your problem right there. Stop striving to be like someone else or have what someone else has, boo-boo. The grass isn't always greener on the other side of the fence." She hoisted herself up from the sofa and began to waddle toward the bathroom. "And the baby's doing just fine, bitch. Thanks for asking," she said sarcastically.

Alex leaned back and considered Jada's advice. Talk to him. It sounded simple enough, but how could she talk to him when all she really wanted to do was run him over with his car? Was she going to be able to hear anything he said over her anger? She didn't want him to take her for some doormat-type of chick and think that he could just treat her however he wanted simply because he'd swept her off of her feet at some point. Wasn't it his responsibility to continue to sweep her off her feet? *Talk to him,* Alex thought. She was going to give it a try. Maybe it was time. Perhaps if they had a civilized discussion they could come to a conclusion about the relationship one way or the other. Either they were going to work it out or let it go. She wasn't sure exactly which way she wanted it to go.

Chapter 22

Clay

Jesus, if you have any mercy please spare me and return my angel, Clay prayed silently as he sat at his kitchen table. *I can't deny that I love this woman, and I know that if we both give it a heartfelt try we can make it work. Please bring her back to me, Jesus. I'd do anything for a second chance.*

It was lonely in the apartment without her. Clay missed feeling her next to him at night, rubbing her feet as they watched television and trying her attempts at cooking dinner. His jones was so bad that he almost even missed tripping over her heels when he walked in his front door each evening. He'd sent her numerous texts and left several voice messages, but she had yet to respond. At some point while he'd been at work he could tell that she'd come in to retrieve some of her things. The gesture pained him. He wasn't ready to throw in the towel on a battle he'd waited so long to be allowed to fight.

In front of him sat a carton of lo mein that he couldn't even stomach. Food had no taste since she'd left. Nothing seemed to feel right. During the ordeal he'd been sure that he was going to be embarrassed as hell upon walking into work the following Monday. But the only thing he'd felt that Monday, and every day since the fight itself, was sadness and heartbreak. He'd never had his heart broken before and felt genuinely sorry if any woman he'd ever dated had felt even an ounce of the pain he was experiencing now.

He heard the lock turn on the front door and thought his ears were playing tricks on him. He stood still for a moment waiting to see what was next. The sound of the door opening and closing made him grasp the Chinese takeout carton tightly. Were things turning around for him? Was his princess actually back? He couldn't move. He didn't know what to expect. He wasn't sure what he was supposed to say after having not seen her for nearly two weeks.

Alex walked into the kitchen and set her purse on the counter. Their eyes locked, and Clay felt his heart melt. Looking at her beautiful chocolate skin, the way she made even some jeans, a long sleeve T-shirt, and platforms look as sexy and glamorous as an evening gown, and the inviting way her lips seemed to pout, made him want to run to her and throw his arms around her. But he remained seated. He didn't want to bum-rush her, not knowing how she was feeling or what her intentions were.

"You look tired," Alex said softly.

Clay shrugged. "Haven't slept very well lately."

She nodded. "Yeah. I know what that's like."

"Where've you been staying?"

"Kacey's."

He'd figured as much but hadn't wanted to just pop up at the old apartment on a whim. He fought the urge to rise up to kiss her and continued to fondle his carton of tepid noodles. "I've missed you."

Alex felt a smile creeping to her lips but fought to keep it at bay. If he thought that a few sweet words were going to work to smooth things over, he had another thought coming to him. "We need to talk," she said.

He lowered his eyes into the food carton. When a woman said those words nothing good could come out of it. "Let me start," he said. If he could lead them off, perhaps things would work out smoothly and he could get his woman back in his arms soon. "What you saw that night was a misunderstanding."

Alex crossed her arms and shifted her weight. Attitude bounced off of her immediately.

Maybe those were not the words to lead off with, Clay thought, taking in his girlfriend's demeanor. "Yes, the woman was kissing me, but that was just it," he said. "She was kissing me. Not the other way around. I didn't invite it. I didn't encourage it. I didn't participate. I wasn't kissing that chick back. I was trying to peel her off of me without creating a huge scene at my man's party."

"Why would some random woman just walk up to you and try to basically ride you on the dance floor?" Alex challenged.

"For one, we weren't on the dance floor," he corrected.

Alex dropped her hands and stomped her foot. "Seriously? You wanna get all technical and semantic with me about this?"

"The truth is the truth, Alex."

"Yeah? And what is the truth, Clay? The honest to goodness truth." She walked over to the table, sat in the chair across from him, and then placed her face in her hands staring him dead in the eyes. "Look me in the face and tell me the truth."

Clay looked into her beautiful round eyes. He reached across the table and touched the softness of her cheek. "The truth is that I love you, and nothing was happening with that woman. She came on to me, I shot her down, and she came harder by trying to force her tongue in my mouth. That's it."

"You're not cheating on me?" Alex asked, leaning her head over to the left, allowing her cheek to be cradled by his palm.

"No, babe. I love you. I've always loved you."

"Then why did you leave me here and go to the party alone?" she whined.

Clay winced. For just a second it seemed like things were about to end well, but now here they were visiting the heart of where their issues really lay. "You were just overwhelming me with your selfishness."

"Selfishness?" Alex repeated the word as if it had been spoken in a foreign language.

"I just felt that you could stand to be a little more considerate of me and a little more of a team player when it comes to our relationship. We need to be on the same page if we're going to work, babe."

Alex sat up straight. "And what page is that? *Your* page? You're not my daddy, Clay. You're my boyfriend."

"I know that, and I never intended to come off like I wanted to be your daddy. Hell, I'm trying to become your husband one day. That ring on your finger symbolizes how I'm in this for the long haul, all the way up to the day that I meet you at the altar, baby."

Alex fingered the diamond solitaire ring Clay had given her for her last birthday. The day she'd opened that box and realized the depths of his feelings for her she'd been sure that she had finally found the man of her dreams. Clay was it. He was everything she'd ever needed and wanted. But even with him she just couldn't seem to get it right. "I want us to work, precious."

Clay grabbed her hands. "Me too. We just have to work together, and baby . . . You have to trust me. I would never ever hurt you."

Alex smiled. "Never?"

He got out of his chair and kneeled down before her. Alex wrapped her arms around his neck and looked him in his pretty brown eyes.

"Never ever ever," he told her before covering her lips with his.

Alex savored his kiss. She hadn't been embraced by him for so long. It was time for them to make up for the time they'd missed. Makeup sex was in order.

Chapter 23

Jordan

"You look nice," Jada said to him from the doorway of the bathroom.

Jordan looked up in the mirror to see his wife looking at him pensively. She hadn't had two words to say to him since the night she'd set their marriage certificate on fire, and she hadn't uttered anything at all to him since coming home from the hospital. He'd been feeling horrible more and more with each day that passed. Being stuck in an environment where you felt like the villain all the time was depressing and exhausting. He was trying his best to take care of her and show her that he was there for her, but Jada was a stubborn one. She hadn't made him feel the least bit at ease with the way she gave him the cold shoulder and continued to make him sleep out on the sofa like a visitor in his own house. Now here she was complimenting him out of the blue. Jordan was leery.

He fiddled with the buttons on his shirt and contemplated what his wife could possibly be thinking. He was preparing to go out for the night. Martin was getting married in a week and wanted to hang out in lieu of having a traditional bachelor party. The two of them and a few friends from college were going to dinner and maybe a club or two afterward. Jordan had mentioned to Jada that he was going to be going out tonight, but she hadn't responded when he did. Now here she was admiring his attire and looking at him as if she was going to try to pull a fast one.

"Thanks," he said trimming the hairs of his mustache.

"Where you going again?" she asked.

"Dinner and chilling with Martin and the guys."

She nodded her head and crossed her arms. "Know when you'll be back?"

"Naw." He put his hygiene bag away and turned around. "It's his night. We just hanging 'til he's ready to call it a night."

"Right." Jada looked skeptical. "We need to talk."

There it was. He knew that she had something up her sleeve. There was no way that he was going to cancel his plans to sit home and argue with her about things that he was ready to put behind them. If she wanted to hash it out it was going to have to wait. "I been trying to talk to you for the longest," he told her as he moved past her to head back into the living room. "Now all of a sudden you wanna have a discussion."

"It's not all of a sudden," she replied. "A lot has been going on, and I was entitled to a time period of sitting with my thoughts."

He rolled his eyes as he sat on the couch to put his shoes on. "Okay, well, I'm entitled to a time period of hanging out and not sitting in here on punishment with you treating me like I'm not shit."

"*Excuse* me?" Jada placed her hands on her hips and stood in front of him. Her belly was in his face. "How am I treating you like shit when *you're* the one running around doing all this dirt?"

"I messed up, Jada. I apologized for that, but instead of forgiving me and working on us, you decided to just shut me out. Well, now, I'm going out so just 'cause you're ready to talk now doesn't mean that I am."

"That's very mature of you," she countered. "How you gonna go out and play with your boys and leave your pregnant wife, who's on bed rest, at home, alone, with all these issues we have looming in the air?"

"Jada, don't do this, okay?"

"You didn't even bother to ask me if I wanted to go. When's the last time I got out of this house and had some fresh air?"

Jordan stood up. "I made these plans while you were busy ignoring me, and I'm not canceling. So, if you're serious about talking things out, we can do that in the morning. I'll make you breakfast, and we can talk all damn day. But tonight I'm going out." He grabbed his jacket from the sofa and stepped close to her. He kissed her forehead. "Good night."

The table was filled with his old crew from college . . . Martin, who was throwing drinks back in celebration of his pending nuptials, Curtis and DeAnthony, Jordan's old college roommates, and AJ, their comrade who had spent more time partying than studying in college and subsequently hadn't graduated. They were all good friends and remembered when Martin and Ashley had first started dating. The two were inseparable from the moment they'd met. The crew had been waiting for years to see the two of them get married. Now the time was upon them, and they were celebrating to the fullest. Sitting around the table at a local

Applebee's they were as loud and belligerent as ever as they recounted stories and memories from years gone by. The seat next to Jordan was empty. They were expecting yet one more person to complete their crew.

"Aye, man, I thought for sure that Martin and Ashley was gon' be the first to tie the knot," Curtis said. "That shit made my head spin how quick Jordan and Jada just up and got married."

AJ had to cosign. "Hell, yeah! It was like one day he was like 'Aye, y'all, this my girlfriend,' then the next day, 'Aye, by the way, this my wife.'"

Everyone laughed, including Jordan. It had happened rather quickly, but he was convinced two years ago that Jada was the woman he wanted to spend the rest of his life with. Even his mother and sister had been shocked, but despite everyone's warnings he'd gone through with it. He'd never been prouder than the day he'd given Jada his last name. It didn't matter to him that no one else understood why they were doing it. All that mattered was the way that he felt when he was around her. It all seemed so simple back then. Now, with the way things were going, he was having second thoughts way too late.

"That nigga ain't been right ever since," DeAnthony said. "All locked down and shit. He don't hang no more. Nothing."

"Dawg used to be a playa for real," AJ commented. "Chicks left and right. Just sniffing pussy from all directions."

Curtis laughed. "Now he only gets to sniff one pussy forever. How's that been working out for you, playboy?" Curtis asked reaching over to slap Jordan on the back.

Jordan looked over and saw Martin doubled over with laughter. "A'ight, man. Laugh on. That's 'bout to be you too, so join the club."

Martin raised his glass of mint julep and smiled drunkenly. "Damn right, and I'm proud of it. I'll just live vicariously through y'all mutha-fuckas."

The crew laughed again.

"So, J, you telling us in all this time you ain't tapped nothing else?" AJ asked. "I mean, *nothing?*"

Jordan chuckled and looked down into his own glass. "Come on, man."

"Aye, J, ain't nobody here but us," Curtis said revving him up. "You know you can talk to yo' boys, nigga. You ain't gotta front over here."

"Yeah, this a no front zone 'round this way," DeAnthony said stuffing his mouth with nachos.

"Well," Jordan said slowly. "I didn't *say* I haven't." The way that he placed emphasis on the word *say* made the others go wild as they caught his meaning.

"That's my nigga!" AJ hollered. "That's my nigga. I knew you couldn't stop being you, nigga. You's a pussy chaser. It's just who you are." AJ shrugged and smiled.

A pussy chaser, Jordan thought to himself. *Is that really what I am? Who wants to live their whole life chasing pussy?* It didn't seem like an appealing trait to have. Jordan wasn't sure that he wanted to be labeled the pussy chaser of their clique.

"Uh-huh, that's just who he is," Curtis said, narrowing his eyes and focusing across the restaurant. "And he been chasing around this one pussy for years."

All eyes darted in the direction of Curtis's glance. They watched as LaTanya made her way across the restaurant in her skinny jeans, crop top, and heels. Her jet-black wavy tracks were pulled back into a loose ponytail, and her full lips parted into a large smile as she took her seat beside Jordan.

She put her arms around him and squeezed tightly. "Hey, booskie! Long time!" She looked over at the rest of the crew and smiled. "Hey, y'all! Y'all missed me?"

LaTanya was cool as hell. She was the one female that had attached herself to their clique.

The others always assumed that she tagged along because she was really trying to hook up with Jordan. Over time, they came to trust her and didn't bother censoring their discussions in front of her because she knew how to keep her mouth closed. Eventually they saw her as just one of them. None of the others ever tried to get with her. She was cute, but something about her just didn't resonate "wifey material" in their eyes. It also didn't help matters to know that she was breaking something off for Jordan every now and then. Quiet as she thought it was kept, everyone knew what was going on.

"What's good, girl?" AJ asked LaTanya, winking at her knowingly.

"Living life, boo-boo. Living life." LaTanya looked over at Martin. "So I hear you finally getting married."

Martin smiled. "Yup. Marrying my baby."

"That's so sweet."

"When you gon' get married, 'Tanya?" Curtis asked.

She shrugged. "I guess when a dude comes around that can handle all *this*."

DeAnthony laughed. "What you gon' do? Wait for Jordan to get divorced so he can handle it?"

LaTanya nudged Jordan. "J don't want none of this."

The crew started laughing. Everyone knew better than that.

Jordan put his arm around her. "I missed you, baby."

"Really?" She frowned at him. "You don't call nobody."

"You know how it is. Been busy with work and—"

"And Jada would cut his dick off if she found out he was kicking it with you," Curtis cut in.

LaTanya shook her head. "That's crazy. Men have female friends. She trips like that?"

Jordan just shrugged. He'd never once mentioned LaTanya to Jada in all the time that they'd been together. He hadn't seen the point. Honestly, once they got together and got married he didn't really see the point in bringing LaTanya up. The crew rarely hung out anymore anyway. He also didn't think that Jada would be feeling the idea of him having LaTanya as a friend. Jada had a way of reading people that was unreal. She could always tell when something was up, and he knew that she'd see right through his bullshit story of the two of them just being friends.

"Hell, yeah, she trips like that," DeAnthony stated. "Jordan don't go nowhere unless Jada's ass is right there. Shit, I'm surprised she didn't end up coming with him here."

"Naw, I wasn't gon' let that happen," Jordan said. "This was for the homies, and I made sure that was known. I wasn't gon' let her mess that up. And shut up, nigga. She don't go everywhere with me."

The crew laughed.

Jordan leaned over and whispered in LaTanya's ear. "You know I wasn't gon' let nothing keep me from seeing you again."

LaTanya giggled. "I know. I don't know why you married her anyway. She doesn't sound nothing like what you need. What kind of wife is so controlling and possessive that she can't let her man hang out with his friends?"

Jordan didn't intend to start bashing his wife. Deep down he loved Jada, but it felt so good to have people on his side, and to have a pretty girl cozying up to him. "That's why her ass is at home. I need a break from all that for a while."

LaTanya squeezed his leg under the table. "Well, anytime you need a break you needa call me. You ain't gotta put up with that mess. That's not a real woman."

Jordan pulled his camera out of his pocket and handed it to DeAnthony. "Aye, bruh. Take our picture."

"Sentimental-ass nigga," DeAnthony said taking the camera. "Snapping pics and shit."

"Memories, man," Jordan stated. "Never know when we'll all be together again."

Jordan wrapped his arms around LaTanya, and together, they smiled wide at the camera clicking in front of them. After that the camera was passed around and everyone was getting caught in fun poses. The night ensued with lots of laughter, drinks, and stories. Finally AJ decided that it was only right for them to take Martin to a strip club. Everyone was down, even LaTanya who had decided that she would ride over with Jordan.

As he pulled into the parking lot of Strokers, LaTanya leaned over and looked at him. Jordan turned the car off and turned to see her staring him dead in the face. "What?" he asked.

"Are you happy?" she asked him.

"Hell, yeah. I'm here with you. Hanging with my boys. Couldn't be happier."

She shook her head. "No . . . I mean, are you happy with Jada? Because from what I've heard you don't seem very happy to me."

"I wouldn't say that I'm unhappy. Marriage ain't easy, though."

"So why'd you marry her ass in the first place? I mean, really. If you were all that thrilled about being her husband you wouldn't have made it sound like being with me is the thrill of your life."

Jordan wasn't sure what LaTanya's intentions were. He was a little tipsy from the drinks they'd had at the restaurant, and admittedly, he was caught up in the moment of being back in his old routine of hanging with his homies. He didn't want to talk about his marriage or his feelings. He just wanted to have a good time.

"We should go on in," he told her reaching for the door handle.

LaTanya grabbed his face and forced him to look her in the eyes. "You don't really want her, do you?"

"Huh?" He could feel that familiar stirring down below and knew that nothing good could come from it.

"You heard me. You don't really want her, do you?"

"I love her. We just . . ."

LaTanya leaned in closer and licked her lips. "You just what?"

"She ain't you, baby," he found himself saying as he crushed his lips against hers.

LaTanya parted her lips so that their tongues could tackle each other. She reached down and squeezed his thigh, then groped his protruding manhood. She knew exactly what kind of pleasure that part of his anatomy could bring her, and she knew that he would be more than willing to go there with her. It made no difference to her who he was married to. If he didn't care about his vows or the woman he'd made them to, then why should she? LaTanya had always assumed that it was she that was truly the apple of Jordan's eye. Timing just hadn't worked out for them. He thought he was ready to settle down at an early age, but LaTanya knew that that wasn't the move for her. Although he'd never approached her with the proposition of them trying to be a real couple she could feel the chemistry between them and knew that he wanted her. Maybe in another time they could have tried to make it work if he hadn't up and married Jada so soon. But now that he appeared to want out, LaTanya was sure that she could be all the woman his current mistake couldn't be for him.

Jordan didn't protest when LaTanya unzipped his pants and reached inside to pull out his dick. It felt good to feel her stroke it. He assumed that she was going to give him head right quick, but LaTanya had other plans. She reached into her purse and pulled out a three-pack of Lifestyle condoms. Hastily she tore the box open, pulled one out, and tossed the box onto the dashboard. Jordan swallowed hard and let his seat all the way back. He pulled his pants down and took the condom from her so that he could slide it on. LaTanya kicked off her shoes and peeled off her skinny jeans and thongs before climbing over and mounting him in the driver's seat.

His windows were tinted, and it was dark so neither of them were worried much about anyone catching them in the middle of their lustful act. The boys were inside the club already and were probably wondering where the hell they'd gone. But then again, the crew knew Jordan and LaTanya's history and wouldn't have been the least bit surprised to know that they were off somewhere sneaking in a quick fuck.

LaTanya grinded her hips and gripped his dick tightly with the muscles of her pussy. Jordan was in second heaven. The last sexual contact he'd had was head from Mona in his office. He was long overdue for some sexual healing. He grabbed LaTanya's breasts as she moved about rhythmically. The windows were fogging up from the heat that their ecstasy was creating. LaTanya's moaning was driving him insane as he bucked into her tight, wet pussy madly. In moments he was grabbing her ass and coming so hard that he thought he was going to break her small, thin body in half.

LaTanya rubbed his head as he released himself while inside of her. A smile crossed her lips,
knowing that she'd just forbiddingly pleasured
this man that didn't belong to her. Now she
could send him back home to his sorry-ass wife
knowing that he'd be thinking of this moment
he'd just shared with her. She lifted her hips,
and his plastic-wrapped dick slipped from her
entrance. She scampered back over to the passenger seat and pulled some baby wipes out of
her purse to clean herself up.

"You came prepared, didn't you?" Jordan
asked, pulling the wet condom off.

LaTanya handed him a wipe to wrap it up in,
and then another to clean himself off. "You just
never know," she said smiling.

Silently they both got cleaned up and redressed.
LaTanya was feeling a sense of accomplishment.
She knew that she had Jordan back in her good
graces and that his wife had better watch out
for her. Jordan, on the other hand, felt a little
guilty. Jada was sitting home on bed rest stew-
ing over the problems that he'd created in their
marriage, and here he was getting his freak on
with a woman that he'd never really see past her
superficial beauty and easily accessible pussy.
He had no business being anyone's husband. He
wondered how he could ever really be the man

that Jada wanted him to be. He looked over at LaTanya, who quickly blew him a kiss. The affection of women just made him feel like something special. Jordan couldn't control himself around a female.

"Come on," LaTanya said. "Let's go see what these fools are doing."

He moved to get out of the car but noticed the box of condoms on the dashboard. Quickly he removed it and tossed it into the glove compartment, making a mental note to get rid of it before going home. Together, he and LaTanya headed toward the door of the popular strip club.

LaTanya grabbed his hand and whispered to him. "When you get ready to get your life together and walk away from that mistake you made, you know I'm here for you."

Jordan remained silent. Had marrying Jada really been a mistake?

Chapter 24

The Girls

Their last impromptu meeting hadn't gone so well so Candace wanted to do something to make it up to her girls. With all of the changes going on in her life she wanted to be able to share her happiness with them versus having any distance between them. She'd talked to Jada already, but she hadn't really been able to catch up with Alex aside from a text here and there. Today they were going to come together and chill the way girls were supposed to.

Zoe was away for the weekend with Candace's parents, who were currently not too pleased with her. Rico was out with his friends at the studio. Candace had the apartment to herself and had gone out of her way to make things comfortable for the ladies. She had her cheese dip on deck already in the center of the coffee table with a bowl of chips surrounding it. For dinner she'd whipped up some homemade Chinese food like only she could do, including veggie egg rolls, chicken fried rice, and sweet and spicy wings. On the dining-room table sat two bottles of wine. She planned for them to drink and talk the night away.

The doorbell resounded, and Candace hurried over to let her girls in. She didn't even stop to check the peephole. "What's up, chicas?" she exclaimed as she threw the door open. Her heart stopped the moment she saw Khalil standing before her in jeans, a solid back shirt, and an expensive-looking leather jacket.

"Hello, beautiful." He smiled at her as if there wasn't anything at all wrong with the fact that he'd just popped up at her house unannounced after being ghost for nearly a month. In his mind he was just doing what he always did. No big deal.

Candace wasn't pleased at all. She hadn't been able to get him to answer his phone lately so that she could fill him in on her life changes. The man couldn't return a call, but he had no problem just showing up. It irked her to no end. "What are you doing here?" she whined looking over his shoulder. She wanted him gone before her girls showed up.

"Came to see my girls."

"*Your* girls? What are you talking about?"

"You and Zoe," Khalil replied looking at her questioningly. "You okay? You look a little flustered."

"You think?" she asked. "Look, Zoe's not here, and I'm about to have company."

"A dude?" he asked with attitude.

"No, not a dude but—"

"Then let me in, woman. I'm not scared of your friends." Khalil pushed past her and made his way over to the couch, helping himself to her cheese dip. "You got it smelling good in here, gorgeous. Looks like I showed up right on time."

"No, you did not!" she snapped. "You should have called first, Khalil. You can't just keep popping up on me whenever you get ready."

"Why you trippin'? As long as my daughter lives here I'm coming by. Long as you don't have some dude laying up in here, everything's cool, baby."

"You're so stupid!" she shouted moving away from her open front door. "You pretend to be all perceptive and shit, but you're so stupid. You just don't get it." She held her left hand up so he could see the faux gold diamond ring she'd purchased at Wal-Mart for herself two days ago. "I'm married, Khalil. I have a husband now. You can't just come up in my house whenever you feel like it, and you damn sure can't come at me like you think you're gon' get any booty."

Khalil dropped a chip back onto the plate and rose from his seat. "You're married?" he asked.

She nodded. "And I don't think my husband would appreciate you coming to our house out of the blue like this. I've been trying to call you. You better start learning to communicate better for the sake of our daughter."

Khalil walked over to her and stared down at the short woman. "What the hell's wrong with you, Candace?"

"*Excuse* you?"

"Explain to me how you marry one out-of-touch brother that can't take care of you, cheat on him with me, and act like you love me, have my baby, then run off and marry the very next dude that smiles at you? You *that* hungry for attention? You just gotta have a man up under you? Damn, baby! You needa fuckin' breathe for a minute. Let your pussy breathe for a second before you let another nigga run up in it."

On impulse Candace reached up and slapped him. Her anger was at full capacity. "What you won't do is come in my house and call me a ho. Not when you're the biggest ho of them all, going around making babies everywhere that you can't take care of."

Khalil shook it off and grabbed her into a tight embrace. "What I know is that this pussy belongs to me. Who you think you fooling, baby? You done went and found you a cheap imitation of me. Some nigga that can't even afford to move you out of this one-bedroom apartment. You made a mistake, sweetheart. How you gon' give my good stuff away?"

Candace was appalled. "Get your hands off of me. We're done."

"We're never going to be done." Khalil held her by the shoulders with one arm and reached down to stick his free hand between her legs. "Nobody can get it wet like me. You know that. You know you like the way I make you scream. You want me to fuck you right now, Candace. I can feel the heat from your pussy."

She struggled to push his hands away. "Fucking with you again was a mistake, Khalil. But I'm over it now. I'm married. You're not getting any of this anymore!"

"Anymore?" Alex's voice shocked both Candace and Khalil.

The couple hadn't noticed Alex and Jada approach the apartment taking root at the threshold of the open door. Jada remained silent as she rubbed her belly, and Alex's mouth hung wide open. This was more drama than they could have ever imagined.

"Um . . . hey, y'all," Candace said, pushing Khalil away. "I don't think y'all have ever officially met. This is Khalil, Zoe's dad. Khalil, these are my girlfriends, Alex and Jada."

Khalil smiled, not the least bit fazed that they'd just walked in on him molesting Candace. "Nice to meet you ladies."

"Um, do we need to come back later?" Jada asked, failing to budge from her spot in the doorway.

Alex moved on into the living room carrying a bag of ice per Candace's instructions. "Why should we leave? It looks like there's a lot going on here to keep us entertained."

Candace rolled her eyes at Alex and motioned for Jada to come in. "Girl, no. Come on in. Khalil was just leaving."

Jada entered and shut the door behind her.

Khalil shot Candace a look. "Was I? I don't think our business is done yet."

"Oh, believe me, we're done," Candace retorted. "We're so done you might as well burn the memories you have."

"A lover's quarrel?" Alex joked.

Candace frowned at her. "Ha-ha. We're not lovers. Go put that ice in the kitchen, girl. It's melting. You're dripping water all over the floor."

"Don't blame me because y'all got it so hot and steamy up in here," Alex shot back before walking off to the kitchen.

Jada took a seat on the sofa. She wasn't sure what was going on, but she had to agree with Alex. It was clear that they'd walked in on a very steamy moment between Candace and Khalil.

Candace turned back to Khalil. "As you can see I have plans, and like I said, Zoe isn't here so you can just go."

Khalil popped his knuckles. "Can I have a word with you in private?"

"Ooh, in *private?*" Alex said coming out of the kitchen. "Why y'all gotta go be in private now? You had the door wide open so the whole complex already knows your business. Now what's this about you being married again?"

"Not now, Alex!" Candace snapped, annoyed that her friend was behaving so childishly during such a frustrating moment for her. She pointed toward the hallway. "Bedroom, now," she said to Khalil.

"With pleasure," he stated, leading the way.

"I'll be right back, y'all," Candace told the girls before scurrying off.

They heard the bedroom door slam, and Alex ran over to the sofa laughing. "Oh my God, girl! What is going on with your friend?"

Jada shook her head. "I don't know. This seems like a whole bunch of mess if you ask me." She reached for a chip and scooped some dip out. "But I know one thing. If she's back there fuckin' ol' boy while we're sitting out here waiting I'm leaving."

"Forget her. I'ma go in there and start making those egg rolls she made disappear." Alex laughed again. "Candace and her baby daddy drama. And do you know anything about this marriage business?"

Jada munched on her chip and screwed up her face.

Alex pointed at her. "Jada! You better tell me what's going on, friend."

"It's not my business to tell, but you gon' find out anyway . . . she married Rico."

Alex frowned and clutched her chest. "Oh God, no. Say it isn't so."

Jada reached for another chip. "Would if I could, honey. They went to the courthouse yesterday."

"Then why the hell aren't they having a honeymoon instead of her having us over here for girls' night and having her boyfriend back there arguing?"

Jada chuckled. "'Cause I wasn't about to come off of any money or my time to throw together no reception to celebrate her haphazard nuptials. Plus you know that dude don't have no money for no honeymoon."

Alex shook her head. "This is like déjà vu. How does one person marry two totally wrong-for-them dudes back-to-back?"

Jada shook her head. "I don't know, girl." She couldn't understand herself how she could be married to a man that had seemed perfect a year ago but was now making her completely miserable. Who was she to judge what Candace was doing?

Suddenly the front door swung open and in walked Rico looking just as hood as ever. His pants sagged, displaying his forest-green-colored boxers, and his hat was pulled low over his eyes. He had to tilt his head back to get a good look at them.

"What's up?" he greeted them before throwing his eyes at the table.

"Hey," Alex stated dryly.

Jada remained silent. After what Candace had told her about Rico not caring much for them she wasn't too interested in exchanging pleasantries with him.

"Where Candace?" he asked.

Jada pursed her lips. She wished that she'd followed her gut instinct and never stepped foot inside the apartment. This wasn't the kind of stress that she needed to be engulfed in. Alex shook her head. She too could feel the impending doom lingering over them.

"Umm . . . she had to handle something in the back," Alex said nervously. "Umm . . . oh yeah. Jada, I think we need to go do that favor she asked us to do."

Jada caught the hint and was glad that Alex had given them a way out of this tragic situation. "Yeah . . . Yeah, you're right." She struggled to pull herself up from the couch. "Come on, let's go before the store closes."

"Y'all still doing your ladies' night thing?" Rico asked.

"Um . . . We were," Alex answered. "But um . . ."

"I ain't trying to interrupt y'all party. I just needa get at Candace real quick, then y'all can get back to ya male bashin' and shit."

"Male bashing?" Alex asked.

Just like Jada hadn't told Alex before about Candace marrying Rico she also hadn't told her about Rico not liking them. The moment just seemed to grow darker and darker. Jada pulled on Alex's arm and tried to get her to abandon the discussion so that they could make a break for it.

"Yeah. You know how y'all do," Rico said smirking.

"And what y'all are you referring to?" Alex asked getting offended.

"Alex, come on," Jada said softly.

"I'm talking about you and your homie," Rico said pointing at Jada. "I don't know what kinda stuff you really be saying to my wife, but I'd appreciate it if you left me out of your discussions."

"What makes you think you're important enough to warrant a spot in our discussions?" Alex shot back.

"Candace tells me everything."

"She does, huh?"

Jada could feel the tension rising. She knew that Alex could get real reckless with her mouth when she got angry, and the last thing they needed to do was add any fuel to this fire that was already about to blaze out of control. "Alex!" she hissed.

"Yeah. So you can keep your opinions to yourself. You and your li'l sidekick. I know how misery loves company."

Something clicked within Jada, and her goal to get out was quickly forgotten. "You calling me miserable? You don't know anything about me, sweetie."

"You don't know nothing 'bout me either. All the more reason for you to fall back and stay out of our business."

"Let me tell you something, you short-ass, insignificant, crusty-ass, self-righteous son of a bitch. Don't nobody care about you. We care about Candace. I could give two fucks about you. So when she comes to me with whatever she wants to talk about, I'ma give my two cents whether you like it or not."

"And you can kiss our ass in the process," Alex chimed in.

"Aye, man, you can—" Rico's words fell short as a crashing sound from the back made everyone turn to look up the hall.

Candace's bedroom door flew open, and she stormed out, hollering, "Hope you remember what it tastes like because you'll never taste it again!" she screamed. She turned to walk up the hall and noticed Rico standing in the middle of the living room staring at her. "Oh my God." It was too late for her to do anything.

Khalil exited the room adjusting his pants and hollering behind her. "You don't have to put on a show for your friends, sweetheart. I'm sure you've already told them how good I put it down, so we all know you'll be back."

"What the fuck!" Rico's young voice barked. Khalil stopped dead in his tracks. Understanding washed over him, and he smiled at Candace. "This must be your new beau." Khalil laughed. "Yeah. Way to marry up, beautiful."

"Shut up," Candace hissed behind her. She hurried over to Rico and placed her hands on his chest. "Baby, I can explain."

He shoved her, and that one act was enough to make everyone else spring into action.

"You punk-ass bitch!" Alex screamed, running over and kicking Rico in the ass with the heel of her shoe.

Khalil stepped forward and literally picked Candace up to spin her around and place her behind him. "You wanna put your hands on somebody, young buck? Put your hands on a man."

"No! No! Don't do this!" Candace cried, trying to pull Khalil away to get him to back down.

Rico looked from Alex to Khalil. He was fuming and the piercing pain from Alex's blow was bothering him. "Get the fuck out of my house, all of y'all."

"Negative," Khalil said. "How you gon' keep a woman when you don't even know how to treat a woman? I'm not leaving. *You* leave."

"You fucking this nigga in *my* house?" Rico yelled at Candace. "You fucking this nigga in the room I sleep in, and now you got him in my face?"

Candace stomped her foot. "I'm trying to tell you it's not what it looks like. He just came over to see Zoe."

"Right. That nigga never comes to see his daughter. That's *my* daughter."

Khalil stepped closer. "The fuck is wrong with you?" He raised his fist to swing, but Candace caught him by the elbow.

"No! Get the hell outta my house." She let go of Khalil's arms. "Please, just go!" she screamed. "You've single-handedly turned my home upside down, you selfish bastard. Get out. Please. I'm begging you to go."

Khalil stared at her as if she was crazy. "I just watched this dude put his hands on you."

"He pushed me . . . That's all." She held her arms out. "I'm fine. Okay? I'm fine, and I can handle myself. Go. Please just go."

Khalil nodded and wolfed up at her. "You're not the woman I thought you were. Don't call me once your husband starts whooping your ass." He took one final look at Rico, then pushed past him to make his way out of the door.

Jada held her stomach and her breath. The shit had certainly hit the fan.

"You told me you was having girls' night," Rico said accusingly to Candace.

She lowered her arms and shook her head. "I didn't know he was coming. He does that all the time. I tried to tell him he can't just disrespect us like that by just popping up. Then he wanted to talk—"

"In the bedroom?" he squealed.

Candace shrugged. "For privacy," she replied weakly.

"Right!" He turned around and looked at Jada and Alex. "Then you got your homies in crime out here listening while you in there getting it on with dude."

"Nothing happened, baby," Candace cried. "Nothing happened."

Rico pointed at Jada. "I bet you practically pulled his dick out and shoved him in there inside of her."

Jada frowned. "You're a demented little fuck. Don't address me please. In fact, Alex, let's go." She turned away to leave.

"Yeah, get the hell on. And *don't* come back." He turned to Candace. "You can't fuck with these grimy bitches anymore. What kind of friend lets you cheat on your husband and don't try to stop you?"

"Grimy bitch?" Alex repeated. "*Grimy bitch?*"

Rico looked at her. "Did I stutter? Fuck out my house, man. Surprised y'all bitches even have a man. Probably why your man didn't even wanna go out with you," he said pointing to Jada. "He probably cheating on yo' stuck-up ass. Told you . . . misery loves company."

"I'm not gon' be too many more bitches and what-not, "Alex said balling up her fist.

"Guys, please," Candace begged them to let it go. Her party wasn't turning out the way she'd expected it to.

Jada walked up to Rico. Her belly nearly poked him in his midsection. "You know what? You ain't shit. What kind of man comes for a chick like this? A pussy-ass punk, that's who. I wish you would say one more word to me. Call me out my name one more time and I promise you my husband will squish your ass like the little bug you are." She reached down and picked up Candace's bowl of cheese dip.

Candace's eyes grew wide, and she held up her hands in fright. "No, Jada. Don't, please don't—"

Jada threw the dip on Rico and tossed the bowl at his head. He lunged for her, but Alex stepped forward before he could make a move.

"You gon' hit a pregnant woman?" Alex asked. "That's the day yo' ass is going to jail."

Rico flung cheese dip from his eyes. "Get the fuck out of my house!" he yelled.

"Gladly," Jada said. "Once you get one, ya' broke bitch." She turned away and headed for the door once more. "Let's go, Alex." She walked out without bothering to say good-bye to Candace. She was eager to leave the girl and her drama behind.

Alex smirked at Rico. "You met the right ones today, sweetie." She looked at Candace and shook her head. "You got some real mess to clean up, friend," she said, *not* referring at all to the cheese dip that was ruining her carpet. Alex exited the apartment and slammed the door behind her.

Candace fell to the floor. She was exasperated. Everything had gone totally wrong, and she didn't know what to do now. She vowed to never have a dinner party at her place again. Every time she did, things seemed to go left. Candace feared that this time she'd lost all of the relationships that were most important to her. All she could do was cry.

Chapter 25

Corey

"What you got for me?" Corey asked his boy. He lit up the blunt he'd just rolled and inhaled the herb deeply.

"Man, I'm telling you I know where their stash house is, but I don't know for sure who did what," Antonio said. "I mean, it ain't like I can just go up there and start asking questions. I heard that Man-Man and Justin are running the block. I can only assume that they're the ones that . . . you know. But they keep a gang of niggas around like they know you 'bout to come for them."

"As they should," Corey said passing the blunt over. "So we gotta see how we can get them two dudes alone without they crew. Gotta figure out how to get them alone where they can get to talking."

Antonio pulled hard on the blunt. "You know they say pussy is the greatest weakness known to man."

"So get a chick to do what? Go over there and front like she buying some shit or something?"

"Naw . . . Get a chick to make them think they gon' get some. They not gon' bring their homeboys through for that."

Corey shook his head and snatched his blunt back. "Nigga, you sound crazy. How the hell is that going to work?"

"What else you got?"

Corey thought about it. He really didn't have a better idea. "Fine . . . sounds extra but find a chick and run it."

"You want me to find a chick? I'on know, man."

Corey leaned back and gave it some consideration. He needed someone who wouldn't be scared to strut their stuff and lead these potentially dangerous dudes on. He needed someone who quite possibly owed him a favor and would feel obligated to do him this solid without him having to offer her anything in return. He could only think of one chick that fit the bill. "A'ight. It's going down tomorrow."

Antonio was high already. He had a lot of things on his mind these days. "What's going down?" His heart was racing thinking that Corey was ready to make a move without having figured out how to get Man-Man and Justin alone.

"The chick, dawg. We gon' send the chick 'round that way tomorrow. By this weekend we gon' get some get back."

Antonio wasn't so sure that things would work out that smoothly, but he was hoping that they'd hurry up and get past this whole ordeal.

He checked the time on his cell phone again. Where the hell was she? She hadn't sounded too happy to hear from him after all that had gone down, but he didn't care. He was on a mission and he wasn't about to be deterred by her feelings. He was about to send her a text to see what was up but an unfamiliar car whipped into the parking spot next to his, causing him to pause. He watched as she got out of her car and slammed the door. She opened his passenger door and slid inside.

"I'm here," Candace said, crossing her arms and not looking him in the eyes. "Now what do you want?"

"Why you gotta be so salty?" he asked her.

"You already know the answer to that."

"No, I don't."

"Did you call me down here to harass me about why I'm unhappy about being in your presence?"

Corey sucked his teeth. He wasn't going to be able to jump to the business without putting her in her place. "We're both grown. Say what's on your mind, Ma. Let's get it all out on the table so that we can move on."

"That's my problem," she said finally turning to look at him. She couldn't believe that she'd ever gone there with him. "I don't understand why we have anywhere to move on to. We don't have no business with one another, so why the hell are you bothering me?"

"You feeling some kind of way about me now?"

"I shouldn't? I mean, if I hadn't been fucking around with you I would have never been there arguing with one of my best friends before she died."

"Check this out . . . I didn't make you do shit. You're a grown woman, and you made a decision on your own free will. I didn't rape you, I didn't beg you for the pussy, and I definitely didn't trick your ass into opening your legs. So don't blame me for how you got ya' self caught up. It is what it is. On another note, don't be making light of this shit and regarding me like it was my fault. Stephanie didn't die, Candace. She was killed. There's a fuckin' difference."

Candace opened her mouth to speak, then closed it. There was no point in arguing with him. Corey was right, to a degree. She'd made a decision and had suffered the consequences rightly so. He saw the change in her demeanor and the anger in her face turn to hurt. He had her roped in emotionally.

"And that's what I called you for, Candace. I'm 'bout to fix the niggas that shot Stephanie," he told her.

Candace frowned. "Why are you telling me this?" she asked softly.

"Because I need your help. I need to get these niggas alone, and I need a chick to do that."

"Why me?"

"Because I know you wanna do something to help avenge your girl's death considering how y'all fell out."

Candace shook her head. "You trying to guilt me into being an accessory to some shit? I have a kid, Corey. I can't be putting myself in no dangerous situations with you. And I damn sho' shouldn't be sitting here with you with the damn feds hounding me to give them more information about them niggas and you and your associates."

"My associates?" His interest was piqued.

"Yes. This agent is gunning for you and wants to know about whoever the hell you hang out with or whatever. I don't like being tied to none of this criminal shit."

It was clear that the feds were trying their best to build up a case against Tommy and BDM. That had to be who the agent was questioning Candace about. Lucky for him no one but Antonio truly knew about his connection to the crime mob.

"I need you in on this, Candace," Corey said. "Help me do this. Help me get revenge for what they did to her."

Candace shook her head. She'd made a lot of bad decisions up to this point. Everything she touched fell apart, even her friendship with Stephanie. If she could take it all back she would, but she couldn't. She also didn't know how to fix any of it ongoing. How could she make any of it right? "What do I have to do?" she asked as a tear trickled down her left cheek.

They'd been sitting down the street from their rival's trap waiting for the dudes to bust a move. The front door opened and two young guys walked out with three other dudes following close behind them.

"That one right there with the hat on is Man-Man," Antonio said. "My cousin fucks with his sister."

Corey nodded. "A'ight, so I'm assuming the nigga beside him is Justin."

"Most likely."

The crew hopped into a black Suburban and drove down the street. Corey tailed them, being sure to stay far enough behind to not raise any red flags. They drove to the BP gas station and parked at a pump. Corey kept going and parked on the side of the convenience store. They watched from the window as the duo got out of the ride and walked inside with only one of their crew members trailing them.

Corey turned around to look at Candace who looked a little nervous. "You know what to do," he told her. "Keep it short, simple, and to the point. Make sure you sell it. A'ight?"

Candace nodded. She slowly exited the car and hurried to the front of the store. Wearing skintight jeans and a low-cut shirt accenting her breasts Candace knew she'd have no problem getting their attention. She could see them on the snack aisle and made her way around to come up the other end of the same aisle. Keeping her eyes low she walked toward them.

"What's up, Ma?" the guy Antonio said was Man-Man eyeballed her like he wanted to rip her clothes off.

She smiled at him. "What's up, Pa?"

Feeling himself, Man-Man sauntered over to her and touched her arm lightly. "Baby, you what's up, for real. What's yo' name?"

"Candy."

"Candy? Mmm, I bet you sweet like candy too, ain't you?"

"You already know."

"How 'bout you show me?"

Candace smiled coyly. "On one condition."

He raised an eyebrow. "And what's that?"

She looked over at the other guy Justin who wasn't paying them any attention. "Bring yo' boy with you."

Man-Man's eyes extended. "Word?"

Candace nodded.

At eighteen, Man-Man hadn't had a three-some yet and was ready to get it popping now if she was down to do it. "Stay right here." He stepped back and slapped Justin on the arm. "Aye, nigga, that girl wanna do a train."

Justin looked at Man-Man like he was crazy. "What you talkin' 'bout, stupid?"

"Ole girl wanna give us some of that good good. She told me herself she wanna fuck with us."

Justin looked over at Candace. She smiled at him seductively. Justin shook his head. "Get out of here. That girl ain't say that."

"I'm dead ass. Come on. What, you don't want no pussy?"

"I ain't desperate for no trim, nigga. And don't you got a bitch?"

Man-Man shrugged. "Ain't no pussy like new pussy."

Justin waved him off. "Man, I'm 'bout to get my shit and go to the car. You trippin'."

Candace approached them. The bigger brother standing behind Justin stepped forward. "Can we help you?" he asked her.

Man-Man gave the big guy the side-eye. "Aye, she cool, bruh."

Candace focused her attention on Justin. "Y'all gonna come holla at me or nah?"

Justin's facial expression was serious. "You just going 'round jumping niggas off?"

"Naw. But I fucks with bosses. You a boss, ain't you?"

Justin nodded. She had a point there. He nodded his head toward Man-Man. "Text my man ya' address and shit. We'll roll through."

Man-Man eagerly gave her his number, and she sent him a text with her address.

"Make sure you come by yourself," she told Man-Man. "Just you and ya' boy. Leave ya' homeboy over there at the house," she said eyeing the dude that tried to step to her.

Man-Man nodded. "We got you, Ma. We gon' roll through around eight. That cool?"

"Yep. That's cool." She reached out and touched his manhood for good measure. "I'ma see you then."

Candace grabbed a Little Debbie cake, went to the counter to pay for it to make her visit to the store seem legit, then hurried out of the store and to the car. She slid into the backseat and leaned back. Her heart was pounding. Corey pulled out of the parking spot and rode off in the opposite direction.

"We good?" Corey asked her looking in his rearview mirror.

She nodded. "Eight o'clock. This ain't gon' be messy, is it?"

Corey shook his head. "Not at all. Get 'em there, we gon' come in and snatch they ass out, then it's over. Simple as that."

"I don't need this shit coming back to me, Corey," she said cautiously.

"I'm on it, Candace. I got this."

She turned away and stared out of the window. Corey knew she was nervous but the hard part of her role was over and done. He was gonna take care of it from here on out. He looked over at Antonio. "Make sure you got two good runners ready."

Antonio nodded. He'd already had two of their men ready for action. The plan was simple. While Corey was handling Man-Man and Justin, the runners would knock off the two dudes they assumed would be left at the stash house, assuming one of their crew members drove them over to Candace's. While Corey was getting his revenge his men would be knocking over the stash house and getting his money back.

What could possibly go wrong?

Chapter 26

Miranda

Six Months Prior

"What's going on with you?" Stephanie asked her softly.

She could hear the sound of the door close behind her, the two men inside wanting nothing to do with this accidental intervention.

"It all makes sense to me now," Stephanie said, brushing back her friend's hair.

She studied Miranda's physique and body language. Her face looked harder than she'd ever remembered, and she constantly kept pinching her nose although Stephanie could tell she was trying hard to appear her normal self. "All this time I thought that you were fucking around with Corey. But all this time you've been fucking up yourself with Corey's shit. I don't know whether to be mad at you for being so *stupid or to pity you for being so obviously lost that you turned to this."*

"Don't judge me," Miranda said curtly. *"Like you're perfect or something. Don't judge me. You don't know what my life is like, what I'm going through, or how I feel."*

"All you've ever had to do is pick up the phone, girl."

"And call you, Steph? You're always too busy worrying about who Corey's under to be concerned with anyone else's problems." Miranda looked down at the ground and sucked her teeth. *"You're probably gonna go run and get on your phone to tell the other girls what you think you know . . . Tell them, then, Stephanie. I'm dying on the inside anyway, so nothing else really matters."* She looked back up and stared deep into Stephanie's eyes.

Stephanie felt her skin crawl and shivers ran up her spine.

"Then again, you practically said it yourself," Miranda stated. *"You're really just glad to know that Corey isn't fucking around on you . . . Well, at least not with me."*

Current Day

She could remember it as if it was yesterday. The way Stephanie had looked at her; the feeling of embarrassment that came over her. The annoyance she felt knowing that Stephanie would run right back to the others and paint her out to be a monster. It was the moment she'd decided that Stephanie wasn't shit. It was one of the memories that had fueled her desire to get even with Stephanie and her dope boyfriend. And she'd done it. But in the end, she didn't feel any better because of it. Thinking about all the lies she'd told and all the mischievous things she'd done while not in her right mind made her shutter. She wanted to not care. None of them cared much about her. They'd all been so much more concerned with the irrelevant drama going on in their own lives to give a damn about her.

"Do you think it's fair?" Doctor Dunham asked her.

Miranda stared at her. "Do I think what's fair?"

She was sitting in her first group session since the time she'd assaulted Missy. Consequently they'd made sure not to seat her next to the girl who was still itching to get even with Miranda.

"We were talking about blaming others for the decisions that we've made. Do you think that's fair?"

She thought back to her previous admittance of having wanted someone to save her from herself. Since no one had done it she felt trapped within her own madness and was upset with the world. She blamed the girls and her family for not being the support system they claimed to be, but she certainly didn't blame them for the decisions she'd made.

"No. It's not fair," she said. "We're all grown. We're responsible for our own actions."

"Hmmm. So do you think it's fair for us to turn our backs on others when they fall short of what we think they should do or how we think they should be?"

Miranda blinked hard. Was it a trick question? "That's called disappointment. People shut down when they've been disappointed so many times."

"So at what point do we start to forgive?"

Miranda shrugged. "I don't know."

"If you hold the anguish in forever you're gon' always need some substance to take you away from it," Stacey, a heroin addict, commented. "Something to numb the pain."

"That breeds addiction," Doctor Dunham said.

"So you're saying we should start forgiving folk that have hurt us so we can kick our habits?" Miranda asked, trying to connect the dots.

Doctor Dunham nodded. "Forgiveness is for you. Not for the other person. It frees you up emotionally and mentally."

Miranda crossed her arms. She was going to have to think about that one. Perhaps it was time to forgive everyone for being absent when she'd needed them present the most. If Doctor Dunham was right she needed that freedom that came with forgiveness.

"The most important thing that you must do is forgive yourself," Doctor Dunham added. "First and foremost, you need to forgive yourself."

Forgive myself, Miranda thought. She needed to figure out how to do that.

Chapter 27

Candace

She was nervous. It was 8:10 p.m., and they still weren't there. It was just as well because Khalil hadn't shown up to pick up Zoe at 6:00 like he'd promised. Candace really wanted to pull out her cell and call Rico to see if they could talk about things. Ever since the fiasco with him and Khalil and her girls she hadn't been able to get a word in with him. He'd packed a bag and walked out of the house without any explanation of where he was going. Candace had been distraught. As she sat there now watching the seconds tick away on the clock above her television in the living room she wondered how she'd gotten herself to this point. Nothing was right, and she had a sense of unrest rooted inside of her that made it almost impossible for her to smile or feel any amount of joy.

Zoe was playing with her rattle in the swing that she loved so much. Candace shook her head. If Khalil was going to choose now to pull a disappearing act she was going to have to put the baby in the bedroom until this whole ordeal was over. She knew that Corey was parked outside somewhere in the parking lot near her building waiting for the dudes to arrive. With the way everyone else was not doing what they were supposed to be doing Candace prayed that Corey was keeping watch and that he'd show up immediately after the dudes knocked on her door because the last thing she was going to do was whore herself out in the name of exacting revenge against Stephanie's killers. That's where she drew the line.

It frightened her to think that the men that had gunned down her friend were going to be standing in her living room. Looking at them up close in the middle of the day earlier nothing about them had struck her as familiar. She wondered just how sure Corey was that he had the right guys. She didn't believe in Corey's method of revenge and tinkered with the idea of calling that GBI agent to come pick up the hoodlums. She dismissed the idea the moment she realized that she'd be questioned about just how they'd come to be in her apartment. She didn't want to implicate Corey in anything, not that she owed him that courtesy. Truth was she didn't want to face any charges of her own for her involvement in this dangerously stupid stunt.

Candace's phone rang, and she jumped. Nervously she picked it up and looked at the caller ID. Great, she thought. He would be calling back at the most inconvenient time. She answered the phone and tried to keep her tone light. "Hey, Rico."

"What's up?" he asked nonchalantly.

"I'm glad you called," she told him. Never mind the fact that she wished he'd waited just a little later to do so. "I miss you, baby."

"You sure 'bout that?"

"Why wouldn't I be? You're my husband." She figured it was a good selling point, even though they'd been married for a very short amount of time.

"So you trying to tell me you ain't been fucking that dude since we've been together?" he asked. "Not just since we been married. Since we've been together. Period."

"No!" she exclaimed, hoping that he believed her. "Absolutely not. It's just been me and you, Rico. You know that."

"No, I don't know that. I know that I saw dude coming out yo' bedroom fixing his pants like he'd just pulled them joints up . . . like he'd just been knee-deep in some shit that belongs to me."

"You have to trust me, Rico," she said watching Zoe swing back and forth in amazement. "Nothing's going on with me and Khalil. It was all just one big ugly misunderstanding. Please . . . come home."

Rico paused. "A'ight. I'ma come."

She smiled, but before she could comment there was a knock at the door. She'd almost forgotten about the plan that was about to go down. She needed to hurry up and get these fools out of her house before her husband came home. She didn't need to have a repeat performance from the last time he'd been there. "So you gon' catch a ride over here?" she asked opening her door and holding up her finger to silence the thugs.

Justin gave her a funny look and hesitated in the doorway. Man-Man, on the other hand, waltzed right in and took a seat on the sofa. He had a box of condoms burning a hole in his pocket.

"Yeah. When I leave the studio with my homeboy I'll be there," Rico said over the phone.

"Okay. See you then," Candace said, avoiding the cold hard stare that Justin was giving her as she disconnected the call and set her phone on her dining-room table.

Justin closed the door and moved to stand by the sofa. He saw the baby amusing herself in the swing and shook his head. "You usually get down with your kid in the room?"

Candace shook her head and tried to relax. "Naw. Her dad was supposed to come get her, but the jerk didn't come."

"So you just gon' leave her there?"

Candace shrugged. "I mean, I planned to just put her in her bed."

"You should do that."

Candace could sense that something wasn't right with Justin. "You okay?" she asked him. "You seem all on edge and shit." She prayed that he wasn't on to her somehow.

"Who's ya' baby's daddy?"

"Why? He's nobody that you know or wanna know. Trust me."

"Aye, man, chill," Man-Man interjected. "We supposed to be having fun with ole' girl. You in here grilling her like you the DA or some shit."

Justin shook his head. "Naw, something just don't feel right."

Candace looked away from him and walked over to Zoe's swing. Where the hell was Corey already? She didn't want this experience or conversation to go any further. Justin hurried over to her and started patting her down everywhere abrasively.

"Hey!" Candace yelled feeling violated and scared. "What the fuck?"

"Just checking," he said eyeing her. "Relax. This what you wanted, right? For us to come fuck the shit out of you."

Candace cleared her throat. "Yeah," she said uncertainly. "I just figured you'd be a li'l more gentle about it and shit."

Man-Man walked over to them and grabbed her ass. "You ripe as hell, Ma," he said. He reached around, placed his hand under her tank top and squeezed her breasts.

Candace worked hard to fight back the tears of fear and frustration that threatened to fall. She didn't want them to sense that she was scared. "Let me . . . uh . . . let me take the baby to the back."

"Naw, you don't needa go back there," Justin said. "What's back there?"

"Nothing. I just don't want my baby exposed to this."

"You a good mother like that, huh?" Justin asked. "Well, your daughter's gon' learn that her mom's a ho sooner or later, so what difference does it make?" He pulled his gun from behind his back out of the band of his jeans. "Get on your knees."

"Aye, man, why the piece?" Man-Man asked his partner.

"'Cause I don't trust this bitch just yet."

Candace was biding her time now. "If you weren't down, then why'd you come?" she asked trying to sound completely legit with her freakiness.

"Curiosity," Justin told her pointing the gun at her forehead. "Now get your ass on your knees. You for real, then show me." With his free hand he unbuckled his jeans and slightly unzipped his pants.

Candace was afraid for her life and Zoe's. She fell to her knees. She was surprised that she hadn't started boo-hooing.

"You should be nicer to the ho," Man-Man stated whipping his dick out quickly and reaching down for her hand. He forced her to stroke him.

Candace wanted to throw up as she slowly unzipped the remainder of Justin's fly while slowly jerking Man-Man's penis. Just as she'd reached into Justin's musty-smelling drawers to pull out his dick, her front door flew open. Corey and Antonio stood in the doorway with their guns drawn and fixated on Justin and Man-Man.

"How 'bout you let the barrel of my bitch right here suck your dick off," Corey said.

"What the fuck?" Man-Man asked, reaching for his piece out of his sock.

"If you move I'm going to shoot your dick off," Antonio stated.

Immediately, Man-Man placed his hands in the air.

Justin smiled at Corey, pushed Candace away, and rezipped his fly. "I knew some shit wasn't right. So what now, nigga? What you gon' do now?"

Corey walked up to the trio and surveyed Candace quickly. "Get up and get the baby," he told her.

Shaking, Candace rose from the floor and fumbled to undo the snaps that held her baby securely in the swing. As she tried to move quickly Antonio walked over to Man-Man and motioned for him to walk toward the door. He did as instructed.

Justin laughed. "Shoulda known y'all niggas would use some pussy to try to come for us. Don't you know if you fuck with me, then Martinez just gon' send some dudes to fuck up the rest of yo' crew and knock off BDM?"

Candace didn't know what he was talking about, and she didn't care to hear any more of their street talk. She freed a fussy Zoe from the swing and moved to walk toward her bedroom.

Antonio was standing at the door aiming his gun at Man-Man's head and looking back at Corey. "Come on, man. Let's go."

"You shot my girl, didn't you?" Corey asked Justin. Everything inside of him told him that this was the exact heartless thug that had taken Stephanie's life.

"I see you got the message," Justin said ruthlessly. "You don't fuck with Martinez's crew. You gon' shoot me, nigga? Shoot me then. I ain't afraid to die. I'm 'bout this life." He then spat in Corey's face.

The sound of his voice as he mentioned Corey getting the message and the way he spat in Corey's face brought back a sudden painful memory. It was like Candace was watching Stephanie being assaulted all over again. The way the man had jumped out of the car and issued the warning to her already dead body, and then spat on her like she was a pile of dirt. She turned to look at Justin in fright. She knew without a doubt that that bastard had been one of the men hurling bullets into her friend that unforgettable night. "Oh my God," she said without realizing that she was speaking at all.

Justin looked over at her and squinted hard. He could see the recognition in her eyes. Before anyone could say a word a bullet flew out of nowhere. Man-Man now had his piece in hand after the two seconds Antonio had slacked in his alertness caused by Candace's exclamation. The baby began to wail loudly, and before Candace could run to her bedroom more gunshots erupted, and she felt a jolt that caused her to drop to the floor with Zoe in hand. The feeling of déjà vu had Candace on the brink of going crazy.

Before Man-Man could bust another shot Antonio put a bullet through his chest. Man-Man dropped to the ground in the doorway and was immediately gone. Antonio then hollered at Corey to come the hell on. His urges were drowned out by Candace's screams and the two more rounds that Corey left off as he placed bullets, one behind the other, between Justin's eyes as the man lay lifeless on the floor. Things moved in slow motion for a moment as a sense of relief washed over him. *This was for you, Steph*, he thought as he closed his eyes briefly.

Candace was distraught. There was blood all over her arm, and Zoe was shaking and screaming uncontrollably. Corey turned around to view the scene. He raced into the kitchen, grabbed a dish towel, and then returned to throw it at Candace.

"My baby!" Candace cried out. "My baby! My baby! You mutherfuckers shot my baby."

"Corey!" Antonio was shaking. He knew the police would soon be coming following all the gunfire.

Corey couldn't afford the repercussions if he was to get caught. He knew he had to bounce. It tore at his heart to watch Candace sitting in the middle of the floor cradling her daughter who had apparently got caught in the crossfire. He touched her head lightly, turned, and ran from the apartment, leaving Candace alone.

"Corey!" she screamed. "Corey! You mutherfucker! Help!" No pain in the world could compare to what she was feeling now. Out of all the things she'd done, agreeing to this scheme had to have been the worst. It was definitely the most costly because here she was sitting with her dying toddler in her arms and no one around at all to help her.

"Jehovah, help me," she pleaded lying down on the floor cradling her daughter as shock began to set in. "Help me. Please don't take my child. Take me instead."

Chapter 28

Clay

Clay was preparing to go home after a long day at the office. As he shut down his computer his office door swung open and his boss, Anthony, walked in with a wide smile. Clay shook his head. If the man was about to ask for a favor he could forget it. All Clay wanted to do was go home, have dinner, and wrap his arms around his girlfriend.

"No can do," Clay said making his position on the matter known. "I'm out of here, Anthony."

Anthony chuckled. "Relax, Clay. I have excellent news for you."

"What is it?" Clay asked grabbing his keys out of his desk drawer.

"That opportunity I told you about in Cali . . . they wanna interview you," Anthony said with his arms opened wide. "This is your opportunity, Clay. They've been going over your portfolio and are very interested in you."

Clay was shocked. Since the Monday after the mishap at Clay's birthday party Clay hadn't heard anything else about this golden opportunity. Since he'd been trying to patch things up with Alex he hadn't had a chance to give it any thought at all. Now Anthony was telling him that the prestigious entertainment agency was considering him for the job of a lifetime. "When?" Clay asked barely able to articulate the word. "When's the interview?"

"In the morning."

Clay stared at his supervisor. He couldn't have been serious. "In the morning? How long have you known this? When were they going to call and actually extend the interview to me?"

"My buddy there called me this afternoon to advise."

Clay shook his head and felt his temperature rise. How could this be slipping from his hands when he hadn't even had a second to revel in the fact that they wanted him? "There's no way I can get a flight out of here on such short notice, Ant. I can't just—"

Anthony reached over and punched Clay's arm playfully. "Trust your mentor, Clay. Harold Remington is flying out here to visit one of their Atlanta clients. He's the one hiring for the position. While he's here placating the outta control rapper he's going to swing by to meet you here at the office. Around one." Anthony leaned back against the desk, crossed his arms, and smiled at Clay. "Relax, brotha. This job is yours. Don't say I never did anything for you."

Clay looked down at the floor, popped the collar of his shirt, and nodded. Anthony had definitely come through for him. "What can I say, man?"

"Don't say anything. Just make sure you're on top of ya' game tomorrow. Don't do anything to piss the man off and get ready to get your stuff out of this office. Trust me. You got this in the bag. Meeting you in person tomorrow is a mere formality. With the research they'd done on you and the reference I've provided, the only thing that can mess this up is if he hates you. So you better be likeable, damn it!"

Clay laughed nervously. "Yes, sir."

Anthony held his hand out. "Good luck, Clay. I'll see you tomorrow."

Clay shook the man's hand. "Thanks, Anthony. I appreciate it."

He walked into the apartment with a bottle of wine ready to celebrate what could quite possibly be the beginning of something wonderful. He wasn't really sure how Alex was going to take the news, but this was monumental for his career. During the ride home he'd mentally gone over ways to make sure that their relationship didn't falter because of his pending location change. He wanted Alex with him, but he knew that she had to finish fashion school. Well, she at least needed to finish out the term. Surely they could find a school for her to transfer to out in Cali.

"Alex!" he called out as he stepped over her heels at the door and ignored the bags she'd dropped on the floor earlier. He hurried to the kitchen where he set down the wine bottle and grabbed two wineglasses from the cabinet. "Alex, baby! What you doing?" He filled the glasses to the top and carried them off to their bedroom.

Alex was sitting on the left side of the bed lacing up her shoes while staring over at the television positioned across from the bed. The sound was muted and the news was on. Clay didn't bother to ask her why she was watching the news in silence. He walked around to her and held out a glass of wine for her to take. Alex's eyes didn't venture over to him. She was too busy staring at the television screen.

"Baby, take the glass," Clay told her. "We need to drink tonight."

Alex nodded. "You're so right." She took the glass and guzzled it down.

Clay's eyes widened. "Um, you could've waited for the toast. And wine wasn't meant to be chugged. It's meant to be sipped, baby. You should know that."

Alex set the glass on the nightstand and ignored her boyfriend's remarks. She was in no mood to be berated by him for her lack of couth today. She tied her other shoe and glanced back over at the television.

Clay was feeling ignored. "So you don't even want to know why we're drinking? Something big happened to me today. Well, not actually today. It's going to happen tomorrow. Well, tomorrow's the start of it." He was rambling, but he was excited, and he desperately needed the love of his life to be excited with him.

Alex stood up and looked him in the eyes. "I can't right now, Clay."

"You can't what?" he asked feeling deflated. "I'm just asking you to listen to me. You can't listen?"

Alex walked away from him. She walked around the bed and got a ponytail holder from the dresser.

Clay was annoyed. He'd been ecstatic the whole ride home; now he gets here and Alex was acting like he was bothering her. He walked around the bed and flipped the light switch on.

Whether she wanted to or not they were about to get to the heart of whatever was causing her to rain on his parade. "I need you to tell me what's up with you! I'm in here trying to share a moment with you and . . ."

Alex turned to look at him and his words trailed off. For the first time he noticed the dark circles under her eyes, the redness taking over the whites of her eyes, and the sullen expression on her face. He set his glass down on the dresser and stepped forward to survey her closer. "What happened?" he asked softly.

Alex's eyes drifted away from his and back to the television. Quickly she walked to the bed, grabbed the remote, and then turned the sound up. Clay turned to see what was so important on the news that his girlfriend was in tears.

"It's a tragic day in DeKalb County for this mother of one, John," stated a reporter standing outside with a grim expression on her face. "Candace Lawson Perry of Doraville is facing a life-changing experience that no mother ever wants to face. We're here at the Children's Hospital of Atlanta in DeKalb County where Lawson's daughter, just shy of turning six months old, was admitted after being shot during an apartment break-in. Perry says she and her daughter were alone in their

home when two men burst into their home. Per Perry, one of the robbers fired shots the moment she tried to race off to the back of the apartment with her daughter. Perry was found in her home several moments later by her husband. Lawson Perry's daughter, Zoe, is not the biological daughter of her husband. Little Zoe was shot in the head and has undergone two surgeries since the horrific event this past weekend. She's here in critical condition in ICU at Children's Hospital. Officials haven't given us any further information about the child's health. Police have questioned the mother about the shooting, noting that nothing was stolen or removed from the apartment. We currently have no information on whether police have a lead on the suspects. Candace Lawson Perry suffered a traumatic labor and delivery earlier this year when she was an eyewitness to the murder of her best friend Stephanie Johnson, the girlfriend of known drug lord Corey Polk, who was recently exonerated for the murder of Montae Stokes. As a result, baby Zoe was born prematurely and is now fighting for her life following this incident. We'll bring you more information once the hospital staff releases an official statement."

The male news anchor shook his head solemnly. "Tragic life this child has had, indeed, Carla. Stay tuned to Fox Five News. This is one story I'm sure many will want to keep up with."

The feeling of déjà vu washed over Clay as he turned from the television and looked at Alex. There always seemed to be some devastating events going on in her circle. It was draining and taxing. The evidence was written all over Alex's face. Clay wished that he could remove her from this toxic circle she was involved in but knew that it was pointless to try to extract her from her friends. But deep down he honestly felt like a change of pace was exactly what they both needed. The possibility of him getting this job in California now sounded even more appealing to him.

He placed his arms around her. He kissed her forehead, then held her tightly. "I'm sorry for your friend," he said softly.

She leaned into his embrace, placed her arms around him, and closed her eyes. "It's so horrible, precious. Nothing's been the same since Stephanie got killed. Really, nothing's been the same since the whole drama with Miranda started popping off. I just can't . . ."

"Some things you just have to pray about and step away from," he said. "When you don't know what else to do, you just gotta pray."

"What is happening? If we pray it isn't going to change what's happened."

"It gives you strength and helps you to deal."

"Poor Candace."

Clay took a breath. The whole story had sounded kind of fishy to him as the news anchor relayed it. He wondered what had really happened in that apartment that night. What kind of mess had Candace been involved in now to cause her daughter's life to be placed in harm's way yet again? He didn't want to bring up his concerns with Alex right now, knowing that she was in turmoil. Instead, he wanted to lift her spirits.

"What if I told you that I have a way to change some things? Brighten the mood and take you away from all of the stuff going on around here?"

Alex pulled away. "I can't do vacation now, Clay. Candace needs us now more than ever. I gotta go. I need the car to go down to the hospital. I'll be back later." She walked out of the room without so much as giving him a peck on the cheek.

Clay sat on the edge of the bed and stared at the doorway as if willing her to walk back through it. He heard the front door open and close and knew that she wasn't coming back any time soon. This should have been a joyous night for him, but instead, he was brooding over the fact that his girl was upset and he couldn't pull her away from the destructive magnet that kept pulling at her. Clay wondered if his feelings were selfish, but then decided that he'd been there for her more times than not. This time he wanted her to be there for him in his moment of accomplishment. *Her girlfriends need her*, he thought. Clay fell back onto the bed frustrated with the course of their relationship. *What about what I need?*

Chapter 29

Jada

The stress was mounting. After the big fight at Candace's place with her husband and with dealing with her own issues with Jordan Jada just couldn't find any peace. She knew that it was affecting her pregnancy so she was trying with everything within her to remain positive. They hadn't really worked things out, but they were at least being cordial to each other. Jada considered it a start. She noticed that Jordan was spending more and more time on his phone but she tried not to let it bother her. He wasn't the one carrying this baby, she was. For the sake of their son she needed to keep her feelings and blood pressure in check. For that reason she was also avoiding her girls. All of the unnecessary drama was driving her crazy and causing her physical issues. She knew all too well how the others couldn't care less about what she had going on or how she felt. It was time for her to start taking better care of herself and looking out for Jada above all else.

She'd returned to work and was trying to get back in the swing of things. Coming home one Monday she realized that she was extremely exhausted. She stopped to get the mail, then walked on slowly back to her unit as she looked through the envelopes. Seeing that their new insurance cards had arrived Jada decided to be nice and place Jordan's card inside of his glove compartment. She used her spare key and unlocked his car door. She slid into the driver's seat and leaned over to open up the little gray door. To her surprise, a green box fell out of the stuffed compartment and onto the seat. Quickly she picked it up. She went to toss it back inside, but her hand stopped in midair the moment she realized that it was a condom box.

Jada looked at it closely and noticed that it was open. She read the front of the box and discovered that it was supposed to be a three pack. Peering inside she saw that there were only two condoms in the box. All of her suspicions had been confirmed within those few moments. She tossed the insurance card into the glove compartment, exited the car, and made her way to her cozy little cottage-style apartment. Jordan was in the kitchen cooking dinner; no doubt he was trying to redeem himself from all the trouble he'd caused. Jada placed her purse on the sofa and waddled into their kitchen.

"Hey, babe," Jordan greeted her as if they were the happily in love couple they'd been just a few short months prior.

"Hello," she answered dryly as she took a seat at their tiny kitchen table. She set the box of condoms on the table in front of her.

"I made some Chicken Alfredo that I think you're going to love."

"Is that right?"

"Once the garlic bread is done it'll be time to eat." He went to the refrigerator and poured her a glass of pink lemonade. Then he walked over and set the glass in front of her. She saw his eyes bulge the moment he took in the box of condoms.

"What's the matter?" she asked him, picking up her lemonade glass. "Cat got your tongue?"

Jordan just looked at her. Once again he found himself trying to figure out a believable story to dish out to her as she stared him down.

"No," she said. "Cat doesn't have your tongue. Your dick got some cat. That's what happened, right?" She gave him a scary smile.

"Baby, that's not mine."

She held her hand up. "Save it. I don't want to hear any more of your tired excuses, your weak-ass lies, or your stupid fabrications. You're a liar, Jordan. You're a cheater and a liar. At least you had the decency to use protection," she said fingering the box. "But it doesn't matter because it'll be a cold day in hell before I let you touch me again." She rose from the table.

Jordan reached out to her. "Baby—"

"Baby *what?*" she snapped. "What can you possibly say to me, Jordan, that you think is going to fix this? Here I am trying to give you a baby, and you're going around making every bitch in the world feel like they're something special *but* me. I really wish I'd never married you." She walked out of the kitchen.

The smell of burning garlic bread pulled Jordan out of his daze. He hurried to remove the pan from the stove and tossed the bread into the garbage. How could he have been so stupid as to forget about the box of condoms LaTanya had left in his car? Since that night he'd talked to her every day, and every day she'd tried to encourage him to divorce Jada saying that he was better off without her. Some days he felt maybe LaTanya was right. Maybe he needed someone a little different from Jada to keep him satisfied. But as he watched his pregnant wife's eyes as she told him she wished they'd never gotten married he knew that all he wanted was his family. He'd fucked up royally, but he just didn't know how to stay away from temptresses like LaTanya that were helping make it so easy for him to ruin his marriage.

Jada's cell phone rang. She looked at the caller ID and saw that it was Alex calling. She didn't have time for whatever theatrics her friend had going on today. She sent the call to voice mail. Finally back at work and off of bed rest, she was finding it hard to focus on anything aside from the fact that her marriage was one big epic failure. She tried to review all the things that she'd said or done that could have possibly made her husband feel that she wasn't worth his love, energy, devotion, or affection. Like everyone else, she thought that they had a stellar relationship. Once she'd finally gotten pregnant all of that seemed to change. At this point, she wasn't sure there was a way to get them back on track.

"Jada, I need that McKenzie file when you get a minute," her supervisor said poking her head into Jada's office.

Jada turned to look at her and offered a fake smile. "Sure thing."

As she pressed the keys on her keyboard to finish the memorandum she was working on she saw the incoming mail indicator for her Yahoo! account at the bottom of her screen. She clicked on her Yahoo! window and saw that she had an e-mail from Jordan. Curious about what he had to say she began to read it. It didn't take long for her to realize that this definitely was not a message from Jordan.

Dearest Jada,

I know you must be excited to be getting mail from your dear Jordan. I hate to break the news to you, but this isn't Jordan. This is your friendly computer hacker doing his good deed for the day. It seems your true love Jordan has been a naughty boy! Not only has he tried to hack into your e-mail, but he has also saved some interesting mail from other women on his Yahoo! e-mail account . . .

Given this, I don't feel that it is a bad thing that you have our dear Jordan's password so that you may see for yourself.

The password for this and probably all of his e-mail accounts is "only me."

Have fun and go easy on him. He is
only a lying, cheating scum who has zero
respect for a lovely woman like yourself!
Love,
Your friend

Jada's eyes couldn't believe the words she'd
just read on her screen. What the hell was happening? Apparently someone had hacked into
Jordan's account, and now they'd felt inclined to
further ruin her faith in her marriage by sharing
Jordan's dirty little secrets. Her fingers trembled
as she tried to type a reply back to let whomever
her informant was know that they could come
on with whatever other information they had.
Jordan didn't know it but his ass was about to be
put out of their home for good.

Before she could hit the send button on the
message she was attempting to compose she
noticed that she'd received another incoming
message. She clicked off of her e-mail and clicked
into her inbox. There was another message from
Jordan's account, but this time it was a copy of
an ongoing chat conversation he'd obviously
been having.

Jordan_Pluv: She wouldn't want us to be
friends. She'd think that you have a hidden
agenda . . . This bitch is crazy.

SexyTJ83: I'm not tripping off her. I don't trip that you have a wife . . . So if you wanna still kick it, it's cool with me . . . It's your call.

Jordan_Pluv: I'm not letting you go, LaTanya . . . You was right, tho. I was better off just being without her . . . I want you!

SexyTJ83: I know it's not right . . . but that makes me feel better . . . I want you too. Some bitches were meant to be wifed up.

Jordan_Pluv: At least thanks to you my dick ain't dry no mo'.

Jada was shaking. She couldn't believe the things that she was reading. Jordan had clearly lost his mind. She quickly printed the two e-mails she'd just received, shut down her computer, grabbed her purse, and then walked out of her office. She stopped by her supervisor's office on the way out the door. "Hey, I have an emergency. Doctor called me. I needa go by the office for some lab work."

Her supervisor nodded. Jada had just come back to work from being on bed rest, now this. But what could she say? "Okay. See you tomorrow."

Jada didn't feel bad lying to get out of work. She just needed a quick excuse so that she could go handle her business. The drive from her office to the downtown building where the radio station was located took a little under twenty minutes. During that time Jada had shed some tears, cursed a thousand times, and prayed to God that she didn't go to jail today. Her anger had reached critical mass, and Jordan was about to be in for a very rude awakening.

She parked her car, found the elevator, and headed up to the floor where the station was located. She knew that he was still on air with about an hour and a half left of broadcasting time. She walked in and went straight past Michelle, the receptionist.

"Hey, Jada. Jada!" Michelle called after her.

Jada didn't give a damn. If the girl called security, then, oh well. It was going down today whether they wanted it to or not. Jordan was in the studio with his sound producer, intern, and other people that Jada didn't know nor understood their purpose. Jordan's eyes lit up when he saw his wife enter the room.

"Hey, look at this," he said into his mic. "We've been pleasantly surprised by the one and only Mrs. Jada Presley."

"Or not so pleasantly," Jada said as she reached over to grab the cup of coffee that he had sitting in front of him. She threw the contents into his lap, and he quickly hopped out of his seat.

"What the fuck!" he screamed in a panic from the sensation of the scalding hot liquid.

"Shoot to a commercial now!" Raven, the producer instructed.

"What the fuck is wrong with you?" Jordan yelled at Jada. "Why you bring your crazy ass down here showing your ass at my job?"

Jada threw the copies she'd made at him.

Jordan grabbed the paper and glanced down at it. "What the hell is this that it couldn't have waited 'til we were home?" He got his answer as soon as he recognized the message strand between himself and LaTanya. He looked up at Jada nervously.

"Because yo' ass don't have a home to go to. Let me be very clear about this, Jordan, so there's no fuckin' misunderstanding. You can have this bitch you talking to in that message and any of your other skanks you been fucking with. I'm done with you. I can raise my baby without you 'cause ain't nothing your lying, pathetic ass can teach him about being a real man. I hope your dick falls off in one of these bitches and you both die from AIDS."

A crowd gathered outside the window of the studio watching the scene play out. Mona sat quietly in the corner on the computer praying that Jada didn't start hurling insults her way.

She hoped that her name had never come up in any of their previous arguments. Secretly, Mona was pleased to see Jordan getting his ass handed to him, especially since he hadn't been giving her the time of day since she'd given him head in his office awhile back.

"Baby, let me explain," Jordan said weakly. He still hadn't recovered from the stinging in his crotch.

"Fuck you. It's over." Jada turned to leave the studio but ran into the station manager just as he entered the door.

"You wanna tell me why you're having a Jerry Springer moment in my goddamn studio?" Raymond belted.

"I'm sorry, Ray," Jordan said. "We're done. We'll take it outside."

"You still have a show to finish. I suggest you handle your family issues on your own time. You're on *my* time right now." Raymond looked at the swell of Jada's belly, and then up at her swollen eyes. "I'm sorry, Jada, but we gotta keep some order around here."

"It's okay, Raymond," Jada said. "I'm done with his ass. He's all yours." She exited the studio and prepared to go home. She had some serious packing to do.

Chapter 30

Candace

Her head was spinning. Way too much was going on for her to handle. People were constantly in and out, and everyone had questions. Doctors, police, her parents, reporters, and even Rico. The one person who had yet to put in an appearance was Khalil. It was just like him to be hiding out somewhere when his daughter needed him the most. With all of the questioning she was enduring, the most frightening interrogation had come from the social worker from the Department of Family and Children Services. She hadn't expected to be paid a visit by DFCS, but it certainly made sense, especially since Candace knew that the story she'd woven together for everyone was a complete lie.

She sat in the small family room at the end of the ICU floor with Rico holding her hand. Her parents were down in the room with Zoe.

The social worker sat at the table with her tan suit and professional demeanor. It was all just another case to her, but for Candace, it felt like the end of her life as she knew it.

"I don't want you to feel like we're trying to make your life more complicated," Ms. Campbell, the social worker stated, without looking up from her notes. "This is just a precaution we're taking. We're working in the best interests of Zoe, therefore, the county needs to be able to assess whether your daughter is safe in your home environment."

"Why wouldn't she be?" Rico asked defensively.

Ms. Campbell looked up from her papers. "The child was shot in the head. She's sitting in a hospital room on life support right now, Mr. Perry."

"Shit happens. It was a break-in."

"You see, that's the thing. Your wife states it was a break-in but the police found no evidence of forced entry and nothing was taken from your home. That doesn't sound like a break-in." Sensing the tension from Rico she hurriedly dressed up her bluntness. "Now, I'm not saying that it didn't happen the way your wife says, I'm saying that the police called us in to make an assessment about your family's environment and background to see if this child is safe based on their speculations about the incident."

Candace raised her tear-swollen eyes to meet the social worker's. "The police called you in?"

Ms. Campbell nodded. "Yes. So I want you to know how this process will work. After I'm done talking to you I'll be interviewing others close to you. The grandparents, any friends you have that are frequently around, the child's biological father—"

"Good luck on that," Candace said sarcastically.

"Once we get a good feel for Zoe's home life I'll turn my assessment over to the police."

"If you don't like what you find out about us, then what?" Rico asked.

"If I find some things questionable or unsafe about your lifestyle, I'll have to give a recommendation to the agency to remove Zoe from the home," Ms. Campbell answered matter-of-factly.

Candace began to tremble as the tears ran rampant once more. That was exactly what she feared, that her child would be taken away from her. She wanted so badly to go back to that moment in the living room when Rico had found her on the floor cradling Zoe's limp, bleeding body. She'd been so scared, and all of the horrible possibilities were attacking her mind at once.

She was afraid that she'd be arrested. She was afraid that Zoe was dead on the spot. She was scared that the bodyguard for Man-Man and Justin would come back and kill her once he realized that something had happened to his boys as a result of her con.

Once Rico had walked in and saw the dead men on the floor he was perplexed. She'd quickly spun a web of lies explaining that the assailant that was with them had shot their two comrades and left. It was the same story she repeated for the police after Rico called them. She wondered why her neighbors hadn't called the police before. Surely someone had heard her cries and the gunshots.

Here she was facing having her child taken away and lying to everyone in sight while Corey was roaming the streets free. It was because of him that she was in this mess. She'd lied for him, but the lie was protecting her too. But while she was so busy protecting Corey and herself who was protecting her daughter? She looked up at the social worker and tried to take a deep breath. The police and the county were trying to protect Zoe. They were trying to protect her from her mother who was constantly putting her in these dangerous situations.

"I've run a background check on both of you," Ms. Campbell stated. "So while I'm waiting for that information to come back I'll be conducting my personal interviews. Do you have any questions for me at this time?"

"How long will all this take?" Rico asked. "'Cause if you haven't noticed we're trying to take care of our daughter and you're kind of making this difficult for us."

Ms. Campbell gave him a cold smile. "Of course, Mr. Perry. I'll try to wrap my visit up as quickly as possible."

There was a knock on the door before Mrs. Lewis stuck her head in. Her eyes were also red and puffy. "Candace, honey, the doctor needs to speak with you."

Candace nodded and looked over at Ms. Campbell. "I have to go. Do what you need to do, but please . . . don't disturb me again." She rose from the table and headed out of the door followed by Rico.

Rico had wanted to ask the woman more questions about the background check she'd requested. He was feeling apprehensive about a few things and didn't want any more stress to be added to Candace's plate right now. He also understood why the police and everyone were giving Candace the side-eye. Her story made no sense, but it was all any of them had to go by. The only other surviving person that had been found in that living room was baby Zoe, and she was too young to say anything to either cosign or negate Candace's story.

The couple entered the room, and Candace almost fainted seeing her tiny baby girl bandaged up and attached to so many machines. She'd seen her like this for the last day or so but the sight never got easier to bear, especially with the massive amount of guilt she was holding on to. Candace was distraught. She immediately walked over to stand next to the tiny baby bed that housed her daughter's suffering body.

"I wanted to get the whole family together to explain what's going on," Doctor Gordon stated. He was a world-class neonatal neurosurgeon, and Candace was grateful to have him caring for her daughter.

Candace's parents, Mr. and Ms. Lewis, stood near the door holding hands. Rico stood next to Candace by Zoe's bedside.

"Your Zoe has really tried to be a trooper," Doctor Gordon stated. "When she came in she'd lost a considerable amount of blood and there was hemorrhaging in the brain. We were able to go in and remove the bullet, but she has since gone into hypovolemic shock."

"What . . . What does that mean?" Candace asked.

"It means that she's not getting adequate oxygen to her other organs." He pointed to a nearby machine. "This machine is basically breathing for her, attempting to give her the oxygen she's not producing on her own. A bullet wound to the head can be very traumatic for an adult so you can imagine the effects it's having on a premature baby. Mr. and Mrs. Perry, you should prepare yourselves . . ."

Rico placed his arm around Candace for support the moment her body began to stagger. Her spirit was telling her that she wasn't going to be able to withstand what was said next.

"Jehovah be with us," Mrs. Lewis prayed from the back of the room.

"Even with the machine providing her the maximum amounts of oxygen we can pump into her, Zoe's organs are already starting to fail." He pointed to another machine. "This monitor is telling us that despite our greatest efforts there is little to no brain activity."

Candace shook her head.

"But she's still here," Rico said. "I mean, you got her hooked up to stuff. None of this stuff can fix the brain activity?"

Doctor Gordon shook his head no. "Unfortunately, there is no way for us to revive her brain. Medically speaking, Zoe is brain dead. Her body is only still here, as you said, because of this first machine. But like I said, her organs are very weak and are already starting to fail despite the machine. Zoe's not going to come back from this. But keeping her on life support is your family's right and decision to make. However, in my professional opinion, no matter if you opt to keep the life support going she's not going to make it to the end of the week. I'm sorry."

Candace was silent. The room went dark, and she felt her body swaying. She could hear the others firing questions to the doctor, but her brain wasn't able to process anything that was being said. She was lost in the memory of hearing the doctor basically tell her that her daughter's life was over. This was the end. She'd never wanted to be a mother, but the moment she'd laid eyes on Zoe she was completely in love. She adored the little girl, and now she'd successfully lost the one person who probably loved her unconditionally. She might as well have pulled the trigger herself because Candace felt that this was all her fault. Her body hit the floor and everyone lunged forward to retrieve her.

"Candace! Baby! Get up," Mrs. Lewis called out as her knees hit the floor.

Doctor Gordon pressed a button on the wall and a nurse ran in. "Get me a full-length gurney!" he shouted to the nurse.

The nurse ran right back out, and Doctor Gordon towered over Candace. He lifted her eyelids one at a time and examined them with his retinoscope. "Candace, can you hear me?"

Rico was stroking her hair. He'd never been so scared in his life. "Come on, baby. Come on."

The door opened. Everyone expected to see the nurse, but it was Alex. She stood in the doorway with her mouth gaping open at the sight of her friend laid out on the floor. "What happened?"

"She passed out," Mr. Lewis said, turning away from the girl he remembered to be one of his daughter's stuck-up friends. He was in no mood to fill any of her wayward comrades in about what was currently going on in their family. "You should wait outside."

"But I—"

"Ma'am, I think it's best if you wait out in the waiting room," Doctor Gordon stated.

Alex nodded and stepped back just as the nurse returned with a tech to help assist the doctor.

Chapter 31

Alex

"Jada, it's Alex. You need to get down to the hospital immediately. I think the baby's in really bad shape and Candace was out cold on the floor when I walked in. Call me back, girl. This is serious." Alex ended her message and took a deep breath. Things were out of control. She had no idea what she should do next.

"Excuse me," a female's voice interrupted Alex's thoughts.

Alex turned around to see who would dare bother her while she was in a moment of despair. The last thing she wanted to do was have casual conversation with someone while her friend's world was being turned upside down. It was as if their circle just couldn't get any peace.

"I'm sorry, I overheard you on your phone," the thin woman with the wrinkled suit stated. "You're friends with Candace Perry?"

Alex nodded. "Yes. Why?"

"Well, I'm Ms. Campbell, and I'm an intake worker from DFCS."

"Intake? What . . . What are you talking about?"

"I'm from the Child Protective Services division."

Alex understood completely. "Uh-huh. And what can I do for you?"

"I'm conducing personal interviews with people that know Ms. Perry and Zoe. We need to be able to get a look at what their home life is like given what has recently happened to the baby."

Alex stared at the woman hard. "You want me to tell you stuff about my girl to help you build a case against her? Are you serious right now?"

Ms. Campbell shook her head. "No no no. This isn't about building a case against anyone. This is about making sure that Zoe is safe when she leaves this hospital."

Alex turned away from the woman and took a seat. She was filled with so many emotions that it was becoming a little unbearable. She wished that Clay had been considerate enough to come down to the hospital with her. She fought the urge to call and ask him to take the MARTA to come be with her. She could really use his shoulder to lean on right now since Jada had yet to put in an appearance.

The social worker quickly took a seat next to Alex. "Look, you care about your friend, I can see that. I'm sure you care about that baby too. So if you just allow me to ask you a few questions, then you can possibly help make sure that your friend doesn't lose custody of her daughter."

Alex thought about it. It was the least she could do. "Fine."

"Great." Ms. Campbell pulled out her notepad. "Okay, so how long have you known the mother?"

"For years. We've been friends for several years."

"And would you say that she's a responsible individual?"

"Yeah, for the most part. She's real big on making a name for herself. Candace always wants to make sure her star is shining bright so she does what she has to do to achieve that. She's been working and taking care of herself for a minute. After she had Zoe she was busting her butt to balance her life."

"What about her decision making? Do you think she makes good decisions as they affect her life and the baby's?"

It wasn't an easy question for Alex to answer, especially given some of the recent events. She didn't agree with Candace's decision to marry

Rico on a whim. She hadn't agreed with her decision to marry Quincy either or to sleep with Khalil knowing that he was married. Alex had been dismayed by Candace's gall to be creeping around with Corey before, but for the sake of burying the hatchet, it was a thing that none of the girls harped on any longer. It was funny how everything they were trying to move past had a way of floating right back to the surface.

"Um . . . I don't know how . . . I guess I'd say . . ." Alex didn't want her opinion about the way Candace conducted her personal affairs to have a negative impact on her daughter's future. She now wished that she'd never consented to answering any of the woman's questions.

"It's really a simple question," Ms. Campbell said growing annoyed with the young woman's hesitance. She took it to mean that the mother was obviously not a good decision maker since her own friend couldn't readily answer yes to the question.

Before Alex could say anything Zoe's room door opened and Rico appeared as he ushered Candace out. She had recovered quickly but was still a little shaky. The doctor appeared behind them. Sensing that her interview with the friend was stalled, Ms. Campbell called out to the parents. "Mr. and Mrs. Perry?"

They stopped in front of her. Candace was staring at the woman but her head was continuously spinning. All she wanted was to lie down and wake up when the whole ordeal was over. Rico had a scowl on his face. He'd just about had enough of the social worker.

"I wanted to advise you that your background checks were back," Ms. Campbell said.

"Um, perhaps now's not the time, miss," Doctor Gordon advised.

Candace's eyes drifted over to Alex who was sitting on the edge of her chair with her eyes wide as a shocked doe's. Candace looked back at the social worker. "What's going on? What are you doing?" she asked in a slurred tone. "What are you doing with her?"

Ms. Campbell looked over to Alex and shrugged off the question. "Personal interview," she stated matter-of-factly. "Which you consented to earlier. Anyway, several things alarm me considering your background check, Mr. Perry, and I thought you two might want to discuss it before I leave for the day."

"If you want to handle this I'll meet you down in my office," Doctor Gordon stated before briskly walking away. He'd never cared much for how the county workers swooped down on the parents of his patients when they were in the midst of dealing with the most tragic experiences of their lives.

"This ain't the time for this," Rico told the woman. "I need to get my wife down to the doc's office."

"I think your wife would like to know about your criminal record, Mr. Perry. That is, of course, unless she already knew that you were previously charged with marijuana possession, obstruction of an officer, and child coercion."

Alex gasped. This day was simply not getting any better. Candace jumped to life and pushed Rico's arm away from her. She was appalled by what she was hearing. All this time she'd been sleeping with this man and had even allowed him to talk her into getting married and she knew absolutely nothing about him. She wanted to kick herself for not having the foresight to have his ass checked out before she'd ever signed a marriage license. She was losing everything today. She needed Jehovah now more than ever.

"You bastard!" she spat out at Rico. "You shady-ass bastard. I knew that you and those drugs were never a good thing. Talking about how you was 'gon' stop.' You never once told me that you had a drug charge against you. And child coercion? Child coercion! You sick mutherfucker! I have a kid. I let you in my home around my daughter, and you're out messing with children?"

"Candace, I can explain all that," Rico said, reaching out for her.

"Don't touch me you sick fuck. Don't you ever, ever, ever touch me again. You're a criminal." She shook her head, and the tears fell hard.

Alex ran to her side and placed her arms around her in a tight hug. Candace looked over her shoulder and stared at her husband through her tears. "I hate you. You're no better than the rest of them. You're a lying, conniving son of a bitch. That's why you couldn't ever get a job, you bum! You obviously have a rap sheet a mile long." She sobbed loudly. "I hate you! I hate you!" Her words turned into screams.

Alex continued to hold her friend but looked up to see two well-dressed men heading their way. Something about them told her that they were official, and she just knew that more trouble was headed Candace's way. "Shhhh," she whispered into her ear. "Calm down, friend. Calm down. Not here, okay?"

"Ms. Lawson, or Mrs. Lawson Perry?" one of the men called out as they stopped in front of the group.

Candace broke Alex's embrace and turned around just as her parents walked out of Zoe's room in tears. "Yes?" Candace asked confusedly.

"I'm Agent Wilbur," the man said.

Candace wiped her eyes and nodded. She recognized him. "What now?" she asked, feeling like the weight of the world was upon her.

"We'd like to ask you a few questions about the incident at your home. The murder of Michael Banks and Justin McClinton."

"Hasn't she answered enough questions about that break-in?" Mr. Lewis spoke up as he moved closer to his daughter.

"I'm afraid not, sir. You see, this series of murders, which your daughter has had a front-row seat for, are more than likely connected. Our sources tell us that Banks and McClinton were the individuals that gunned down Stephanie Johnson. The streets are talking. In fact, all of these incidents have Mafia ties, and your daughter here is the key to getting the answers that will help end the madness."

"Mafia?" Alex asked. What in the hell was going on?

"What are you talking about?" Mr. Lewis asked.

"Damn, shawty," Rico exclaimed, feeling as if anything he'd ever done was miniscule next to whatever it was that Candace was involved in.

Ms. Campbell silently jotted down notes as Mrs. Lewis clasped her hands together and prayed for them all to be delivered from this hell.

"If you don't mind coming with us, Mrs. Lawson Perry," Agent Wilbur stated.

Candace was shaking. It was all making sense to her now. Apparently Corey was in some shit with whatever Mafia the agent had referred to and now that she'd allowed him to use her she was caught up. There was no way she could tell the truth now. Not only did she fear the legal ramifications, but she also feared that whoever these Mafia people were they might be somewhere lurking and waiting to pounce on her if she said the wrong thing. She didn't know exactly what Corey had going on, so there wasn't much she could say, but she figured it was best for her to keep his name out of it. The moment she let it be known that she had any connection to Corey it would be over for her.

"I do mind," Candace stated. "My daughter is in there practically dead. I'm about to go sign papers to terminate her life support and finally end what's left of her sickly little life. I can't help any of you right now because I need to take care of my daughter. Please . . . Let me grieve in peace and handle this before you try to hit me with anything else because I can barely handle this as it is."

Alex was crying now. The pain Candace was harboring was rubbing off on her.

Candace looked back at Alex. "Walk me to the doctor's office," she said through her tears.

Alex nodded. She held Candace's hand and looked up at Agent Wilbur questioningly. She wasn't sure they were going to allow Candace to just walk away, but no one made a move as they inched their way down the hall. She could hear Candace's heavy breathing as the girl fought to hold it together. The moment they turned the corner Candace's legs gave way and she wavered.

Alex was right there to catch her. *Where the hell is Jada?* she thought as she leaned against the wall holding Candace in her arms. *I can't do this without her.*

Chapter 32

Jordan

"How's Jada?" Mrs. Hood, Martin's mom, asked Jordan.

They were all enjoying the reception at the Othello Event Hall which Ashley's parents had rented out for the nuptials. The wedding party was small and consisted of only the bride and groom and Martin's nephew as the ring bearer and Ashley's niece as the flower girl. The reception was taking place in the venue's green room. The walls were painted a mint green that made an interesting contrast to the baby blue and white wedding colors that Ashley had chosen.

Jordan forced a smile as he placed his cup under the fountain to get another drink of peach punch. He was growing weary from answering the same question over and over again. "She's fine."

"Why isn't she with you today?" Mrs. Hood probed deeper. "Martin mentioned something about complications with the pregnancy, but I thought she was out of the woods with that."

"The baby's fine. Jada just decided it was best for her to stay home and rest." It was a lie, but he couldn't very well tell his homeboy's mother that his wife had actually thought it best to stay away from him because he was constantly making her life miserable in every way that he could.

"Hmmm. Well, we're wishing you both all the best." She pecked Jordan's cheek. "It's good to see you again. Don't be a stranger."

"Yes, ma'am." Jordan took a sip of his drink and scanned the room for the guys. He'd made it to the wedding late and had ended up sitting in the back while the others sat together up front. Part of him hadn't even wanted to show up. How could he sit there and watch his boy start his happily-ever-after knowing how he'd recently messed up his own?

"Looking for anyone in particular?"

The voice behind him made Jordan close his eyes tightly and wince. The one person he did not wish to see today while he was mourning the death of his marriage was LaTanya. But, of course, she would be there to torment him further about his relationship with Jada. He turned around and gave her a polite smile thinking he'd just be cordial, and then get the hell on. "What's up, 'Tanya?"

"You and your disappearing act," she responded, smiling wickedly. "You haven't hit me up lately. What's going on?"

"Just been busy." He stared down into his cup and wished that there was some alcohol in it. Damn Martin and Ashley for having a dry wedding.

"I see you didn't bring your wife. Calculated move or nah?"

"She didn't want to come."

"I bet. I bet her ass never wants to do anything."

Jordan shrugged. "I'ma go find DeAnthony and them."

LaTanya placed her hand on his arm and gripped his bicep. "I'm sure wherever those fools are they are just fine. I know you not running away from me."

"Naw, it's just that I probably shouldn't be over here looking like I'm booed up with you."

She frowned. "What? You think somebody gon' go back and tell Jane . . . June . . . Judas . . . whatever her name is that you were talking to me?"

"Really, 'Tanya?"

"Really what? You're the one that said she'd never want us to be friends, which I think is stupid. Anyone that's that insecure with herself needs to have several seats."

"I'm not trying to make things worse than they are."

"What are you talking about? It ain't like she knows anything."

Jordan's eyebrows rose, and then fell. He remained silent.

LaTanya studied his facial features. "She knows? About us?"

"She knows."

"How the hell did that happen?"

He shrugged. "I'd rather not talk about it."

"So now what? You just gon' pretend like I don't exist? Fuck her, Jordan."

"Shh!" He held his index finger up to his lips and took a look around the room to make sure that no one had overheard her outburst. "You need to watch your mouth. If Ms. Hood hears you showing out you know she's gon' hand you back your feelings."

LaTanya was disinterested in who was listening to what. "Jordan, I hope you aren't trying to tell me that you're gon' kick me to the curb over your silly little wife's insecurities."

Jordan looked at LaTanya as if she'd lost her mind. The girl was speaking as if she hadn't been present the night they'd screwed in his car. "I have to do what's best for me and my family right now."

"Really? Well, you and I both know that you might be faithful to her for all of two minutes before you come calling me again. And if not me, I'm sure it'll be somebody else."

Jordan set his cup down on the table. "Thanks for the vote of confidence." He turned to walk away.

LaTanya followed him. "Am I lying? You don't wanna be married to that bitch. You said it yourself. Why don't you do yourself a favor and divorce her ass before you spend the next ten years of your life in a miserable situation?"

They reached the outside and Jordan quickly turned around to face her. "Are you trying to embarrass me?"

She shook her head. "No, I'm trying to save you." She calmed down and moved a step closer to him. "Look, I'm your friend, and I care about you. Despite any of the other stuff, I'm your friend, and as your friend, I'm telling you that being married to this woman is going to ruin your life. If you wanted her you would have never sniffed around my way."

Jordan didn't have a response. He felt like he wanted Jada, but LaTanya was saying some things that were logic. If he loved his wife why did he feel the need to seek pleasure anywhere else? It wasn't a question that he readily had an answer to. Before he could speak Curtis walked over and patted him on the back.

"What's up, man?" Curtis asked. He winked at LaTanya knowingly. "'Tanya. You over here hogging ya' boy?"

LaTanya shook her head and smiled. "Nope. He knows he's free to go whenever he wants 'cause he knows exactly where to find me when he's ready to come back." She looked at Jordan and dared him to break the stare she initiated. "Call me," she told him before walking away.

Curtis chuckled. "What the hell was that about?"

Jordan shook it off. "Nothing."

"Uh-huh. I know a lovers' quarrel when I see one, homie. You ain't slick. You ain't bring Jada either 'cause you knew ya' girl was gon' be here. But you know what? I woulda gave you mo' props if you had been able to handle both of 'em in the same place. That woulda been some real playa shit."

Jordan sucked his teeth. "Man, fuck being a player. That shit's getting old."

"Like hell," Curtis responded. "Everybody knows ain't no pussy better than new pussy. Ya' boy right here gon' be a player for life."

"Yeah, until you find the woman that locks yo' ass down."

"Ha! They ain't built a pussy yet that can put my ass on lock." Curtis laughed at his own joke. "Come on, man. Martin and them waiting in the back to take a shot together."

"A shot? Where they get alcohol from?"

Curtis shot him a look. "You know AJ ain't going nowhere without some shit in his trunk. Let's go."

Jordan followed Curtis back into the event hall in search of the fellas. He considered telling them all how he'd fucked up and how Jada had put him out, but the moment he saw the extra cheesy grin on Martin's face he decided against it. It was his boy's day, and he was thrilled about the possibility of everlasting love. Jordan didn't want to ruin Martin's high and his positive feelings about marriage by imparting news of his failure. Now wasn't the time. As they took their shots Jordan's eyes met LaTayna's across the room. She was cute, but she wasn't the type of chick that he could see himself spending a lifetime with. She lacked the qualities he wanted in a wife. It was funny because the one woman he'd found that had those qualities was the one woman he was giving the least respect to. He just couldn't understand how things had gone so wrong.

He didn't want to be disrespectful by using his key to let himself in. A part of him was sure that she'd changed the locks by now anyway. Jordan rang the doorbell and waited with his hands behind his back for his now estranged wife to let him in. His stomach felt knotted, and he was nervous about how she would receive him.

Jada opened the door slowly and shot him a "what the hell" look. "Is there something you need?" she asked.

He looked at her and felt as if he would cry. She was beautiful. She didn't have on any makeup and her hair was pulled back and partially covered by her scarf. She was wearing an oversized T-shirt that read "too blessed to be stressed" with leopard print lounging pants. She was completely tacky, but her skin glowed so angelically and her eyes were bright and radiant. The swell of her belly made him want to reach out and touch it, but he restrained himself. He didn't want to upset her, but he was so taken aback by the wonderment of his pregnant wife. It was as if he was seeing her for the first time.

"Um . . . I wanted to get some of my things . . . and talk," he told her. "Well, I mostly wanted to talk."

"You couldn't have just called?" she asked.

He shrugged. "I figured you wouldn't have answered the phone anyway so what would be the point."

"You figured right." She took a deep breath before stepping back and opening the door wider.

Jordan stepped in, then handed her the flowers he'd been hiding behind his back as she closed the door. Jada slowly took the flowers and eyed him suspiciously.

"You didn't think that you could bring me some roses that are just going to die in three days and that everything would magically be okay, did you?" she asked. Her tone was harsh and her look was deadly.

"No, but I was hoping it would be a start," he answered honestly as he moved to sit on the couch. "Can you sit with me?"

Jada laid the flowers on the coffee table and took a seat on the sofa, making sure to leave some space between them. "So what now, Jordan? You wanna convince me that I misunderstood everything that's been going on? You wanna tell me that it's all in my head and I'm tripping?"

"No."

"You wanna tell me that I might as well take you back because who is going to want a ready-made family?"

"Of course not. I know that you're a good woman and any man would be lucky to have you. But the thing is, I want to still be your man. I want to be the one to have you by my side."

"No, you don't. You specifically told that chick that you don't want me. If you said it to her, then I'm sure you've said it to others, including your boys. So why the hell should I want to be with someone who thinks so little of me and trash-talks me every chance they get?"

Jordan finally reached out to place the palm of his hand on her lump of life. "Because we're a family. I made some mistakes, Jada. I can admit that. But I love you, and I want our family to work. I want *us* to work."

Jada wasn't convinced. "If you wanted us to work you should have worked on us instead of going outside doing all this other extracurricular shit."

"You're right. And there's nothing I can say to that. But I'm here now, and I want to try now."

"Why?"

"Because I love you, Jada." His eyes grew misty, and he didn't care about looking like a punk. "I don't want to be without you, baby. I know I messed up, but I'm begging you . . . Please give me a chance to make it right. Please give me the chance to fix it."

Jada was tired. With the stress of going back to work and trying to figure out how she was going to make it as a single mother, the hurt she'd been feeling over Jordan's betrayal, and the horrible ordeal that Candace was going through, she felt completely overwhelmed. So much was happening at once, and it seemed that everyone's lives were being rocked in one way or another. She loved Jordan, but she didn't want to deal with a lifetime of drama. For the longest she'd been the one everyone turned to and looked up to; the responsible one who could show them all how to love and how to carry themselves. Jada was sick of being the responsible one. She was sick of being taken for granted. She wanted the others to know what it was like to feel half of the things that she'd experienced over the years so that maybe they could appreciate the kind of friend and wife she'd been to them all.

"Baby, please, let's try to make this right," Jordan begged as he fell to his knees, threw his arms around her, and buried his face in her belly. "I need you."

Jada rolled her eyes to the ceiling wondering which of them would regret the decision first. "One chance," she said softly. "One chance, Jordan. I swear to God if it wasn't for this baby and the fact that deep down I really do love you I'd spit in your face."

He held her tighter. "It's going to be better," he told her. "I'm going to be better. You'll see. I'm going to be a better man for you."

She touched the top of his head and closed her eyes. She knew that some things would never be the same and wondered if they were fooling themselves to ever think otherwise.

Jordan lifted his head and looked into his wife's face. "You're beautiful, woman. For every day that I failed to tell you and every moment that I caused you any pain, I'm sorry. All I wanna do is love you, Jada. That's all I really wanna do."

Jada remained silent. It was time to show and prove. The time for talk was well over and done with for her.

Jordan rose from the floor and cleared his throat. "I'm gonna go take a piss, and then if you're hungry I'll go out and grab something to eat."

"Krystal's," Jada said. "I'm in the mood for some Krystal's."

Jordan laughed. "That's random. You gon' have bubble guts messing with that stuff."

Jada rubbed her belly. "The baby's craving it so . . ." She shrugged. "Besides, I just cleaned myself out real good before you got here so you might wanna spray when you go in there."

"Ewww," Jordan laughed as he walked to the bathroom. He closed the door and said a quick prayer of thanks before relieving himself. As he pissed a vibrating sound caught his attention. Jada's phone was lying on the vanity counter near the sink and was constantly buzzing. Jordan flushed the toilet, and then washed his hands. The phone buzzed again. Someone was really trying to get ahold of Jada.

Jordan picked the phone up mindlessly to take it to her. Reaching for the doorknob he looked down at the screen as the phone buzzed again. The name caused him to stop. Amir. Who the hell was Amir? Insecurity and curiosity caused him to click on the text to see what was being said. The conversation strand made him put down the toilet lid and take a seat. He scrolled up to the top and held his breath as he read.

Amir: Hey, sexy. What you doing?

Jada: Watching TV and enjoying the quiet.

Amir: You ain't let that man come home yet?

Jada: No.

Amir: You got room over there for me to lay down too?

Jada: Next to me and my big belly?

Amir: I'll rub it for you . . . and your feet . . . and that clit.

Jada: Really?

Amir: You think I won't?

Jada: It kinda scares me to know that you will.

Amir: Don't be scared, sexy. Just be ready. I'm glad you found me on Facebook. I been looking for you for years.

Jada: You ain't look too hard.

Amir: Water under the bridge. I found you and I don't intend to let you go.

Jada: You do know I'm still married.

Amir: You do know what he don't know won't hurt him . . . but I'ma hurt that pussy again as soon as I get back to the A.

Jada: LOL. You just know you gon' get this, right?

Amir: I'm your first love, boo. I'ma always be able to get that.

Amir: Where you go, girl?

Amir: You done fell asleep on me over there?

Amir: A'ight, hit me when you wake up. I love you, sexy.

Jordan couldn't breathe. It was clear that in the short time he'd been gone Jada had wasted no time in moving on. Here she was having a nigga tell her what he was going to do to her and she was still carrying his baby. His blood was boiling. Jordan didn't know whether to call the dude and curse him out or run out of the bathroom and shake Jada to death. He was livid. How could she want him to be faithful and true to her when it only took the slightest bit of turbulence for her to run off and start messing with someone else? He rose from the toilet and gripped the phone tightly. He guessed that the saying was true. Once a good girl's gone, she's gone forever. He only had himself to thank for that.

Chapter 33

Miranda

Miranda slowly walked to the private visitation room. Who in the world would show up out of the blue like this was beyond her. She'd purposely distanced herself from everyone and hadn't asked anyone to come out. She walked into the room and was confused. The only man present was a heavyset balding guy in a cheap suit. She turned to leave the room.

"Miranda," he said. "Surely you aren't going to just turn your back on me again."

Again? She turned around to look at him. She didn't recognize him at all.

"Please, take a seat," he encouraged her.

Miranda didn't budge. "Who are you and what do you want?"

"It took us a long time to find you. Somehow we weren't able to find any identifying information about you from the myriads of databases

available to us. No information about your birth.
No vehicle registration or voter registration info.
Nothing. I wonder how that came to be when we
were able to trace your name and phone number
the day that you called me."

She was nervous. It was clear to her now. She
hadn't given them any more thought since the
night that she'd tried to end it all. She pressed
her hands together and tried to think clearly.
Time wasn't on her side now, that much she
knew. She wasn't afraid of the thick guy full of
his own self-importance. It was the man that
was surely trailing him that she was concerned
about.

"Why'd you run?" he asked her.

"Huh?"

"We had a deal. You were supposed to come to
the office, sit down with me to get your statement
out, and then we were going to throw the book
at Polk and ultimately get the real bad guys."

"The real bad guys," she repeated, shaking
her head. She was the addict, but she seriously
wondered what the hell he'd been smoking.

"Why'd you run?"

"Who said I ran?"

"You didn't show up. I pulled strings to get
Polk taken in, and you didn't show up."

"Who told you to get ahead of yourself? I didn't tell you to run out and arrest the man without any concrete evidence, asshole."

He banged the table with his fist. "I had a good feeling about you."

"You were a little too overly optimistic, huh? Bet you won't do that again."

Agent Wilbur looked into the short woman's eyes. Her hair was plaited in unruly cornrows, and she looked as if she could stand to eat a couple of more meals. Her eyes were cold and unfeeling. Even her tone was harsher than he'd remembered. It had taken forever for his team to track her through her ER visit which had ultimately landed her at the treatment facility. He had been completely surprised to find out that his eyewitness was nothing more than a stoned out crackhead. Still, it didn't mean that her testimony wouldn't be able to help them.

"It's not too late," Wilbur told her in a calmer voice. "We can still get your statement. Maybe you saw something, anything, that'll help us pin a conviction against the others."

"The others?" She wanted to hear him say it. She wanted to force him to say that which the media continued to gloss over every time they ever mentioned Stephanie's death and even recently the unfortunate demise of baby Zoe.

She wanted him to say that which she'd found out the hard way.

Agent Wilbur leaned back in his chair and cracked his knuckles. "This is a big deal. Your friends have suffered a great deal. Anything you know . . . Anything would be helpful, Miranda. Just tell me about the execution of Stokes."

She shook her head. "I can't," she said giving a throaty gulp at the end of the statement.

"Can't or won't?"

"I can't," she repeated backing up until her back was completely against the wall with the exit just to her right.

Agent Wilbur leaned forward and placed his elbows on the table with the fingertips of both hands pointed at Miranda. "Do you have any idea how important this is? How many more have to die, Miranda?"

She shook her head again feeling tormented and helpless. "I can't." They were the truest words she'd spoken in ages.

He rose from the table and walked around to the front of it. Several feet stood between him and the fragile woman. "Do they have you that scared? You're safe here, Miranda. Tell me what I need to know, whatever you know. My original promise still stands. I'll make sure no one bothers you. I will personally make certain that you are safe."

She covered her face with her hands. She just wanted him to go. The more he spoke the more she realized how useless and detrimental her existence was. He brought back memories that she was now forced to act upon sooner than she'd wanted to. She just wanted him to leave her alone with her thoughts.

"Say something!" he yelled. "You can't continue to say nothing! You just may have the power to stop this."

She didn't have the power to do anything. He was giving her far too much credit. Miranda slid to the floor and buried her face in her hands, feeling herself about to lose it.

"This is ridiculous," Agent Wilbur stated. "Citizens complain about us not keeping our communities safe, but people like you allow the villains to scare them into silence. Silence kills, Miranda. Zoe is dead! Stephanie is dead! Montae Stokes is dead! Justin McClinton is dead! Michael Banks is dead! That's five bodies attributed to this drug war. *Five* murders, Miranda. If you don't want there to be another you better start talking! Tell me something."

"I can't!" Miranda screamed looking up at him with hazy eyes and tears escaping rapidly. "I can't tell you anything because I don't know anything. I . . . lied! I lied. I didn't see anything! I was never there! I lied!"

Agent Wilbur stared at her in shock. He hadn't considered the possibility that she had played him to this extent. He'd been sure that Tommy Castello's crew had silenced her. He had been a little surprised that they hadn't killed her. Now here she was telling him that she'd been yanking his chain the entire time. He massaged his forehead. "What do you mean you lied? Why would you call the GBI to make a statement if you had no statement to make?"

She leaned her head back against the brick wall and closed her eyes. "I'm a crackhead, Agent Wilbur. I'm an addict. I'm liable to do or say anything. Corey was my dealer. He pissed me off. I wanted to piss him off. Mission accomplished."

Agent Wilbur was disgusted. People were dropping like flies around them, and she thought that it was funny to call and make a false report. She knew that they had bought every word she'd fed him over the phone that day. He could just imagine the sound of desperation she'd picked up on in his voice as he'd continuously begged for her assurance that she'd come in the next day. He was going to be the laughingstock of the bureau for sure once word got back that he'd made a pointless arrest of Polk to begin with; that he'd had no merit at all behind his arrest.

Then another thought occurred to him. "But you knew about the wallet."

"Luck," she told him. "I'd honestly just happened to be following Stephanie that night and saw her toss something. I'm telling you I didn't see the murder." Telling the truth felt like a burden had been lifted. Even her breathing felt different.

None of it made sense to him. He'd been certain that Tommy's crew had been on to the girl and had eliminated her. But here she was overcoming addiction and admitting to him that she was simply full of shit. There were no other words to say. Without so much as a good-bye the agent exited the door, allowing it to slam loudly behind him.

Miranda bit her bottom lip. She had moves to make. She rose from the floor and left the room, intent on heading to the shrink to make a request. But as she passed the nurse's station a thought occurred to her. She stopped at the desk and smiled nervously at the receptionist. "Um . . . May I have a sheet of paper, please?"

The receptionist looked at her inquisitively.

"I want to write a letter to my folks," Miranda explained.

It seemed like a healthy gesture considering everyone there knew that Miranda was distancing herself from everyone she knew on the outside, even after being encouraged to reach out. The receptionist handed her a sheet of stationary and a pen with a smile. "Here you go. Good for you."

Miranda gave her a half smile in return. She knew the receptionist was thinking positively. If she only knew the truth about the words that were about to be penned she would have prayed instead of smiled warmly.

Chapter 34

The Girls

Alex was the first to arrive. She'd borrowed the car and left while Clay was still in the shower. It was easier that way. Lately it had just been too difficult to have a conversation with him. Nothing she seemed to say or do was ever right, and he didn't seem as interested in her life as he used to be. Something was missing for them, but Alex didn't have the time to stop to figure out what it was. Between school, work, and staying most days with Candace she just didn't have much time to nurture their relationship.

She sat in a meeting room looking around at all the sofas and chairs wondering where the hell everyone else was. She'd been surprised to get a call from the rehab facility. Miranda had been very clear early on that she didn't want any of them around while she tried to get herself together. Alex wondered if this meeting was

Miranda's way of showing them that she was in a better place now.

"Hey, you," Jada said entering the room. Her stomach kind of led her, and the rest of her body followed.

"Hey, yourself," Alex responded.

They hugged and Jada joined Alex on the couch.

"Miranda hasn't come in yet?" Jada asked.

"Nope. Not yet."

"I hope she's good. I can't wait to see her. It's been too long."

The door opened, and they both turned around to see Candace stagger in with a thin white woman behind her. Candace wore dark shades and didn't move with her usual diva strides. She gave her girls limp hugs and sat next to Jada on the couch.

"You okay, girl?" Alex asked, looking over at her.

"How okay is one supposed to be after burying their six-month-old daughter?" Candace asked.

It was a sad time in Candace's life. The family had wasted no time in funeral arrangements for Zoe. The only thing Candace had left of her were her baby pictures and clothes. Every night she was tormented by the memories of the deaths of her only child and one of her closest friends. The images that ran through her mind made her want to die and never again have to feel the pain that was ripping her heart apart. She wanted out.

Jada grabbed Candace's hand. She could feel the tremble running through the girl's body. No parent ever wanted to succeed their child in life. Jada couldn't imagine the hurt Candace was feeling.

Doctor Dunham cleared her throat. "Um, ladies, I'm really glad that you could make it out. This is very important to Miranda, and I know that she's kind of a bundle of nerves over seeing you all again."

"Who are you?" Alex asked bluntly.

"I'm the center's therapist, and I've been working with Miranda to come to terms with certain things . . . so this is a very huge step for her. I'd like to ask you all to bear with her and have an open mind. I'm not sure what will be said. Miranda's kind of a live wire."

"She is?" Alex asked thinking about the meek, timid woman that had once sulked on Candace's living-room floor and softly admitted that she just needed to feel loved even if it was a lie.

The door opened and the three girls were speechless as a different version of Miranda entered. She took her time walking across the floor and taking a seat in the chair across from them. She was so thin that they could see the bones of her skeleton. Her eyes were dark, and her face looked sadder than they had ever seen. It was a heartbreaking sight, and no one said a word. They didn't have to. Miranda knew exactly what they were all thinking.

"I'm a little skinnier than usual," Miranda voiced. "But this is nothing compared to my coked-out look. So you can stop staring at me like I'm the ghost of Miranda."

"Your friends came out to support you, Miranda," Doctor Dunham stated to deter Miranda from going into defense mode off the bat. She took a seat in a chair beside the girl. She looked at her to see if she was calm. Sensing that she was okay Doctor Dunham looked over to the girls on the couch. They all appeared stunned. "Okay, to kick-start things I want to say this. Miranda once made a very striking statement in group. She said that no one understands. She feels no one understands her or what she's been through. There are a lot of things on her heart and mind that she just never shared with you for fear that you didn't care or wouldn't understand."

"When did we ever give you the impression that we didn't care?" Alex asked. "We've always been tight. What couldn't you say to us?"

Doctor Dunham was a little nervous about the way Alex snapped at Miranda, but Miranda responded before she could intervene.

"There are just some truths that you're not ready for . . . that I knew you wouldn't have been able to handle," Miranda answered. "That's also why I didn't tell you about Norris hitting me. You proved your inability to understand by badgering me about how I could stay with him that night we had girls' night after he'd put me in the hospital."

"Is that not a logical question?"

"Someone who's being domestically abused doesn't really wanna hear, 'Girl, why you staying?' They want to be loved on."

"You needed help," Candace said dryly. "We were telling you what you needed to hear not what you wanted to hear. Tough love."

"Tough love? Hmmm . . . Maybe I could have used someone going to my meetings with me. Maybe I could have used someone calling me to see how I was and if I was still alive while stuck in my situation."

"You weren't stuck," Candace countered. "You chose to stay. There was nothing holding you there. Not even the man. Didn't he leave you?"

Jada squeezed Candace's hand that she was still holding. She was stunned by how snarky

Candace was being. Candace responded by snatching her hand away.

"Why don't we go about this a different way," Doctor Dunham stated. "Miranda, why don't you tell the girls what you want to say."

Miranda bit her lip. She was having second thoughts about this. She just wanted it to be over with. She'd already sent out copies of her letter, and they would each have them by morning. This meeting was just a way for her to lay eyes on her circle one more time. "Alex . . . I love you, girl. But your whole life you've just been so absorbed with Alex's world that you really never had a moment to open your eyes and see anything or anyone else. Kinda explains why you never realized Clay was in love with you."

"I saw you," Alex argued.

"You judged me."

"I stood up for you when Stephanie sat at Jada's table that night downing you. I've been your friend from the jump. Don't try to paint it any other way."

"You've been my friend . . . when it was convenient for you. When it didn't interrupt the Alexandria Mason story."

Alex crossed her arms. "I resent that. What did you want from me?"

"You. You act like you were so concerned, but you never once came knocking on my door to see if I was still alive—did you?"

Alex wanted to snap back and tell her that she probably would've been too stoned out to know if she had but realized that it would have been catty. Miranda was clearly purging. If this was a part of her treatment process she would just take it. She didn't have the energy to go back and forth, not when she had to figure out what was going on between her and Clay.

"So this meeting was designed for you to hand us back our feelings?" Candace asked. "Because I'm fresh out of those, and I don't want to waste your time."

"You have this air about you, Candace . . . this air like you're so perfect when we all know that is not the case. I don't have to remind you of your shiftiness. I think that you've strived so hard to be the perfect image of yourself that you created and see in your head that you just destroy everything in your path. I think . . . I think you've been trying for the longest to be Jada."

Candace pulled her glasses from her face and slid to the edge of her seat. She looked at Miranda through the stingy redness of her eyes. "Are you high right now? The only thing I strive to be is the best me that I can be. I don't want to be like any of you. Have I made some mistakes? More than I care to mention, and trust me, I'm paying for them all day, every day. The memories that I have . . . The pain that I'm suffering is killing me. But I own it all, Miranda. Don't sit here and try to point blame at any of us because of what you've done or been through. We've all made choices that we just gotta deal with."

"Exactly," Miranda agreed. "We've made choices that we have to deal with and not play the victim because of them. You got that victim thing down pat, don't you? Wanting folks to feel sorry for you because you got knocked up by your married boyfriend. You shouldn't have slept with him. Wanting folks to feel sorry for you because Stephanie died hating you. Again, your doing."

Candace rose from the sofa. "I don't need this."

Jada stood up and grabbed her. "Wait, don't go. Come on. We're all friends. What are we doing here?"

"Stop it," Miranda said.

Jada looked at her. "Huh?"

"Stop it! Stop pacifying folks. Stop trying to hold it all together. Shit falls apart sometimes, Jada. Let it and just pick up the pieces later and move on but don't put a fuckin' Band-Aid on it and pretend like everything's coming up roses."

Jada was shocked. "What are you talking about?"

"You're so busy fixing it all that you're really fixing nothing. We don't even know you. Candace is trying to compete with the perfect front you show us, but nobody's perfect. She's competing with a phantom Jada. A Jada that doesn't exist."

"I never said I didn't have issues," Jada responded. "I just never had time to address them because of you heifers and all of your drama. It is tiring being everything to everyone. I am tired."

Miranda nodded. "As much as you tried did any of it work?"

Jada looked around at her friends and considered their lives. So much was wrong. So much was beyond her grasp. Nothing she'd said or done along the way had stopped them from ending up at this moment of total despair. No one was okay. She took a seat on the sofa and looked at Miranda. "We all could have been a little better to one another . . . a lot more real with each other."

Candace returned to her seat as well. "So you've told us all how you feel about us. What about you?" she asked Miranda. "How do you feel about yourself?"

Miranda's right brow rose. "I'm not my favorite person. We've all been harboring secrets and behaving horribly to some degree. I'm not exempt."

"Your secret's been out," Alex stated.

"Not all of them."

The others looked at her expectantly.

"I was mad at Corey for refusing to sell to me," Miranda said slowly. "I was mad at Stephanie for looking down on me. She was so mean and judgmental. I wanted to get back at them. Both of them. I was following Stephanie one night and I saw her throw away Montae Stokes's wallet. I was the one that tipped off the GBI. I told them where to find the wallet, and I told them that I'd seen Corey kill the Stokes dude."

"What?" Alex exclaimed. "You never . . . You never told us that."

"Because it was a lie," Miranda said flatly. "That's why Corey was picked up. After it happened . . . after the call and after they got Corey I called Stephanie and left a message for her to watch the news. I was gloating about how I got her boyfriend caught up. But that was the night she was killed."

"She was at Corey's getting his things," Candace stated. "Corey must have sent her there to clean the place out after you dropped the dime on him. If you hadn't done that . . ." Her thoughts trailed off.

Miranda had considered the possibilities herself many times. "If I hadn't done any of it she would have never been there, and those men would have never gunned her down. But then again, who knows? They could've picked her off at any time."

Jada was in shock. The secrets kept among them all were outrageous. Anyone on the outside looking in would surely wonder how the hell they could call themselves friends.

"I just wanted to tell the truth," Miranda stated. "I've been lying and stooping to all kind of lows for the longest. I just wanted the opportunity to come clean."

Candace considered sharing her truth but she looked up at the therapist and realized that it was best for her to keep quiet. None of it mattered anyway. None of it was going to bring her daughter back. "So you've let it all out . . . Now what?"

"Now I pray that you'll all see yourselves and each other differently," Miranda stated. "Really be there for each other, not just Jada trying to be the glue, and not just falling together after the shit has hit the fan."

"We needa be better friends," Jada stated. "Point-blank."

"And be better to yourselves," Miranda added.

"Why are you talking like you don't need to do these things too?" Alex asked. Something didn't sit well with her.

"I do. I just wanted to make sure that I give you guys something to think about. I did a lot to create the problems in our relationships. I just wanted to do something to work on fixing it." As the words left her lips Miranda realized that she honestly wanted to leave them with something good to repair their friendship. It was the least she could do considering all the trouble she'd caused.

Chapter 35

Alex

Feeling completely drained and wanting only to sink into a hot lavender-scented bubble bath Alex slowly made her way inside of the apartment. She could hear the low lull of the television coming from the bedroom. Kicking off her shoes she took a deep breath and headed toward the back. She hoped that Clay was awake. She could really use some comforting. As she entered the room the wind was knocked out of her and she gasped. Clay was not only awake but he was packing a suitcase.

"What are you doing?" she asked nervously, trying to recalculate everything that had happened between them in order to figure out how they'd gotten to this moment. "Where are you going?"

Clay didn't look at her as he placed a suit into the garment bag that was lying on the bed. "Business trip."

Alex clutched her chest and sighed. With the year she was having her emotions were all over the place and she was apparently paranoid. "Oh my God. You scared me," she said walking over to the dresser and taking off her jewelry. "For a minute I thought you were leaving me."

"I am leaving," he said slowly and almost inaudibly.

"Excuse me?" His tone wasn't low enough because Alex heard him loud and clear. She stared at the back of him holding and toying with the promise ring he'd given her.

"I've been trying to tell you this for a minute. Everything has been moving so fast and you've been so caught up in other stuff."

"Tell me what?" she demanded. "Precious, what have you been trying to tell me?"

He finally turned to face her. "I had an interview with an entertainment agency in Cali."

That was news to Alex. "You did?"

"Yeah, I did. And they offered me the job. I'm going there for two weeks for some training, fill out some paperwork, and handle some other business."

"And then?"

He sighed as he turned to zip up his suitcase. "And then I'll come back for the rest of my things."

Immediately she felt as if she couldn't breathe. Alex clutched her shirt with her right hand while her left hand lingered by her side as her thumb nervously fondled the solitaire diamond resting on her ring finger. "What about me?" she asked softly and innocently. "What about me?"

Clay turned and sat on the edge of the bed. He looked at her with gentle eyes. "What about you, Alex?"

"You're just going to leave me here? Is this job a permanent thing? I mean, can't I come with you? How are we going to maintain a long-distance relationship? That's not what you had in mind, was it?" She was rambling, and she knew it, but she needed him to put to rest her greatest fear.

"I'm not asking for us to have a long-distance relationship," he told her.

She nodded and held her hands out. "Good . . . good. Then I can start looking for schools out there so I can transfer next term. And I can put in my notice at the boutique. Shoot, I'll have to let the girls know ASAP. They're probably gonna go crazy."

"Alex . . ."

"I really should be going with you now because don't we need to find a place? Surely you don't wanna find a place that I end up hating. Not that you have bad taste or anything but—"

"Alex."

Alex turned around and rummaged through her drawer for a notepad. "I need to make a list. There's so much to do, and I don't want to miss anything."

"Alex!" Clay raised his voice.

Alex stopped talking, but she was too afraid to turn around to face him. She knew in her heart what was coming next but didn't want to see it in his face as the words escaped his lips.

"I'm not asking for us to have a long-distance relationship," he repeated. "And I'm not asking for us to have a relationship anymore. Period." He rose from the bed and started to walk over to her but stopped midway. "I love you, Alex. I've loved you for a long time. I don't think that's going to ever change but . . . I need someone that can love me the same way that I love her, and I just don't think you're ready."

Alex set down her notepad, took a breath, and then slowly turned around. "How can you say that? I'm here with you. After everything that's happened I'm here with you."

"You're here physically, Alex . . . at times anyway. But you're not here with me," he said motioning his hand between the two of them. "You're caught up in Alex-world, baby, and I don't think there's any room for me."

"That's crazy," she said choking back tears. "I love you, precious. There's always room for you."

"I think you need some time to figure out what you want out of life. I think I need to go on and pursue this dream, and you need to figure out what you want; see if you can tear yourself away from being the center of attention, if you can make a move without being glued to your girls."

Alex shook her head and reached out for him. Clay pulled her toward him, held her tightly, and kissed her forehead. She closed her eyes and cried into his chest.

"Please don't leave me," she begged. "If you leave me I don't know what I'll do."

He took a deep breath. "If it was meant for us to be together we'll find our way back to each other, Alex. But right now I feel like we're forcing this, and you're just not ready for the type of relationship I need."

She looked up at him. "But I can try harder. I promise, precious. I can do better."

He kissed her lips, and her tears dripped onto his mouth. He ignored the saltiness and relished in the moment of their final embrace. "We need time," he told her as he pulled away. "We need time."

Alex buried her face back into his chest and cried. He was right. She hadn't been the attentive girlfriend he needed. She didn't even know what was going on in his life. But she wanted him so badly that losing him was tearing her apart. Maybe Miranda had been right. She was just a little too self-absorbed, and now it was costing her the love of her life. Her only hope was in his statement that if they were meant to be they'd find their way back to each other. Alex prayed that it would all work out for them.

Chapter 36

Corey

"You killed a baby," Knuckles said. "How could you have been so stupid?"

Corey took a deep breath and tossed the trash bag of bills into the trunk of the car Knuckles was driving. While he was busy shooting it out with Man-Man and Justin, his boys had taken over their rivals' stash house. They'd only been able to secure one bag of money, which was only half of what Corey owed Tommy, but some money was better than none. They didn't dare touch the product that was in the house, knowing full well that Martinez's product was of no use to their hustle.

Corey was worried about what would happen to him next. He'd gotten even with the fucks that killed his girl, and he'd gotten lucky that Candace hadn't fingered him in the shoot-out at her house. He didn't understand why she wasn't snitching. He knew that she'd been interviewed half a dozen times by the county police and the GBI. They wanted badly to pin Martinez's boys' murders on him. The only thing keeping them from it was Candace's testimony. He owed her his freedom. It hurt him that she'd lost her daughter in the process.

Although he was free now he didn't know for how long. Surely Martinez wasn't going to take too lightly the fact that he'd wiped out the strongest members of his Atlanta street force. The war between Tommy and Martinez was sure to escalate now, and Corey was right there in the line of fire. If Martinez didn't get to him Corey feared that Tommy might retaliate for the money he still owed him. But even if neither of them came gunning for him he still had to face the drug charges that the state was pinning against him. There was always something.

Knuckles took a look at the kid and shook his head. He'd shown so much promise. To Corey's left stood Antonio, quiet and watching. He was a good kid. He did whatever Corey told him to do, and he kept up that front of loyalty. It was too bad that his esteemed leader wasn't as on top of his shit as he thought he was.

Knuckles nodded in their direction. "You know what needs to be done now," he said before getting into his car and pulling off.

Corey sighed and nodded toward Antonio's whip. "Let's ride." He knew what needed to be done, he just didn't want to do it. He was sure that the night Montae was killed there had been no one in sight, but the fact that Miranda had contacted the GBI claiming to be an eyewitness disturbed him. How was it possible? It simply wasn't. But no matter what he thought he was sure of, he knew that Tommy didn't want to risk the chance of him being wrong. With all the blood that had been shed already Corey knew that this wouldn't be the end of it. He just wondered when his turn was coming.

Chapter 37

Miranda

It was time. She clutched her hands by her side as she made her way down the hall to her room following the center's final roll call. Her roommate, Alicia, had left the program a week ago. She'd decided that it wasn't for her and checked herself out. Miranda was going to check out as well but in a different way. The plan was simple. She would wait until the final room checks, then unscrew the lightbulb from the lamp in her room. After breaking it she would then use the shards to cut herself in various places. By the time the nurses rounded in the morning she would have bled out and all the pain would have evaporated from her body.

The plan was very simple indeed, but as she entered her room she knew that things were not going to go accordingly. She closed the door slowly and quietly. Honestly, she had to admit that she was surprised he'd waited so long. She'd been fooling herself to think that she could kill herself before he showed up. She faced him with his stone-cold expression and waited for him to speak. The last time they'd seen each other he'd given her enough coke to kill two people. But as luck would have it, Jada had to come and save the day, thus sending her to the hospital which ultimately landed her right here in this dorm room at the rehab center.

"I see you're still with us," he said.

She shrugged. "Not my fault."

"You said you wanted it to be over. I thought we had a deal."

"Again, it wasn't my fault," she said sounding agitated. "But maybe you can help me with something."

He crossed his legs. They had very little time, but he didn't mind entertaining her thoughts for a bit.

"I've told you that I was lying . . . only trying to get even because I was caught up in my feelings. I didn't go through with my story, and even after the GBI found me here I still didn't say anything because I have nothing to say . . . because I know nothing."

He nodded his understanding.

"Okay, so then why is it that you still feel inclined to do away with me?" She was genuinely curious about their interest in her.

"Because we can't leave anything to chance," he told her in an even tone. "Maybe you were lying, maybe you weren't. Maybe you know something, maybe you don't. But the easiest way to make sure that the possibility of you knowing something is no longer a factor is to do away with you altogether."

"And that's just it? No loose ends, huh?"

He smiled, pleased to know that she under-stood. "That's right, Miranda. No loose ends." He opened his jacket slightly to reveal the pistol covered with a silencer.

Two swift pulls of the lever and her chest was burning with bullet holes. He watched as her body fell to the floor and her eyes stared at the ceiling as she took her last breaths. It reminded him of the day he'd paid her a visit at her modest apartment following the tip they'd gotten from Royce. Tommy watched her take hit after hit until her body had convulsed and she began to spasm on the floor of her bathroom. He'd been sure that there was no coming back from the damage she'd done to her body and had left her to die alone on the cold tiles. He should have fol-lowed through. Leaving her as a potential loose end had been just as much his fault now as he had been Corey's. The difference between them though was that he had no problem effectively correcting his mistakes—all of them, including bringing Corey on as well.

Chapter 38

Candace

It was quiet in the house. The silence forced her to be alone with her thoughts, and that was killing her. She'd been packing up the remainder of Zoe's things and just couldn't do it any longer. Throwing down a plastic bag she lifted herself from her Indian-style position on the floor and started to head out of her bedroom. Her cell phone rang from its place on her dresser. She turned around and picked it up, being careful to read the caller ID before answering. If it was Rico she was going to send his ass straight to voice mail. She didn't have time or the energy to deal with him. As soon as she was able to think clearly she was going to file for an annulment. Staying married to his criminal behind was not an option. But it wasn't Rico calling. It was Khalil, which wasn't much better.

"What do you want?" she asked him. Now that they no longer shared a child together she figured they really didn't have any further business with each other.

"I just wanted to check on you, beautiful," he said. "How you holding up?"

"I wish people would stop asking me how I am. They should already know how I am. What do you want?" she asked again, in hopes of moving the conversation along.

"You need anything? I can come over."

Candace walked out of the room, through the living room, and out into the hall of her apartment building to go to her mailbox. Khalil's request was insane, and she didn't feel like entertaining it. "No. You have no reason to be here."

"We lost our daughter, Candace. We're both grieving."

Candace thought about the way Khalil had showed up just before the memorial service for Zoe had started. He hadn't paid for anything, and he certainly hadn't been there to hold her hand through the process of getting everything together. Now that their baby was returned to the earth she certainly had no use for his "help" or his false sense of unity. She returned to her apartment and sifted through the mail. "Khalil,

I'm only going to tell you this once. I have no need or desire for you in my life. We're done with each other. Done."

"You don't mean that. I know you're hurting right now, and you don't need to be alone. We're in this together, gorgeous."

Candace's eyes fell upon a letter addressed to her from Miranda. They'd just had their little powwow the day before and now she was looking at an envelope that Miranda had sent to her. The meeting had been tense and cutting at best. Candace wondered what could be in that letter that would be any different from the tone of their meeting. Khalil was still rambling on in her ear about how they needed to lean on each other as Candace ripped open the letter. She sank down onto her couch cradling the phone with her shoulder as she read the first few lines.

Dear Chicks,
    You're not going to believe this. I don't even believe that I'm writing it so I know you're not going to believe it . . . or maybe you will. But I don't love myself. I look in the mirror every day and want to just shatter the glass. I smile, I say the right things, I make the right moves, and I play the game. And I think I've done it all this

time so that you all, everyone around me really, could be more at ease. At first, I thought that being honest with you would help free myself of some of the anguish that's been built up inside of me for so long. This letter is proof of what I thought . . . but with each word I write I realize more and more how empty I am, whether you know the truth or not. And that's all about me. So I've made a decision that I'm sure you're not going to like or agree with, but for once, I am not hiding what I think, feel, or do.

Candace gasped as her spirit picked up on the sadness and despair laced in the words written on the page. By the time she got to the end and realized what Miranda had planned to do she'd dropped the phone and her tears were smearing the ink of the letter. It was too much. Death was all around her, and sorrow consumed her. Quickly she grabbed the phone, hung up on Khalil without a word, and dialed Jada's number. They had to do something before it was too late.

Chapter 39

Antonio

They sat in the car in silence for a moment. Corey was ready to go, but Antonio had other things on his mind. He looked over at his buddy and shook his head. Some careless decisions had been made, and it simply wasn't going to fly any longer.

"Aye, come on. Let's go, man," Corey snapped. "We needa handle this ASAP before Tommy has another reason to be pissed with me."

"Naw, he ain't gon' be pissed with you no more," Antonio said reaching under the seat.

"Yeah? You think this shit gon' smooth over in my favor?" Corey asked hopefully as he lit a blunt.

Antonio sat upright and turned to face him. "I think it's over for you."

Corey looked over to ask him what he was talking about and could only process the silencer pointing in his face as his joint dangled from his lips. Antonio didn't give him a moment to speak. They didn't have any more time to waste. He shot him once in the head and once in the chest. There was no way he was going to survive that. The joint fell into Corey's lap as his blood splattered the window and his body slumped over in death.

On cue, a car rolled up beside the old Mustang. Quickly, Antonio wiped the steering wheel, driver's seat, and the door down before getting out and hopping into the ride that awaited him. His breathing was heavy but not as weighed down as his heart. He'd been rocking with Corey for a minute, but he knew that the man was going to be his downfall with all the careless moves he was making.

Antonio had helped Tommy clean up the mess surrounding Montae's death. Everyone was gone. The niggas that retaliated and now the dude that had pulled the trigger and was going around acting on impulse. Antonio looked over at Knuckles wondering if he had confirmation on the last piece of the puzzle.

"Boss handled it himself," Knuckles said, noticing Antonio's pensive look. "Ain't nobody left to talk about nothing, and if Martinez wants to run up again, he better watch his back. But I have a feelin' he's got the message that Atlanta belongs to BDM."

Antonio nodded. Things were about to change. He was about to fill Corey's shoes and run the streets of the A as BDM took over. He didn't have a girlfriend getting in his business and clouding his judgment like Corey did. He knew that he was better suited for this life than Corey was. He wasn't flashy, and he was loyal to the game, no emotions involved whatsoever. Antonio felt bad that so many lives had been destroyed surrounding Corey's dealings, but so be it. What's done was done. Everyone's dirty little secrets had to catch up with them at some point. Now he needed to focus on making sure his never did.

Epilogue

The Girls

Jada sat on the front pew massaging her protruding belly and staring forward. It took everything in her to regulate her breathing and avoid having a panic attack right there in the small viewing room of the funeral home. She couldn't believe that they were doing it again; burying another friend.

"Here you go, girl," Alex said, handing her a small plastic cup of ice-cold water. "The director said they may have some crackers they can give you."

Jada took the water and shook her head. "I'm fine. Thank you." It was a lie. She was anything but fine. From the moment she'd read the letter sent to her from Miranda she hadn't been okay. Truth be told, since all the drama began to pop off over a year ago none of them were okay.

Alex took a seat next to her friend on the pew and looked up at the casket that held the lifeless body of their previously troubled homegirl. It was surreal. Alex reached over and grabbed Jada's hand. "You did good," she commented in regards to the outfit that Jada had chosen for Miranda's funeral.

Jada simply nodded. Miranda's parents had been shocked to learn about their daughter's original suicide attempt which had landed her in rehab to begin with. It appeared that they hadn't been in contact with her for quite some time and had no idea about the physical abuse the girl had suffered at the hands of her husband or the drug abuse she'd turned to as a defense mechanism. The fact that Miranda had been killed while presumably in a safe haven while trying to overcome her issues was even more shocking. The center had contacted Jada immediately with the news and promised the family that a full investigation would take place. Jada had kept Miranda's letter a secret from her parents. Knowing that their daughter would have ended up dead anyway, only by her hand, would have only made matters worse. To help the family, Jada had chosen Miranda's pale pink casket, the black slacks, and pretty pink blouse she was being buried in, and the flowers that would cover her casket the next morning as they laid her body to rest. Yes, Jada had done well. She always seemed to be able to come through for everyone else, but how on earth had she managed to find herself in an unhappy life situation with no clear plan as to how to turn things around?

The duo heard the sound of footsteps behind them. Alex turned to witness Candace approaching them. Jada didn't budge. Candace wore dark shades and failed to remove them as she took a seat on the pew directly behind her girls.

Alex let go of Jada's hand and shifted her body to address Candace. "You know there's no sun in here, right?"

Candace sighed. "I can't mess with you today, Alex."

"I'm just saying."

Candace reached into her pocket and pulled out the letter she'd received from Miranda. On the day she'd first read it, she'd called the girls after getting herself together and learned that they'd each received a copy of the exact same text. With everything that was going on in Candace's life, she felt as if the wind had been knocked out of her. She couldn't breathe the majority of the time. Given the incident with Zoe and not being completely over the loss of

Stephanie, Candace just couldn't cope with the death of yet another person close to her.

"I keep going over and over this," Candace said, looking down at the letter in her hand. The paper was crumpled badly from the many times she'd read it and refolded it. "I keep going over it and I just . . . I just don't get it. I don't understand how she could just . . . how life could be that bad that she'd just kill herself. Like, why not call us? Why not come to us? Wasn't that the point of the whole group meeting thing we had? And who would have any reason to sneak into the center and just . . . just bore holes into her like some . . . target dummy?"

The others remained silent.

Candace reread the letter for what felt like the hundredth time and felt her eyes tear up. Sighing deeply, she refolded the paper and stuck it back into her pocket. "I don't get it."

"I get it," Jada whispered after taking a sip of water.

"Well, please clue me in."

"We keep parading around here like we're some solid sorority sisters or something, and that couldn't be any further from the truth."

"Jada," Alex said in an astonished tone.

Jada turned her head to the right to meet Alex's eyes. "You deny it? I mean, really . . .

How much do we know about the other these days? Friends are honest with one another. Friends look out for one another. Friends notice when something's not right with the other. Hell, friends care enough to check in to see what's up with the other. Honestly, we haven't been that close-knit in a long while, especially since . . ." Her words trailed off, but the others knew where her thoughts were heading.

"Stephanie's death shook us up a little bit, but we're still here," Alex stated. "We're still friends."

"Are we?" Jada countered. "The relationships in your life are supposed to help build you up. It seems like our relationships only help to tear us down."

Candace felt as if the last statement was mostly targeted at her. "Why don't you just say what it is that's on your mind, Jada."

Jada looked at Miranda's casket and didn't bother to wipe away the tears that freely flowed down her cheeks. "We're horrible friends. We're not people that Miranda felt she could turn to. She was filled with so much turmoil and found absolutely no security in coming to any of us. What does that tell you? Some of the shit that's been done is deplorable. I can't breathe," she said, placing her right hand over her chest. "I can't breathe from being suffocated by all of the lies and secrets that linger between us all. Hell, even I don't feel comfortable coming to you guys about the things in my life . . . keeping it all bottled up. From the panic disorder that none of you knew about until all the drama before Steph died, to the fact that my husband had been cheating on me and my marriage is practically a joke."

Alex gasped and reached over to grab her friend's hand. "Oh my God, Jada. I'm so sorry. I didn't—"

"You didn't realize," Jada interrupted and finished the girl's sentence. "Exactly."

Alex's bottom lip trembled. "I'm so sorry," she repeated. "If anyone deserves to be happy it's you. You two seemed so perfect together. I guess no relationship is perfect." She paused for a moment. "Not even mine. Clay left me. That's why he wasn't at Zoe's funeral," she said looking back at Candace. "He took a job in Cali and left me."

"I was helping Corey." The confession came out of nowhere. She hadn't planned to ever tell anyone the complete truth, but it was eating her alive. "He wanted to get back at the dudes that killed Stephanie and guilted me into helping him. Things got out of control at my place, and that's how Zoe got shot."

Alex stared at her in disbelief. "Are you crazy? What the hell would possess you to get involved in that? And with your kid around. Have you lost it?"

"Don't judge me." Candace's voice quivered as she used her index finger to push her shades up on the bridge of her nose. "Trust me, I constantly beat myself up about it so I don't need to hear it from anyone else."

"I can't understand how it is that you're always finding yourself in these damning situations where someone ends up dead. Damn!"

Candace finally removed her shades from her face to reveal her red, swollen eyes. "You think I'm happy about any of this? You think I *wanted* to help Corey? You think I *wanted* Steph to die? You think I *wanted* my child, my own flesh and blood, to be killed over some foolishness? You think I wanted *any* of this?" she asked, spreading her arms wide. "I'm dying on the inside." She looked over Jada's shoulder to gaze at Miranda's casket. "It should be me being buried tomorrow. I should be the one dead."

"So what?" Jada broke in. "You going to go home tonight and kill yourself now?" It was a crass response, but Jada didn't care. She was over the bullshit. "This is over."

"What are you talking about?" Alex asked, feeling a little nervous about what was to come.

"Tomorrow we're saying good-bye to Miranda. I'm done burying people, keeping secrets, being lied to, being hurt, and being caught in the middle of an emotional wreckage that just can't be fixed. This friendship, this whatever it is we're supposed to be to each other, can't be fixed. It's over." She rose from the pew and turned to walk away from the girls.

Candace quickly stood up and grabbed Jada's hand before she could bypass her. "Wait, wait! Don't do this, Jada. We need each other." Her eyes were grew big and pleading as she spoke. "This isn't the time to turn our backs on one another."

"You really don't get it. We've already done that, Candace! Because of this friendship and the crap between us all, two of us have died. Enough is enough. I'm getting off of the roller-coaster ride. I have enough of my own issues to sort through. I can't carry the burden of all the extra drama anymore."

"But I need you. You can't walk away from me when I need you the most," Candace cried. "Please! Please don't do this."

Jada was unmoved. She was convinced in her belief that they all needed to go their separate ways and work on themselves. How could they be good friends to one another when they had so much personal stuff of their own to deal with? It seemed that nothing but hurt and heartbreak surrounded their friendship, and Jada no longer felt it was a healthy situation.

Jada snatched her arm away from Candace who looked as if she was about to crumble to the floor at any moment. "Sometimes friendships end, Candace. Sometimes the end is merely the beginning." Without another word she walked away, failing to so much as throw them a final glance over her shoulder.

Candace fell to her knees and screamed. Her heart was broken into a million pieces. Everything she'd ever had was gone—love, friends, family. It was all destroyed. "Help me, Jehovah," she prayed aloud. "Help me. Please help me." Feeling completely lost, she turned to the only source she felt could give her an ounce of strength to carry on. Perhaps it was time for her to rekindle her relationship with her Savior.

Alex stared into space as Candace continued to cry and pray on the ground. The shift in her life had happened so quickly that she was unsure of what to do or say next. She could have gone after Jada and tried to smooth things over, but a part of her felt that Jada was right.

Perhaps they'd all gone as far as they could in their relationships with one another. Just like her relationship with Clay, sometimes it just wasn't meant to last forever. Everything in life happened for a reason or a season. Maybe the season of their bond had expired, and it was time to move on. Together they'd learned a lot, lost a lot, and grown a lot. Alex wasn't sure what the future held, or if they would ever be able to repair their friendships later in life. But today, she was grateful for the time she'd had with the girls, and she knew that she'd never forget any of the lessons learned during their era.

THE END